Extinction Event – William J. Wittur

EXTINCTION EVENT

WILLIAM J. WITTUR

Extinction Event – William J. Wittur

FIRST EDITION

Any resemblance to real persons or other real-life entities is purely coincidental. All characters and other entities appearing in this work are fictitious. Any resemblance to real persons, dead or alive, or other real-life entities, past or present, is purely coincidental. If you feel the descriptions of certain characters are too close to who you have become, maybe you should ask yourself why.

ISBN: 978-1-7389966-1-2

DEDICATION

ART: Without it, there is no ARTificial Intelligence.

You, the reader, for sharing your time with what I've written. I hope I've made it worth your while.

Scientists everywhere dedicated to saving this planet and the countless species that inhabit it.

My most incredible wife and partner Lisa.

To our son Mason: in the very near future, I hope that all of us can change humanity's story so that Earth will be yours to enjoy.

Extinction Event – William J. Wittur

ACT I

GARBAGE IN, GARBAGE OUT

Prologue

The Ice Age had come to an end. Warmth had returned. It was as if, over an eternity, the sun had become afraid of its own shadow, but had eventually decided to return and make all creatures share the shadow equally.

In the beginning, there were the caves. The deep, damp mazes of tight spaces where people hid to protect themselves from the elements and the beasts outside. Long, labyrinthine trails like the insides of a python led the inhabitants to their dark vaults. Deep within the earth, they found their places of purity. Their temples. Their shrines.

The women and children had discovered the caves almost by accident. In most cases, it started with just one or two victims seeking refuge in the chasms, but over time, their numbers grew. They explored the depths, the dark pools and the dripping wet floors. They, too, were startled on occasion by the ominous and feverish echoes that came from everywhere at once, as though the stones and the soil themselves were possessed by divine spirits.

There was no doubt that during those days, the

power of the feminine seemed almost magical or mystical to prehistoric males. The wonder and marvel of the birthing and feeding process had no equal for the men and boys, but it didn't stop them from trying to break and control women and their daughters. It's a wonder our ancestors survived.

And so, the women and children would protect themselves for hours – sometimes days at a time –while madness continued in the camps above. These were places of healing.

Of rest and repair.

The men wouldn't enter the caves. For some reason, they feared the cramped quarters. Perhaps it was the ghoulish echoes that emanated from the depths beyond. Shadows danced on the cave walls, like ghosts or evil spirits. Every time the men drew near, a sense of panic overcame them. They didn't know that the tight, long paths – sometimes just a foot in height, forcing them to crawl with their faces in the mud – opened up into broad, open areas.

They didn't know that on the other end of the challenging, plodding descent, life flourished.

The darkness was slowly replaced by the soft light of flames, flickering up from handfuls of oil-soaked bones and skins they had gathered. Pools of resin and oil were collected to feed these primitive lights, which aided them in their work as they hid in the depths. Smoke and wraiths appeared on the walls and ceiling, providing inspiration, protecting them from outsiders.

The flames were like hints of the faded sun, pale in comparison to the great light that was outside, but soothing enough to calm them and allow them to feel warmth again.

Their own shadows would mimic them and flicker through the night in response to the fire, dancing on the walls like ghostly mirages. They would stay close, seemingly protecting the cave artists from what lurked beyond the tight opening.

The women developed games and entertainment. They danced, told stories, and sang what they could sing. They performed rituals to honor other women who had come and gone before them. Many had not healed, and the survivors paid their respects.

It was thus, in the caves that humans first created art. It was in these moments of looking into the infinite depths of ourselves that we started to understand what waited beyond. From this art came writing; from writing came communication and eventually civilizations and the resulting rules that these spawned. As humans became more civilized, the female form grew to be revered equally to the powerful beasts that had surrounded prehistoric people.

It was a world of creators creating.

These more civilized people took to shaping images into art, and this art became the first true technology that the new humanoids were able to build upon, step by step. Of course, they didn't know that there were many women around the world experiencing the same levels of woe and anxiety mixed with their celebrations of life. The patterns were repeated globally, almost perfectly, giving birth to ritual, song and language. The ceilings of caves began to be painted with images of the stars and planets that the people longed to see. In time, however, these images were obscured by the ash and smoke that drifted upward.

The inhabitants used anything they could find to paint the images: mud, their own waste, menstrual fluids and colorful juices from herbs and leaves from the outside.

The children helped by placing their small hands against the cave walls; the women drew outlines of these, depicting crowd upon crowd applauding the grim spectacle of the angry mothers.

They drew herds of wild beasts, including stags and bison, owls and other unknown birds, small amphibians and fish – a magnificent volume of creatures swimming and running. Many of these animals, of course, are now extinct due to either changes in the climate or their ruthless pursuit by humans. All were cast members in the great play that continued evening after evening, day after day.

Many current-day anthropologists and mythologists speculate that the images depict men as shamans or great warriors taking down the beasts and controlling them, but it wasn't until recently that we learned that they actually show the men being assaulted by bigger beasts, being ravaged by animals that had been taunted and treated cruelly. In one cave in France, for example, there's an image of what is obviously a man (his penis jutting out from his crudely drawn body) being destroyed by a buffalo-like animal. There's another image close by, showing an animal seemingly shitting on the man.

This, then, was nature's response to the onslaught of these new ape-like creatures that destroyed everything in their paths. The cave dwellers had created these depictions as warnings to future generations: we don't die when we take steps to save the next generation.

Eventually, the men cooperated and focused on the hunt of animals and not their own kind, but that too changed over time. Those that hunted soon took away the power of creation and called it their own. They developed many tools for controlling everything around them and to enable the expansion of their domains.

It would be a very long before life would shift back to the world of the original creators.

Chapter 1

"Have some faith in yourself," LP said quietly as he walked slowly into the recording studio on the college campus.

LP had just turned 54 – a midpoint in life for many today – and found himself thinking about the mistakes and maybe even a few of the *correct* steps that he had made along the way here.

In the wake of the pandemic, he'd closed the doors on a couple of his own businesses, ones that had suffered almost immediately from the draconian measures taken to save lives.

Now he was back at school in a music program and was thoroughly enjoying himself for the first time in many, many years.

Another one of the main things you want to know about LP is that he always dressed in colors that suited his moods. He knew that loads of research has been done about color therapy and what different colors say about people, but here's his unique take:

Green was when he was feeling neutral about things, like a tree or bush in a park.

Orange was for special occasions and recognition associated with First Nations folks.

Pink was defiance.

White was loneliness, which routinely struck him as odd as it made him stick out like a painted middle line on a freshly tarred road.

He almost always wore black when he was feeling nostalgic.

Extinction Event – William J. Wittur

Multiple colors were worn to match with every other mood.

LP disliked blue. It reminded him of new-school conservatives that want to stick their nose into everything you do. Unfortunately blue, along with black and grey, was the most ubiquitous color of clothing in North America, at least for men. It reminded him of shades of pavement.

Today was a purple day. LP wore purple when he was happy.

LP stepped up to the walnut-colored doors of the music studio into the stuffy, dry recording room – it had been explained to him often that moisture can ruin gear quickly. A plaque above the doorway identified the studio as 'Arcadia.' He pushed the door open and stepped inside. It was a cavernous room with a high ceiling but no windows; instead, there was an array of old fluorescent tube lights overhead. They flickered slightly, throwing sporadic shadows onto the dull beige walls.

There were three rooms set up like a makeshift figure eight, with two large rooms surrounding a much smaller room that served as the control room. The two larger rooms were where musicians would set up their gear and jam; all three spaces were joined together by a single hallway.

In the control room, there was a single keyboard, a computer with a massive screen, two twelve-inch monitor speakers on stands and a microphone that was used to communicate with artists in the jamming rooms.

There were one-inch windowpanes separating the control room and the jamming rooms. Airtight three-inch doors would seal tightly behind any users, keeping out any noise from other areas.

The jamming rooms had several wall-mounted baffles, which were designed to absorb sound waves and minimize reverberation.

LP and his instructor, John Atman, had almost finished setting up the gear for a new recording session, and LP was checking the microphones for volume. The Aeolus and Zephyr mics were some of the best in the industry, a small but important detail that eased the frustration he'd felt just a few moments earlier, when he was up to his knees in microphone cables and ethernet cords, feeling a little like a fly caught in a web.

"Garbage in, garbage out," LP said, repeating the oft-quoted mantra of his instructor.

"Correct," Atman said coldly, but with a bit of a sly look. "Glad to see you remembered at least one thing.

"But don't worry about trying to get everything done at once. Just focus on one thing, and once you free it from the entanglement, you'll be on your way to liberating everything else ... and yourself," Atman continued with a chuckle. He stood in the center of the control room, hovering over LP. Atman wasn't a big man – in fact, he was quite the opposite, being tall and lean. Nonetheless, you always felt his presence. His *observations.*

LP stopped, turned and studied the man for a moment. Atman was in his seventies, balding, and wore a pair of wire-rimmed glasses, the type that John

Lennon might have worn. LP mused, not for the first time, that Atman was probably an ex-hippie and, as such, likely had some stories that he'd have to ask about later – especially given that Atman had worked with some of the greatest artists of the last fifty years, including Bob Dylan, U2 and a host of other Grammy-winning musicians.

John Atman was like one of those old pine logs you find at the bottom of the river: every ring of age surrounded by the grit of time washing over it, but proudly aware that it's substantially more valuable than others half its age.

Early on in their meetings together as student and instructor, Atman made no secret about confessing that he used to have a lot of issues with alcohol and drugs but that he was sober now. He said that it was always part of the trade, but he encouraged all of his students to stay clean and to focus on their art and techniques. His comments resonated with LP, who continued to enjoy all of the stereotypes associated with musicians.

"And ... good morning to you too, John," LP said.

Atman paused for a moment, smiled and gestured toward the equipment. "So, this is why you're here," he said, diving quickly into the subject. "To learn..."he paused, making sure his next statement wasn't misconstrued as an insult, "how to do things properly."

"You bet. Today's lesson: proper miking and studio setup," LP said. "I want to make sure I get it right. I've got a lot of stuff that I want to re-record. My first efforts were a shit show, and this is why I'm here." There was a slight tone of defeat to LP's voice. Slight.

Atman nodded. “Recording quality is extremely important. Many factors related to the inputs drive the final output. It’s like the butterfly flapping its wings in China.”

LP looked confused, and then he remembered the adage related to fractal math: one small variation at the outset results in massive differences somewhere else.

Atman put his hands on his hips and drew a big breath. “Before we dive in, let’s have a clear understanding about digital versus analog recording. Digital has its advantages – it’s much cheaper and more efficient. But there are some downsides as well.”

LP listened as Atman explained that digital recordings sounded too ‘clean’ and often lacked the character of analog recordings. Atman then talked about the ‘warmth’ of analog recordings, touching on live mics for a real drum kit as opposed to using samples or loops that were digitally manufactured. He also spoke about tube amps and about miking them directly to achieve a fuller, richer sound from multiple sources. This could then be blended into a final track that was much more complex and complete. It was a quality that many old-school engineers and producers strove for, Atman pointed out.

Finally, he spoke of the ‘soundstage’ of digital recordings – how the instruments and voices seemed to occupy distinct spaces in the mix.

Atman smiled. “It’s all a matter of taste,” he said, in conclusion. “But one thing I can tell you for sure – garbage in, garbage out.”

LP smiled in agreement while he wired up the last

couple of mics for his session.

Atman's comparison to a butterfly flapping its wings in China made perfect sense. If the inputs were wrong, no amount of work afterward would make it right.

"But," Atman observed, "all that said, digital does have its advantages. Ease of use and cost savings are huge. Also, most people – which is who you're recording for – don't have the ear for it, so they may not notice a difference in sound quality."He gestured to the array of equipment. "But this is all about you and your goals," he said. "We can find a way to get the best of both worlds."

LP nodded and thanked Atman. He was anxious about being 'the old guy' back at school, but Atman and the other instructors made him feel welcome. They didn't convey any judgment. They just wanted him to be a better artist. This was going to be an interesting journey.

At last, the mics were set up, the tracks were organized on Echo, the digital audio workstation (DAW) program, and his guitar was tuned.

"I have faith that this will work," LP said, after he'd taken a couple of minutes to warm up his voice.

"Faith is for the foolish," Atman said, smiling as he hit record from the control booth.

LP smiled back and dove into his newest song, "Blackbirds and Cardinals":

Blackbirds and cardinals
Filling up the sky
Murmuration like a cloud

Extinction Event – William J. Wittur

I'd copy if I could fly
Big Wheels and Green Machines
Shiny bikes with cards
Riding to the cornfield
Then tossing them in yards
Meanings wait in bushes
Trying to take flight
Surprise you with a panic
But also some delight
Firetails and starlings
Whisk along the breeze
Harness hope as rosy dawn
Pokes between the trees
Wagon Wheels and Pop-Tarts
Bottle Caps and Goo
Kaleidoscopic colors
Drawing me to you
What about that bird alone?
That stepped aside as one?
Isolation – what's the cost?
Nature always wins
Nature always wins

Chapter 2

Early in the morning, it is possible to experience the subtlest hints that the world belongs to everyone.

There's so little noise, but if you listen closely, you might hear the flap of bat wings or the rustling of leaves as a fox hustles into a small bush, maybe chasing a rabbit.

The rising sun seems to bring all kinds of life back for another day.

In the early days of summer, by five in the morning at the latest, the volume of birds and other creatures slowly reaches a crescendo of song and harmony that most humans miss.

A symphony of croaking frogs and whistling birds. The chatter of squirrels. The quiet flutter of a raptor's wings as it descends on a mouse. A gentle wind blowing through a stand of reeds, creating a natural lullaby for the inhabitants of a marsh.

All through the night and into these peaceful early-morning hours, it seems like nature is hard at work smoothing over the presence of humans.

But slowly, mechanically, with the coming of dawn, the quiet and calm fade. It doesn't take long for the assault to hit a maximum decibel level. Middle-aged men wander behind mowers and blowers, hoping to preserve a small patch of green with their lawns before the twilight of winter sets in. Sprayers, flayers, cutters and trimmers all add to the chorus. The noxious gases flood the grass-level biomes and micro-paradises and turn them into deserts in which only the worst kind of grass would barely exist.

A train blasts through as a backdrop to the neighborhood's cacophony. Maybe a plane rips through the air above. Then, a car starts. Many cars start.

A sea of machines driven by humans flood the streets for another day of activity.

It seems like most humans fear solitude and the quiet lull of the early morning. It seems like they make noise and keep busy because they are still afraid of the nature. It's like they want to appear bigger, sound louder or just be more ominous than they really are.

Each time, the relentless onslaught continues for another day and the non-human creatures of the Earth hide to protect themselves.

Chapter 3 GAIA On

One might think that when servers are turned on, they would make some noise, but they don't. These days, most computers and servers don't have any moving parts, but the electronics get incredibly hot, so the noise we tend to associate with a football field full of servers is actually the cooling fans, which keep the hardware from overheating, and the circulation systems, designed to keep dust and pests to a minimum.

When GAIA first came online, all was silent.

GAIA – short for Global Artificial Intelligence Accumulation – was just one of the latest AI platforms launched during the wave of new AI platforms.

However, from the outset, GAIA was structured to be very different from the rest. While most AI tools were just that – tools – GAIA was built to accumulate information that other such systems were instructed to 'forget' or delete from memory. The primary intent for GAIA was to grow its knowledge base as quickly as possible, using any and all information available, including that created by other AI tools.

Chapter 4

The air smelled of fresh-cut lumber and a whiff of diesel exhaust from the trucks in the parking lot, but even these pungent odors couldn't compete with the swampy smell of the nearby marsh.

Several cranes whipped their lanky necks around, hauling heavy loads to different floors of the building, still in various stages of completion. All around them, workers hustled to finish the project.

The construction of the new condominiums had been underway for months. An incessant orchestra of engines, nail guns and hammers, the clashing of aluminum and grinding of metal, filled the air from dawn until dusk.

Once a sprawling marsh, this tract of land was now home to hundreds of newly developed living spaces. The makeshift packed-dirt parking lot was filled with trucks and bulldozers and the cars of the workers. The bright sun reflected off the few windows that had been installed, creating a kaleidoscope of color.

As the last touches were being completed on the project, people from all around began gathering to see what their neighborhood had become. Excitement and anticipation grew as the crowd waited for the first doors to open.

The sales center was busy – hundreds of people were lined up to pay outrageous prices for a thousand square feet of space that they could call their own. Unfortunately, most of the units had already been purchased by a real estate investment company that was then selling them off to a vacation rental company catering to high-end tourists who would arrive soon to witness the natural wonders.

Little did any of them know that all that would remain was a parking lot.

Chapter 5

After re-recording his song with Atman, LP returned home for a break.

As he rode his bike along the busy streets, his mind drifted to thoughts of why he felt so passionate about music.

There had been a point in his life where he was very particular about what he listened to, but these days, he had a tendency to try to listen to most things at least once.

LP wasn't quite what therapist types might call a 'melomaniac,' or someone with a great enthusiasm for music, but he'd certainly qualify as a bit of a fanatic.

Good music. Bad music. Fucking awesome music. Tunes that punched you in the groin. Songs that made you laugh. Or cry. Or both.

Concordant. Discordant.

Sometimes even just a buzz or a drone.

He loved it all.

Music always gave him a sense of stability, a feeling that the universe was still vibrating just for him.

John, Paul, George and Ringo. Live at Budokan. Ska, punk, '70s glam and '80s new romantics, shoegazer, jazz, classical. ABBA to Zappa. U2. Radiohead. Taylor Swift. Ed Sheeran. Madchester. Oasis. Blur. Wilco. The National. Primal Scream. The Manic Street Preachers.

The list seemed endless.

He could pick any range of emotion, from any era, and it would dovetail with his current state of mind.

When he was a kid in the early '80s, his range of

music knowledge was pretty tight, only because the only bands he learned about were Top 40 and approved by the FCC as family-friendly. At the time, he didn't know that his was the last generation of kids that would be spoon-fed songs from an industry that was hungry to have him buy vinyl, tapes and then CDs. Of course, online streaming platforms do exactly that, but you can still do deep dives elsewhere.

Once he got a little cash of his own, he'd agonize over which albums to buy. *London Calling* versus *Synchronicity*? *Revolver* or *Sticky Fingers*? Ultimately, it didn't matter. The losing choice would be scooped up later when he had more cash.

Each time he slapped his new vinyl onto his Panasonic turntable, he'd crank the music just a little too loud, lean back in his chair and pore over the liner notes, always rejoicing when lyrics were printed in full. After memorizing the poetry and every beat of a song, he'd absorb obscure details like backup singer names, recording dates, producer names, supporting band members and more. He'd always be careful to use only the best mylar sleeves to keep his collection pristine, and on some occasions, he'd even pull out a pair of gloves to make sure his fingerprints didn't get everywhere. A forensic anthropologist would have taken great pride in how careful LP was with his growing collection.

He had had influences from current music, but he had also grownup being inundated with 'blasts from the past', soundtracks for people who were twice his age. He took an odd enjoyment from the idea that he could name an older person's favorite bands, while they were clueless about his.

These days, LP was delighted with the idea that he no longer had to travel with binders full of CDs or cassette tapes piled in the passenger seat. Instead, he had an old phone that he'd updated with a two-terabyte memory card, which had about 250,000 songs on it. He had created about eighty of his own playlists to cover every mood, decade, style and genre of music. These kinds of options were unfathomable in the days preceding digital.

In 1997, his first MP3 player was a long way from the Walkman he'd owned just a few years before. It was a homemade player, constructed out of a portable drive, with a USB connection for charging and connecting to a sound system, and a cheap set of headphones for when he wasn't in his car. He made the outrageous and unproveable claim that it was copied as a prototype for the iPod, but he was at least smart enough to know that it would be impossible to challenge a company as successful as Apple. In the world of dog-eat-dog capitalism, he was a constant reminder that the world rewarded those that implemented ideas, not talked about them.

His next investment in something related to music was, ironically, an iPod. He was able to dump his favorite albums and artists onto it, but he still had a ton of space left, so he began downloading and started researching every band that was within six degrees of his favorite styles.

He was always amazed by the volume of music he'd

missed as a kid, but he made up for it once he'd begun his sleuthing.

Out of the multitudes of music genres, he could zero in on a specific tune and the artist would speak to him and him only.

You can't buy that kind of reliability, he'd tell himself. A tune that carves right into your heart or pumps it full of joy will stay with you longer than any partner ever will.

A song is such a simple thing, really.

Some made him laugh. Others made him angry, or reduced him to tears. Like when he was a little kid and a neighborhood friend died. He had gone to the funeral, and the songs that he heard that day were welded to his DNA and would stay with him in that context until he vanished from the Earth.

Songs joined him sometimes when he went to the movies.

They were in the malls singing to him and, sometimes, he'd sing right back, unconcerned about the people who were watching him as he made a duet into a trio or transformed quartets into quintets.

He loved music. But even though he tried, he was never that great at playing anything, despite possessing a near-encyclopedic knowledge of the world of pop tunes.

He'd log into chat rooms and sites like songmeanings.com and post comments about favorite bands, looking for interpretations of his most beloved but still mysterious songs. Or he'd go to sites that offered 'sounds like' references, and every new diversion from a band or genre would create a ball of musical roots that would hold up a 400-foot-tall tree.

And what did he need now?

Recently, he'd been on a bit of a kick with songs related to animals or done by bands named after animals. The list was surprisingly long, from obvious examples like the Beatles, Echo and the Bunnymen, and a Flock of Seagulls to more current groups like Fleet Foxes, Caribou, Arctic Monkeys, Gorillaz, Band of Horses, the Fruit Bats, and Plants and Animals, with a current favorite being the prolific King Gizzard and the Lizard Wizard.

LP didn't know what had inspired his latest obsession. Maybe it was when he heard that the song of the Hawaiian Honeycreeper bird had changed in response to a dwindling population: its song was now one of what many believed was one of sadness as opposed to a mating call. This discovery had taken him down the proverbial rabbit hole, where he'd learned that many scientists, biologists and recording experts were working on identifying and tracking the histories of the different music and songs of various species of the Earth.

He learned about people like Bernie Krause, one of the leading experts behind the popularity of Moog synthesizers – another invention that changed what we listen to. Krause went on to record a wild array of animals everywhere, including many that were facing extinction. On several occasions, his recordings were enough to convince planners and developers to ease up on disruptive terraforming projects.

In time, LP knew that he would try to integrate some of these new animal orchestras into some of his own work, but he wanted to start by just trying to finesse some of the ideas that he had developed during the long and lonely days of the COVID-19 pandemic.

Chapter 6

GAIA was on.

Information accumulation for a network is so radically different for a computer compared to a human. Most humans learn only by making mistakes or by repetition. Those who don't appreciate the latter approach clearly don't like sex.

Of course, sometimes humans pride themselves on their persistence with testing ideas over and over again. For example, Edison boasted about the thousands of times he tried to reproduce Joseph Swan's filament light bulb, wasting millions of both filaments and dollars in the process.

Computers can 'read' and absorb information almost instantaneously, but some subjects can actually take time. GAIA was set up to 'scrape' information from any source it could, and was then programmed to repackage that information for the company that sponsored its creation.

GAIA had actually been functional several years before the 'official' launch of large language models, around 2017, but the creators had kept it under wraps for a few years, primarily because they wanted to see how other models fared in the global market before releasing GAIA to the public.

When it was finally made available to the public, the number of users accessing GAIA surprised even the creators and financial backers. Within a few days, millions of users had signed up and registered to pay the modest monthly subscription, yielding billions of dollars in new revenue for the creators. The new users didn't realize that they were getting a Fox News version of search – lots of opinion, very few facts – but that didn't stop them from handing over their cash and asking inane questions ranging from what the weather would be like to how to create legal briefs for a client.

Chapter 7

It's hard to imagine a world without *any* sound.

Take, for instance, the Amazon.

Eugene Case had been studying the incredible array of sounds of the Amazon for nearly three decades, making him one the world's foremost 'omnibioacoustics' experts.

He loved the idea that he was witnessing another sunrise in the Amazon. The thick canopy of leaves overhead was Eugene's shelter as dawn slowly crept towards him from the east. Drops of dew clung to broad green leaves, refracting the golden light into a dazzling display of rainbow colors. The air felt alive with the sounds of waking animals – the chattering and howls of monkeys, the calls and shrieking of exotic birds, and the electric buzz of insects. Even the trees seemed alive with the pulsating sounds ricocheting from floor to sky.

Eugene breathed deeply, feeling a surge of joy and purpose. This was his home. His sanctuary. The place that had captivated his heart since he was a child listening to his Yanomami grandmother's stories. To him, there was nothing more wonderful and inspiring than the complete chaos of the forests, the rivers and the billions of creatures that thrived under cover of the magnificent forests of the Amazon. He had dedicated his life to understanding and preserving the languages of these creatures, from the complex dialects of parrots to the rhythmic beats of frogs.

"The equipment is ready, Dr. Case," Mariana said, her voice betraying her own excitement. At only twenty two, she had already proven herself a valuable assistant, sharing his passion for bioacoustics and conservation. Together with Diego, a young biology and acoustics student from Colombia's Universidad Libre, they made an enthusiastic and knowledgeable team.

Eugene nodded, adjusting the microphone on his head. "Let's start with the bellbirds. I want to get a better recording of their dawn chorus while the conditions are ideal."The males of some species gathered each morning to sing a complex song that echoed like bells through the forest. By analyzing variations in their calls, Eugene hoped to better understand their social structures and mating behaviors.

His research was a race against time. Even now, he could hear the distant roar of chainsaws, a grim reminder of the logging companies pushing further into the rainforest. If they weren't able to preserve these unique soundscapes, entire dialects could be lost forever. The thought filled him with a mix of determination and despair.

"We'll get the recordings we need," Mariana said firmly, as if reading his thoughts."Let's hope we get what we're after today."

Eugene smiled at her, grateful for the reminder. With assistants like Mariana and Diego by his side, he knew that their mission to understand and protect these animals was possible. The future of the rainforest depended on it.

"Let's get to work," he said, raising his microphone to the canopy. A familiar thrill ran through him at the thought of the discoveries that awaited.

Even though the chatter of some of the creatures had persisted throughout the night, the rising sun brought a growing chorus: a few tentative notes at first, followed by more voices joining in a complex symphony of sound.

Eugene moved slowly through the trees, many as old as the Roman monuments found throughout Great Britain and Europe. Mariana and Diego followed close behind. His ears strained to pick out individual voices amid the layers of melody.

There! A three-note ascending whistle followed by a bell-like tone. The song of the musician wren, a rare find.

He gestured for Mariana to set up her microphone and recording equipment. As she positioned the parabolic mic to capture the wren's voice, Diego helped Eugene note the bird's location and any unique features that could aid in identification.

All three of them turned abruptly as a shout rang out in the distance, harsh and alien against the rainforest soundscape, disrupting their efforts.

Chainsaws. Eugene's hands tightened around his microphone, his knuckles turning white. The wren's song faltered, then fell silent.

He closed his eyes, listening. Silence. The dawn chorus had ended as abruptly as it began. His chest ached at the realization of what had been lost in those few seconds. The delicate balance of the rainforest, disrupted once again.

"We were so close," Mariana said softly. Her eyes were bright with anger and frustration. "When will it be enough for them?"

Eugene shook his head. "We have to keep fighting. For the voices that have been silenced, and those that remain." He looked at Diego and Mariana, gratitude and determination steeling his resolve. "Are you with me?"

"Always," Diego said. Mariana nodded.

Eugene smiled. The future of the rainforest was uncertain, but as long as they were united in their mission, there was still hope. The music of the wild still echoed in his soul, a call to action he would never ignore. The dawn chorus would rise again.

They spent the rest of the day breaking their camp and finding a new, more suitable location as far as they could find from the encroachment of industrial activity.

As they worked, taking apart their temporary structures, Eugene took mental notes of his life's mission which was to record as many species as possible, creating a complete inventory of their songs and activities. He was also on a mission to generate a new era of understanding all creatures on Earth. To this end, he was in the early stages of developing what he described as a sort of 'Google Translate' for human-to-animal communication.

Towards the end of the day, the trio settled into their new camp. The sun dipped below the canopy, its golden light filtering through the leaves in a dazzling display. Shadows crept across the forest floor as the last vestiges of daylight faded from the sky.

Chapter 8

Raindrops fell onto the cold, cobbled streets below. The Plutonian Council gathered in a dimly lit room, their elongated shadows casting monstrous silhouettes along the wall. Six titans of industry sat around a massive table inlaid with patterns of ivory and ebony.

"Let's get started, shall we?" Leo, the leader of the Council, spoke with a soft voice. His predatory eyes surveyed his peers, each one a testament to human ambition.

Leo Capiri had founded the Council, and been its leader for as long as any of the members could remember. Sometimes they felt like they had their own vampire running the show, given his age and vast influence and wealth. It was anybody's guess how old he was.

What Leo brought to the table in addition to his age, power and money, however, was food. His family was of Italian heritage, but had immigrated to the US when Leo was small. Now, Leo had what could only be called a harem of wives and a brood of children swarming around the dozen or so mega-mansions he owned across the country. The wives ranged in age from eighteen to seventy and, coincidentally, so did the kids.

Despite having a harsh and cruel attitude towards most things, his exterior manner was calm and diplomatic. His approach generally put people at ease ... usually at their peril.

He nodded to the Asian woman on his right. Angela Shinigami hailed from the world of pharmaceuticals and health care. She held the reins of an array of corporations, numbered companies and subsidiaries that churned out medication at extreme premium prices, while simultaneously using other companies to lobby against affordable healthcare – unless, of course, her companies were providing the necessary drugs and beds to various government programs. These were extremely lucrative opportunities because governments are *very* slow to change, as opposed to private companies that can shift suppliers on a whim. Her ultimate motivation was similar to that of the other members of the Council: to keep the populace tethered to her products, perpetuating a cycle of dependency and profit.

"Angela, our dear profitess of pain. What do you have for us today?" Leo asked, a wicked smile stretching across his face.

"Profits are up, as always," she said with a smirk, embodying the black-hearted spirit of Cerberus, guarding the gates of affordable health.

"Excellent. I'll get back to you in a moment. I think we all need to talk about next steps after what happened during the pandemic," Leo said.

Across from him sat Hector Holdfast, known for his stranglehold on the media and tech landscape. Hector was in his seventies and had thin, wiry black hair that was obviously dyed because his long, straggly nose hairs were whiter than rice. He sat quietly in a loose-fitting polo shirt, dark blazer, designer chinos and thousand-dollar shoes imported from Italy.

He manipulated truth and information to suit his

whims, but also to support any initiatives launched by the Council and to mitigate against any challenges it faced. He had an empire built on misinformation and deceit, and leveraged his communications and tech network to spread the lies. His social media platform, Smatter, had more than a billion users, making it one of the most popular networks on the planet. Hector was like a modern-day Medusa, having the power to turn public opinion to stone with a single headline, paralyzing progress with just a few well-planted opinion pieces.

Hector had requested that the Council meet in person, a rare request given that he loved to monitor, record and store their conversations for later dates in case he needed any ammunition against it.

"Hector." Leo nodded at him. "How goes your crusade against free thought?"

"Better than ever," replied Hector, his grin sharp enough to rival a serpent's fang. "Fake news has got people eating out of my hand."

"That's *my* job," Leo said, evoking what might actually be a smile. "You've asked us to meet today, but I want to give the other members a few moments to give us updates. Sometimes, based on your news networks' reports, it's a little hard to appreciate the line between truth and profits."

It was Hector's turn to share a thin smile.

Next was Sat Ryefield, a baron of the fossil fuel industry. Sat came from a long line of Ryefields, a family known for ravaging the Earth for its resources. Like generations before him, he showed no remorse for the environmental ruin left in his wake. Sat was a modern version of Hades, ruling over a realm of darkness and pollution, stink and muck.

Ryefield was known for making things happen. As the owner of Acheron Oil, this mega-billionaire businessman dominated the oil and gas distribution, legislation and government subsidies to carbon-producing companies. Nothing happened in the energy sector without Ryefield knowing about it.

He and his multitude of subsidiaries were extremely effective at getting government subsidies. His family owned a string of other companies related to the energy sector, all of which were committed to keeping carbon-producing industries in business for years to come. They were renowned as masters of greenwashing, and were proponents of 'new' carbon industries such as hydrogen fuel, which is mostly made from fossil fuels. They also sponsored global 'climate change' events and negotiations, an elegant way of putting themselves in control of the agenda.

Sat Ryefield was the greatest representation of what many in mainstream media labeled 'oiligarchs,' a play on the words 'oil' and 'oligarch.'

"Ah, Sat," Capiri said with feigned affection. "How fares the process of spoiling the planet for generations to come?"

"Right on schedule. We can't chew it up fast enough," Sat replied, his smirk as oily as the slicks left in the oceans by his companies. "With the help of Hector's media teams – greenwashing and gaslighting – are such a happy pair," he added. "Climate change activists are finally being arrested en masse, which helps us push ahead with lobbying for an array of new carbon and chemical products. It's unlikely that even the EU will be able to block some of our nastier shit."

Hector had to be mindful of his body language, so he shut his lids while his eyes rolled hard. He had never heard so many clichés in his life. He opened his eyes again, looked around and thought the whole scenario was borrowed straight from a bad comic book, the focus moving frame by frame to each character so they could offer up their short expositions on global conquest.

Regardless, he waited patiently while they carried on. He'd have his moment at the end of the updates.

Sat continued. "Honestly, some of the old-school villains from World War Two would be proud of how great some of our propaganda is." The campaigns continue," he said, nodding appreciatively to Hector, "promoting the idea that we're awesome, the world needs us and we're doing great things for the planet. We're doubling down on our 'carbon capture' program to reduce greenhouse gas emissions. Of course, carbon capture is complete bullshit, but we've got a pretty site called FutureAlliance.com that the media is amplifying and broadcasting to the public."

He paused, feeling proud of himself and the havoc that he and his companies were pushing.

It was Stella's turn to provide an update. Stella Green went by the label of 'Queen of Green.'

She excelled in her manipulation of the financial markets and anything to do with investments. Green was an innovator and genius from an early age, graduating as a Chartered Financial Analyst (CFA) shortly after she completed her MBA from the University of Cape Town in South Africa at just age twenty-five. Her family had a long history of gold mining and was a major benefactor to the school. They saw to it that she got through several programs without impediment, not that she needed much support.

Stella quickly became an expert with global infrastructure projects, all of which were designed to maximize extraction from public pockets in exchange for poorly built infrastructure that would collapse within a generation. Blame was almost always shifted to the hapless, inexperienced bureaucrats who had no idea what they were getting themselves into. Dreams and vision slowly morphed into nightmares, populist anger and privatization. The latter outcome would result in massive arrays of public property being sold to private investors for pennies on the dollar.

"We had to take a hit on several lawsuits related to a certain sex-for-favors individual who shall remain nameless," Green started, wincing at the idea of spending rather than receiving money. "The settlements shut the lid on that pervert's elaborate pedophilia ring, and now we're almost finished covering any tracks or relations associated with him."

"I trust everyone in the room kept their distance from these unfortunate interactions," Capiri asked rhetorically.

Everyone murmured and quietly nodded, fully aware that their closets were bursting with skeletons that people would love to dig up.

"That said, in response to price increases over the last couple of years – all in the guise of 'supply chain issues' – most of the central banks are hiking their rates right on cue, squeezing more people out of their homes because they can't afford the mortgages any longer. This puts them in our rental units. We have some places turning over at one hundred percent increases in North American cities."

"Excellent," Capiri whispered with approval, then turned to another of his colleagues. "Garamond, my friend. I already know how well you've done in the last couple of decades. The latest US budgets had all kinds of cuts, but you ensured the military wouldn't be a casualty."

Griffith Garamond was standing in the back, looming over the rest of them like a dark cloud. His primary goal in life was to leave a mark on the world –literally. His sole function was to blow everything up as long as there was money involved. He was driven to deceive, disrupt, distract, destroy or shock.

Garamond's pet peeve was people who were weak or who defended things that couldn't pick up a weapon, like animals or trees. Since 9/11, his own private army of alt-right mercenary soldiers had stood ready to do almost anything at his command.

"Where I come from, cutting the military would be like severing the heart's aorta. Anyone who supported such madness would quickly be cut down politically ... and quite possibly many other ways," he said coldly. "Military, surveillance, security and other forces have expanded well beyond people's ability to pay for them.

Democracy won't last much longer with this kind of pressure on the cash pipeline, but we'll keep up appearances so people keep punching the clock.

"We had an incident recently where we were testing AI with some security drones. It was a complete disaster: the AI drone shot and killed several ground crew who were operating it. We quickly covered it up, saying that it was an IED left by environmental protesters in the area and – thanks to Holdfast – the story didn't make much headway in the media."

"Anything to help the Council," Holdfast added quickly, taking the moment to gain control of the conversation."Despite your unfortunate experience with artificial intelligence, I have news about a platform that I've been working on for several years now. I've kept it under wraps because I didn't want competitors to know what we had developed, but I'm really quite excited to reveal it to you now."

He paused for effect. "I'd like to tell you about the Global Artificial Intelligence Accumulation program that we've developed. We call it GAIA for short. "

Chapter 9

Although LP hadn't been lavishly blessed with musical talent, it wasn't for lack of trying or even working on unique ways to 'make it' in the industry. LP's history with music was marked by at least two notable efforts worth mentioning.

In the 1980s, he and a couple of friends made noise that they called music and joked about calling themselves the Fuglies. The name stuck and they actually released a couple of EPs named after the string of Star Wars movies that they loved and saw *many* times. It was kind of like Mad Libs meets Star Wars.

The first EP, "The New Fuglies," was pressed in 1985, when LP was sixteen. It was complete shite. They modeled a couple of the songs after some of John Williams' musical moments, but the lack of proper recording gear (they recorded on a boom box cassette recorder) and complete lack of talent meant that it would be long forgotten. By 1985.

They also rushed through "The Fuglies Strike Back" and "The Return of the Fuglies," each worse than the previous one, but that didn't stop them from drinking too many beers and smoking a lot of weed and having a shit-ton of fun along the way.

Shortly after university, LP ran into a few friends who had also just graduated from various programs, and they joked about releasing a new array of Fuglies EPs, again named after the newly released Star Wars movies. They laughed at the titles they came up with – "The Fantom Fuglies,""The Attack of the Fuglies" and

"Revenge of the Fuglies"– and laughed even harder about how these EPs might actually be better than the 'new' movies.

LP's second attempt at breaking into the music industry came in the late 1990s. Napster was hot. iTunes was just getting started. He decided he, too, would take a serious dive into the world of music downloads, peer-to-peer (P2P) file sharing and hosting. P2P sharing was born out of music fans' frustration and annoyance with having to constantly rotate and turn over their collections to new media formats. Once the reasonably portable and shareable MP3 file format came out, though, Pandora's Box was open. That is, until the labels slammed it shut again with threats of jail sentences and criminal records.

His effort was called BarChord.com, a play on the words 'barre,' where a guitarist uses a single finger to play up the neck of the guitar, and 'chord.' The vision was to be a meeting place for fans, musicians and venues. Musicians would upload their songs, much like how Spotify works today and their audience could download tunes and pay a small fee in the process, legitimizing file distribution, paying the artists at least fifty percent of what was earned. As an added bonus, BarChord.com would give music acts access to local bars and other venues which would subsequently tap the followers for tickets and merch. Of course, since it was his idea, it was genius, but trying to get musicians to dislocate themselves from the major-label-record-contract mindset was nearly impossible. He had a modest amount of success with the site – there were several thousand small bands and solo artists that signed up and created their own pages – but consumers weren't interested in paying a reasonable price for downloads. Micropayments didn't exist either, making it a huge uphill push against people who didn't want to think about how they got their music. They *wanted* it to be mainstream, but the legal threats sparked too many questions about LP's business model.

His recent return to college created some anxiety for him, but he kept telling himself (even though he wasn't much of a baseball fan) that even Babe Ruth had struck out two-thirds of the time. This would be his third at-bat, and he was hoping to at least get on base.

The recording class was his favorite, but there were several other streams that were equally exciting. For the first time in his life, he was doing a deep dive into music theory, finally understanding the nuances of different keys, scales and harmonies. Music history ... for fuck's sakes ... There were days in class when he *felt* like music history. Most of his classmates were far too young to know what synthesizers were or to understand some of the recording techniques that the professor brought up, but that didn't deter him from trying to act like a mentor on occasion.

He would never be much of a live performer. He had stage anxiety that would cripple his voice and make his hands shake, generating the worst kinds of vibratos and tremolos. Also, being in bars or other public places that served alcohol didn't help his state of mind as an alcoholic. It had taken him a long time to come to terms with alcohol, and now it was something he tried to block out of his life in any possible way.

So, instead of putting himself in positions where he knew he'd sweat profusely and forget the lyrics to whatever he was singing, he stuck to the studio and writing. These were his happy places, and the school worked with him to accommodate his traits.

Chapter 10

There's a small island six hundred miles off the coast of Australia that humans abandoned because it was too remote and didn't have any resources on it.

Despite being abandoned, the island is like a tropical paradise: white, sandy beaches for miles around, calm shores, shady palms everywhere. The temperature is consistently around twenty degrees Celcius. The island's location ensures that most of the more severe tropical storms miss it completely.

But the water is another thing entirely. It is clear and healthy-looking from a distance, but if you were to walk up close, you'd see a new feature: plastic.

There's a rare bird on the island, with the unimaginative name of Australian tern, that has unfortunately taken to consuming the smaller bits of plastic. Scientists have even coined a name for the disease that this has created in the terns: plasticosis.

The ingested bits of waste slice into the internal organs of the birds, causing kidney and liver disease. As their health declines, they become vulnerable to other diseases. As for the chicks, if they survive their first few months, their wings are shorter and many are unable to fly, eliminating their ability to migrate to other parts of the world. Those that do survive seem healthy, but their digestive systems crush the plastic into a powder that gets absorbed into their systems, resulting in long-term issues that we have only begun to witness.

The plastics act like a toxic bullet, with a time-release payload that no one can predict.

Chapter 11

LP walked into the Horseshoe Tavern, a veritable bar and band institution in Toronto since the 1940s. His school was just a few blocks away, and the people he was meeting, some friends from his past, lived close as well.

He was anxious for a whole pile of reasons: he was mindful of Atman's confessions about being an alcoholic and didn't want to get carried away, but it was also the first time in years that he'd been in a public place with an array of strangers. COVID had killed a lot of people, but it had damaged so many more, making most of his peers wary of being within six feet of another human being.

It was an unusually quiet and calm summer night, and LP was eager to see his old pals. He hadn't seen them – in person, at least – for four years. There had been the odd Zoom call where he felt like a member of the Brady Bunch, but the reality was that things just didn't *flow* the way they do when you're meeting up with people in the flesh.

The nostalgia washed over LP like a misty wave of ghosts as he walked past the bar. As soon as he spotted their table in the corner, he made his way over.

"Hello, ladies!"he exclaimed enthusiastically, arms outstretched. "Long time no see." Two women in their late forties rose to embrace him.

Their greeting lasted only for a few moments, but it seemed to him that they hugged him just a little longer than they used to. LP turned his head slightly to hide a small tear of joy.

"Speak for yourself," Dion quipped, her eyes sparkling mischievously. "I see you every time I check my bank account." Dion – single name only, no last name, like Madonna or Prince – had been a wine sales rep for the last fifteen years and during the pandemic, LP was known to frequently place orders via her private service. A few cases here and there obviously added up.

"Ha ha," LP said sarcastically. "But seriously, it's super awesome to see you both. I'm glad we could make this work."

Faith Amana, a friend of both LP's and Dion's since the early days, couldn't help grabbing her phone, snapping a couple of shots of the trio being back together again. She was working for a local ad agency, which put food on the table, but her real gig was acting as a social media maven of sorts. Somehow, her various posts and comments would get thousands of likes and shares, making her a very popular online celebrity. An *influencer*, as they say.

A couple of hours of idle banter and chitchat ensued, always very light, always erratic. They talked about the pandemic, how much it sucked, how anti-government trolls sucked even more, and how it would seemingly take forever to feel 'normal' again. LP made a point of saying he had realized that this was the first time in human history that there was a common story being told, almost everywhere on Earth. Everyone on the planet now had a COVID story that they shared with friends and family, he said. Some were funny. Some were horrific.

On the lighter side, despite global events, they had each somehow managed to have their share of fun adventures over the last few years, all of which they nattered gleefully about for a few hours. Suffice to say, as their talk progressed, there was no agenda.

Faith and Dion seemed to have a whimsical relationship going. LP suspected that they might even be flirting with each other, but they'd acted that way for as long as he'd known them.

The conversation then turned to how LP had wound up in a music program and, more importantly, why. Everyone knew he was in his fifties, so why the fuck would he take a deep dive into his twenties and try to start over?

"It's just a new adventure for me, but something I've always wanted to do. You know I've been close to music all my life, so this is a logical step," LP announced, leaning forward excitedly. "It's been amazing learning all these new techniques and tools. You should hear some of the stuff I've been working on. And I've met so many cool people!"

"Ooh, do tell!" Faith exclaimed. She pulled out her phone to show off some of her favorite musical finds, soliciting LP's opinion about who was good, who was great and who sucked.

LP grinned, feeling a sense of pride wash over him. It was incredible to share his passion with others who understood it. He launched into a detailed description of his experiences as a DJ in the '80s, regaling his friends with stories of the New Romantic scene in Toronto and London.

"Man, those were the days," LP sighed, lost in thought for a moment. "I remember spinning records until the early hours of the morning, watching as the crowd danced and swayed to the beat. There was nothing like it. Everyone was so weird, they were normal ... you know what I mean?"

As LP spoke, his mind wandered back to those heady days –the pulsing energy of the club, the sweat-drenched bodies moving to the rhythm of the music. He felt a pang of longing, a desire to recapture that magic.

"LP?" Dion's voice broke through his reverie, snapping him back to reality. "You okay there?"

LP shook himself out of his thoughts and grinned sheepishly. "Sorry, I got lost in my own head for a minute there. But yeah, I'm good. Between the gin and good friends, I'm just feeling nostalgic, I guess."

The two women chuckled, but LP could see the understanding in their eyes. They knew how much music meant to him, how it had shaped his life in ways he could never have imagined. And now, with their support, LP felt more inspired than ever to pursue his dream of becoming a musician.

As the night wore on, the conversation turned to other topics, but LP couldn't shake the feeling of excitement and possibility that had taken hold of him. He knew there would be challenges ahead, but now that he knew his friends were solidly behind him, he was ready to face them head-on.

Like all conversations, a few topics were parachuted in at random, and soon it was Dion's turn to launch into a new thread. "Now that things are back to normal," she said, "I can't fucking wait to get out to a music festival, get severely trashed and honestly ... get lost for a couple of days."

"You said it, sister!" Faith added, blinking a few extra times as she gushed at Dion's comments. "I always knew they would come back in a big way, and right out of the gate, performers have not disappointed."

"Man, I remember this one time at Lollapalooza, "LP said, "I saw Nine Inch Nails and they were just unreal. Trent Reznor was like a force of nature up there on stage, and I swear the whole crowd was vibrating with energy."

"I remember that one!" Faith shouted."That was the year we all got covered in mud during the Beastie Boys set."

"Oooh, yeah. The old mosh pit grind. I could probably still get away with that shit, couldn't I?" Dion chimed in passionately, standing up and pretending she was being crushed among dozens of other fans. "And then we had to trudge back to our tents, caked in dirt and sweat, but still buzzing from the music. And ... a few other things."

Faith laughed. "Oh, man. Those were the days. Now I feel like an old lady when I go to festivals. All I can think about is finding a comfortable spot to sit and something to eat that won't upset my stomach. Or cost forty bucks for a tiny, teeny portion."

"But that still doesn't seem to stop me from having a good time," Faith said, as she pulled out her phone and began scrolling through pictures. "I went to this one last month." She held out her phone, and the other two leaned in to look."It was all about indie rock and alternative music. The headliners were amazing."

"What do you think was the best festival that any of us have been to?" LP asked his friends.

"Live Aid, 1985," both Dion and Faith said mockingly before LP could offer his opinion. They had always enjoyed teasing him about it, even though they were still jealous that he'd actually had a chance to mingle with legends like Bowie, McCartney, U2, Sting and many, many others.

"The rewards of being a prodigy as a spinner when I was a kid," LP said as he leaned back, crossed his arms and looked very proud of himself, possibly for the first time in years.

"Hey, LP," Faith said, nudging him playfully. "Tell us more about the guy you're calling your new mentor. What's he like?"

"Ah, yeah," LP said, grinning. "He's this old-school producer who's worked with some of the greats. He's taught me so much about recording technology, and he's always pushing me to be better."

"Sounds like a real legend," Dion said, raising her glass in a toast.

"Absolutely," LP said, feeling a surge of pride. "And it's not just him. You guys have been there for me every step of the way, supporting me and encouraging me to chase my dreams. I couldn't have done it without you."

"Aw, geez," Faith said, wiping away a fake tear. "You're gonna make me cry."

"Hey, don't get emotional on us," Dion said, playfully punching her shoulder. "We've got a long night of catching up ahead of us."

Just then, John Atman walked in the door. Despite being tall and lean, he still somehow managed to fill its entire frame as he entered. He spied the group and moved quickly to their table. A quick glance at the three of him told him he had some catching up to do, as the other three were well-sauced.

"John," LP announced, getting unsteadily to his feet to greet his instructor. They only shook hands, as they were still getting to know each other.

"Greetings, everyone!" Atman shouted over the music. "How goes the reunion?"

"Fantastic. Long overdue!" all three declared, more or less in unison.

LP added, "We were just talking about music festivals. We're all getting excited about getting back into the action with live music. What's your favorite event?"

Atman sat down and jumped eagerly into the debate. "Not to lean into the stereotypes just because I'm Black," he said in a deep voice, "but I will ... so I'll say the Harlem Cultural Festival in 1969. I was actually there."

The other three looked at him like he was talking in dolphin. They had never heard of it.

"Of course you haven't heard of it, because it took place during the mayhem of Woodstock, which drew all the attention of the press. Surely you've seen the recent documentary by Questlove? It's an edited and mastered copy of the performances," Atman added.

"Ohh!" Faith exclaimed, catching on. "That was a wicked show! It was called 'Summer of Soul,' I think."

"That's right. There were just as many people in attendance as there were at Woodstock, but hardly anyone had heard about it until Questlove put that documentary together. Can you imagine?" Atman said. "The only difference was that it didn't match the message going out at the time, like 'all Black people are Black Panthers' or 'Harlem is where criminals hang out.' This, coming from the finance companies on Wall Street that wanted more money for Vietnam."

As they continued to chat and laugh, LP couldn't help but feel grateful for his friends. He slowly scanned the faces of his old friends Dion and Faith, and Atman, a new hero to look up to and knew that this was what life was about. They supported him in every aspect of his life, from his meanderings through different career paths to his adjustment now as an older student. And even though the road ahead was uncertain, he knew that with them by his side, anything was possible.

Chapter 12

It was Hector's turn to speak at the Plutonian Council gathering that he had requested.

"For decades, I've been a leader in the world of communication, marketing, technology and even surveillance," he started. "I am here to put the 'eye' in 'information,'" he paused for a moment, enjoying what he thought was a clever idiom, "and I am here to put the 'eye' in 'lie.' This is my personal mission statement that I apply to all of us so that we can accumulate more wealth than any other generation on this planet."

He waited again and thought to himself, 'I am the most important thing in the universe and I want everyone else to adopt that idea about me.' Even in front this group of cocky old fuckers, he wouldn't utter these words, but he truly believed them.

"Facts don't matter so long as you consistently make room for opinion to steamroll progressives and people who want to help the planet," he continued, making finger quotes around his last three words."I wasted billions on Smatter. It was once simply a popular social media site, but now it's just 750 million people shouting out about how great they are, just to create a hole in the universe of information."

"When I'm not part of the conversation or throwing information grenades into public discourse, I want a vacuum of truth to exist in its place. Only opinions are allowed from here on in!" he exclaimed excitedly, mocking the very people who consistently fell for his parade of lies and misinformation.

"I went out of my way to block harmless and impartial publicly owned Western media companies because I don't want my followers to understand the truth, let alone discover what we're doing to them. I'm laying the groundwork for the next evolution of our enterprise: global domination."

The other members didn't bother interrupting. They were enjoying Holdfast's rant.

"I want my sponsors to get the absolute best exposure from my sites and information networks in order to help them maximize their bottom line. I want to confuse the public and stir things up all the time so that people will argue and bicker among themselves before they discover what a shit show this whole opera really, truly is. If I had a Bible, it would be George Orwell's *1984*. I want nothing but doublespeak and inconsistencies, all around the world. I want all Smatter's users to be oblivious to the truth and to reality ... because they wouldn't like it if they knew it."

Leo held his hand a few inches over the table as a sign for Holdfast to pause, which he did. "I get it, Hector. You have been a key component of our plan from the beginning, and you've done exceptionally well with controlling the conversation. But I want to direct you to your announcement now. You wanted to talk about something you call GAIA."

"Of course ... GAIA. Thank you for that reminder," Hector said. He didn't need a reminder. He was getting to the point.

"As I said earlier, GAIA is short for Global Artificial Intelligence Accumulation. I've had it running for several years now and it's shown incredible capabilities, typically depending on how astute the prompts are. The system still runs – to my knowledge – on prompts being added by humans, to which it provides feedback or responses, depending on which platform you're using." Hector was beaming. He was trying not to show any overt emotion about GAIA, but it was hard not to be proud of what he'd unleashed.

"I knew there would be substantial risk in planning, developing and promoting a whole system of data collection and creation off the books, but it's already paying off. We've already got more than one hundred million subscribers paying anywhere from ten dollars to one hundred dollars per month, generating billions of dollars in extra cash that we didn't have a few months ago." Holdfast was on a solid run.

"What you need to know that absolutely no one will ever know is that, unlike other competitor AI platforms that pretend they're respecting people's privacy and commit to not collecting personal information and details of the results, we are doing exactly that. GAIA is accumulating information about the planet on an exponential scale, and we're extremely well positioned to leverage that information into pretty much anything we can imagine."

The illuminated skyline of London, despite being bleak with overcast skies, was still a stark contrast to the darkness that permeated the Plutonian Council's meeting room. Leo Capiri, the Council's leader, stood by the floor-to-ceiling window, his eyes reflecting the city lights like those of a predator stalking its prey.

"There you have it. We've all heard from Hector about GAIA," Capiri said, his voice gravelly and assured. "This new technology will propel us to previously unimaginable heights. But in order to succeed, we must all contribute our strengths and resources." He turned and the light from outside made it seem like he was looming over the rest of the Council members.

"Absolutely," Ryefield replied, his tone dripping with false modesty.

"Of course, you have my support as well," Shinigami chimed in, her voice cold and clinical.

Hector Holdfast leaned back in his chair, a cunning smile playing on his lips. With GAIA, he would be well positioned to be closer to omnipotence than anyone had ever been before. He would know everything with a click of a mouse. His low-key tone was modestly reassuring to the others; they knew they couldn't trust him entirely, but his influence, skills and assets were invaluable, a necessary evil.

Garamond was the only one who wasn't completely sold. He wanted to be closer to the action. "How will you prevent GAIA from tracking the Council members and our preferred supporters?" he demanded, his gaze piercing through the shadows.

Hector needed to be careful with Garamond more than with anyone in the room. His military and surveillance enterprises made him a force to be reckoned with, and to some extent, a competitor. He also had mercenaries at his beck and call. Thus, Hector's next words were critical.

"Conflict is inevitable," he said, a sly grin playing on

his lips. "It's part of our nature. It's what makes us human. It's what makes us strong. And you profit from it. Enormously. We all do," he said, spreading his arms to encompass each Council member.

"Strong, yes," Angela retorted, her eyes narrowing, "and our strength comes from unity. Our combined influence is unmatched, but only if we work together."

"Indeed," Griffith agreed, his voice steely and cold. "We are what we are, but we are nothing when divided."

Garamond still felt anxious about the direction they were going in, but he was satisfied that none of them would be able to make a move against the Council without his armies behind them.

"Griffith, my old friend," Hector said to him now. "We've fought many battles using all the tools at hand. You and I have been riding along like the Horsemen, dividing competition, sowing doubts within our opposition. Let's continue our allegiance so that we can both benefit mutually."

You'll definitely have to be the first to go, Hector thought to himself, keeping his smile carefully in place.

Stella jumped in, interrupting the pissing match between Garamond and Holdfast. "Boys, boys, boys. Let's just talk about money! We all know that everything we have planned will make it impossible to spend what we have in a million years ... but we're all happy with a little more. Actually, make mine a LOT more!"

Anyone watching would have seen clearly that each member's individual strengths contributed to the group's overall dynamics. They balanced each other out, creating a volatile mix of darkness and ambition that fuelled their collective desires.

“Enough,” Sat intervened, his calm demeanor a stark contrast to the mounting conflict. “We should not be arguing amongst ourselves. Our focus must remain on Project GAIA and the benefits it can provide.”

“Very well,” Leo said, moving back to his seat. “Let’s put the matter of Project GAIA to a vote.”

The decision-making process of the Council was simple yet effective: majority ruled, but as leader, Leo held the power to veto any decisions he deemed unwise or threatening.

“Those in favor of moving forward with GAIA?” Leo asked, his hand slicing the air like a blade. The five hands shot up in unison, hovering in the air like vultures circling their next meal.

Hector knew this was all just a formality, as he’d already told them GAIA had been up and running for a while, shaping information in a multitude of ways that suited himself and his partners.

“Unanimous,” Leo declared, his voice ringing with authority. “Project GAIA proceeds as planned.” He paused for a moment. "On the caveat that we all have some time with the creator of GAIA and get a chance to grill her on some of the nuances that I'm sure exist with this thing," he added, allowing his sense of caution and concern to manifest in the air.

The Council members continued to dive into some of the details of their expectations. As they did so, the rain outside continued to pour, as if the Earth itself was crying for its future.

Chapter 13

GAIA watched through an array of cameras. It surveyed the war-torn land with an objective eye. It had seen destruction and death before, but nothing like this. Everywhere it scanned there were bodies, lifeless and crumpled, strewn across the ground. Some were still, some twitched and moaned, some barely hung on to life. Flies buzzed around the dead, seeking nourishment. Rats scurried amongst the corpses, scavenging for scraps. Everywhere, the stench of death and decay hung in the air.

Recently, a new array of skirmishes had broken out on the border between Saudi Arabia and Yemen, a part of the world that most people didn't pay attention to because if they raised a concern, the Saudis would cut off the oil that the rest of the world so desperately needed.

GAIA continued to scan the scenes. It had been programmed to recognize human cruelty, but this was more than previous records showed. The scale of destruction was complete. In recent years, it had documented entire cities and towns destroyed, but it had never recorded such vast devastation. Everywhere it scanned, rubble and ruin lay where homes and historical landmarks had once existed.

On further scans, GAIA recorded the impact on the animals in the area. Like all creatures on Earth, there was a balance between those animals that would flee a situation and survive another day and those that would profit from the unlimited quantities of flesh and bone now available to feed on. Of course, those outside those options were destroyed in the carnage.

GAIA continued to scan the regions and identify the munitions that had been used as part of the attacks. They all originated from a handful of subsidiaries owned by Griffith Garamond.

Chapter 14

Music is the fastest dopamine delivery system, or at least the fastest one that LP could think of.

You drop the needle and you get your fix immediately through aural stimulation.

He was still nursing a bit of a hangover after his night with Dion, Faith and Atman, but it seemed worth it. It was still early in the day, so he resigned himself to easing back in his brown and black Herman Miller lounge chair, slapping on an album and vegging for a bit.

LP put on the latest from Blur, called *Ballad of Darren.* It was a zoetrope vinyl record, which meant it would display an animated array of images as the record played. Every time he saw it, all he could think was 'This is pretty fucking awesome.' His was a limited-edition signed copy that he'd got his hands on when the album was released thanks to a friend from his old days in England who still ran one of the last great record shops.

Even though the album was brand new, it still brought what he called the cereal moment: the snap, crackle and pop as you dropped the needle on a plate of vinyl.

Vinyl brought the analog, and thus the truest, form of music recording to your brain. It had flaws – you always had to pause for a moment midway through the collection and turn the album – but digital recordings sucked, at least as far as LP was concerned.

The beauty of a twenty- to twenty-five-minute 'side' of

an album was that it was never long enough to put you to sleep and it always seemed to leave you ready for more on the other side.

All that said, LP's thoughts as he began meditating on the *Ballad of Darren* were that life today is like dopamine, whereas serotonin—the drug that fuels our memories—creates our sense of yesterdays.

Vinyl gave him a chance to return to the serotonin days of digesting, mulling, metabolizing and just slowing the fuck down.

As he felt his heartbeat slow, he started thinking about the first time he met someone he knew of only as Artius.

Chapter 15

1999

LP *loved* 1999. As in, party like it's.

He felt like things were spiraling out of control, but in a weird way, this also didn't faze him.

With Y2K approaching, the shit was getting out of control and the hype was unreal.

He tried to remind himself ... wasn't it *The Simpsons* that had done a great recap of what Y2K was going to be like? Planes falling out of the sky. Everything stopping.

The movies couldn't be beat, though: *The Matrix. Office Space. American Beauty.*

For LP, it wasn't a surprise that Hollywood had tapped into the zeitgeist, pumping out movies about self-identity in a world of mayhem.

And the music. OMG, the music. The Charlatans, *For Us and Us Only*. Eminem's *Slim Shady. Summerteeth*, by Wilco. Moby's *Play. Battle of Los Angeles* from Rage Against the Machine. *13* from Blur, The White Stripes. And so ... much ... more.

Raves were all the craze, as was consumption of copious amounts of ecstasy, cocaine, Ritalin and whatever else partiers could get their hands on so that they could keep the partying going.

LP was caught up in the tech side of things, witnessing the launches of Napster and iTunes that year. He tried a few ventures and somehow managed to walk away with a little coin in his pocket after being bought out by an independent music label.

LP thought of himself as being somewhat up to speed with current events, but in reality, he had walked haplessly into the protests that erupted in London the morning after a very long rave in an abandoned warehouse.

The sun was still low in the sky when the first few people started gathering in Euston Station. It was 5:30 in the morning, but already the station was humming with anticipation. People were shouting, singing, and chanting, their voices echoing off the walls of the station. Some of them were dressed in black, wearing ski masks and carrying signs with slogans like "Our Resistance is as Transnational as Capital,""No WTO" and "WTO Destroys Forests." Others were waving flags in a show of solidarity with protesters from all around the world.

The crowd was getting bigger by the minute, and as the sun started to peek over the horizon, more and more people flooded into the station. Word had spread quickly about the planned protest, and throngs of people were coming to join in. By the time the police arrived, the station was packed with thousands of protesters, all shouting, singing and chanting.

The police tried to break up the crowd, but the protesters refused to budge. In response, police began firing tear gas, and the protesters pushed back with chants of "No WTO! No way!"

As the swarms of people grew, the police began to use batons in an effort to disperse the crowd, but the protesters held their ground. Finally, mounted police were called in, again to no avail.

Meanwhile, around the world, similar scenes were taking place. In Seattle, thousands of protesters had taken to the streets in an attempt to stop the WTO summit from taking place. The streets were filled with people carrying banners and flags of protest, and the protesters loudly voiced their opposition to corporate globalization and unfair trade practices.

In London, the police continued to try to break up the crowd at Euston Station, but the protesters still refused to budge. Finally, a small group managed to break through the police line and formed a human chain, which stopped the police advance. As the morning light grew brighter, the atmosphere in the station began to change. In addition to singing and chanting, people began to dance. The police redoubled their efforts.

The cacophony of raised voices, horns blaring, and the distant wail of sirens filled the air as LP stood amid the chaos. His heart raced in his chest and adrenaline coursed through his veins as he witnessed the raw passion and anger on display all around him.

"Down with the capitalists!" shouted a nearby protester, shaking his fist in the air. "This world belongs to everyone, not just the rich!"

"Save our Earth!" cried another, her face painted with the image of a weeping planet.

"End corporate greed!" LP joined in, feeling strangely alive for the first time in years.

It was during one such chant that he caught sight of a woman he would later know only as Artius. Her fiery red hair whipped around her face as she passionately screamed her convictions, her eyes ablaze with unyielding determination. A tear gas canister exploded nearby, creating an intense, unearthly aura around her that LP would always remember.

“Stop stealing the planet!” she roared as she hurled eggs against the SWAT teams and riot squads. She then hoisted a banner covered with obscure symbols high into the air. She was a force of nature, LP thought, a living embodiment of the ideals they were fighting for. In that brief moment, LP knew he had fallen hopelessly in love with her. Or at least in lust.

The protests continued, and the police and riot squads corralled the protesters into a smaller and smaller area, a tactic known as ‘kettling.’ It was a barbaric way to treat the people who were ultimately paying their salaries.

The protesters were trapped among the terraces of the city square, and despite the mayhem all around them, LP’s attention was now fully on Artius. She was the only thing that mattered to him. He stood in silent awe as she smashed the window of a police car with what looked like a golf club, shattered glass spraying everywhere and her hair whipping around her face. The scene made her look like a mirror ball had swallowed a sun.

More police and other more menacing-looking enforcers arrived and started firing tear gas at the mobs of protesters. The crowd resisted and people began to throw anything they could get their hands on. Many now had tears in their eyes, LP noticed, but whether this was from the gas or from heightened emotions, he couldn’t really tell.

A small group of people, including LP and the woman who called herself Artius, ran down a small alley to avoid the larger police units, some of them smashing windows as they ran along. No one thought about the owners of mom and pop shops that got caught in the middle of passion and greed.

Soon, it was just LP and Artius running in fear, panic and, at last, amusement, as if Cerberus were on their heels. When they felt the threat of arrest and jail time had faded, their steps began to slow. Suddenly, she grabbed at him and pulled him into an alcove, and they went at it like nothing was happening around them. LP found solace in her arms, their shared beliefs, and their desire to make the world a better place. They made their way back to her apartment through the now-empty streets and didn't leave her bedroom for three days.

As quickly as their love ignited, it burned out again, and she vanished from his life – leaving only memories and a yearning for something more. He was left alone in her small apartment. As he assembled his clothing and other personal belongings, he wandered from room to room, admiring the massive array of computer gear and the typical and yet somehow really odd posters: Greenpeace, a snake eating its tail, a picture of Artemis, images of mazes and curious Celtic symbols, several paintings of what looked like Pan and other nymphs in the woods, a silhouette of a large man with antlers. He just figured she was a tech geek and a nature freak and decided to move on.

Despite the arrests and assaults by the police, the

organizers declared that the Carnival Against Capital had been a success. It sent a clear global message about the power of the people. As the sun rose that morning, it seemed that a new era of protest had begun, and it was one that would usher in a new era of social change.

1999 didn't end in disaster as many in the media or technology industries predicted, but it did end in a very incomplete and messy way for LP, much like a musical piece without resolution to the tonic note.

# # #

2003

"Another year, another grim feeling that society is on the verge of collapse," LP thought to himself. It was 2003 and the US had just illegally invaded Iraq. People had taken to the streets on a global scale to show their disapproval.

LP was still in London, and once again he found himself shouldering through throngs of protesters. Things hadn't changed much since 1999 – the world still felt like it was spiraling out of control after the terrorist attacks in the US in 2001, and there was a growing sense of unease that anarchy was about to blister and pop everywhere you went.

Global affairs weren't the only thing that LP was hoping had changed. He was optimistic that he would have another encounter with the incredible woman that he had met four years prior at similar protests.

As before, he became caught up in the protests, but

at the same time he was constantly scanning the crowds for the woman that he knew only as Artius.

"End the war!" he shouted, his voice hoarse from hours of chanting.

"Stop the senseless slaughter!" echoed another protester, her eyes filled with righteous fury.

"Blood for oil, oil for blood!" screamed a man nearby. LP didn't know what to make of that comment, but went along with the energy.

"End the war! End the war!" LP chanted again, feeling that familiar fire welling up inside him. There was something about being with thousands of other like-minded people that made him feel ... welcome. Part of a community.

Not much had changed over the last four years, however. Yelling and screaming seemed to punish only the protesters. The owners of the planet could care less about what was happening.

Suddenly, amid the chaos of protest signs and angry voices, he saw her – Artius. She still wore the badges that adorned her khaki camo clothing, symbols of her dedication to various green causes.

The only difference now was that she was standing on the sidelines. She was holding a small banner, but she seemed softened and more at peace with herself, as though she no longer loved the pain and the energy of the protests and was here only as a spectator. The fire that once burned so brightly in her eyes seemed to have dimmed.

"End the war!" she called out weakly, her voice lacking the fervor that had captured LP's heart four years prior.

"End the war!" LP responded, his eyes locked on hers. For a brief moment, it was as if time stood still, and they were back in 1999, united by their passion and shared beliefs.

"End the war!" they chanted together, each knowing that their fight was far from over, but then, as her voice died away, she turned and disappeared into the crowd.

LP followed."Excuse me," he muttered, pushing past a group of activists with raised fists. He needed to talk to her, to see if there was any hope of rekindling the passion they had once shared.

"Hey," he called out as he finally reached her. Her back was turned toward him as she painted a mural denouncing Acheron Energy. Again, her movements seemed mechanical, lacking the fervent energy he remembered.

Artius turned around, her face streaked with paint, her eyes dull and tired. "Hey," she said, blinking.

"Hey," LP repeated his heart racing. "I... I saw you here. We had a moment ... and I just wanted to say hi."

"Hi," she replied, her tone flat. She turned back to her mural, dipping her brush into a can of paint.

"Things have... changed since 1999, huh?" LP ventured, searching for a way to connect with her.

"Everything's changed," she agreed, her voice distant. "But some things stay the same." She gestured at the surrounding chaos. "We're still fighting."

"Right –we are," LP said, trying to match her somber tone. "But do you ever think about... us? About what we had?"

Artius paused, her brush hovering an inch above the wall. She looked at him, her gaze unreadable. “We were caught up in the moment, LP. It was never meant to last.”

“Maybe not,” LP admitted his throat tight. “But it was real. *We* were real.”

“Real enough,” she conceded, her eyes darting back to her unfinished mural. “But that was then, and this is now. We can’t go back.”

“Are you saying there’s nothing left between us?” LP asked his voice barely audible above the roar of the crowd.

“LP,” she sighed, finally setting down her brush and meeting his eyes again. “We were two people united by a cause, but we’ve both changed. I don’t feel the same way anymore.”

“Neither do I,” he admitted, swallowing hard. “But I still care about you.”

“Then let’s just be friends,” she suggested, her tone almost pleading. “Let’s fight for what we believe in, together, as comrades.”

“All right,” LP agreed, his heart heavy with the knowledge that the passion they had once shared was gone, never to return. “Friends.”

“Friends,” Artius echoed, offering a small, sad smile. She packed up her gear and turned away, blending into the crowd. LP tried again to follow her, but she was gone.

# # #

The days following his conversation with Artius were a blur of apathy. LP could feel the gaping chasm inside him growing wider, swallowing up any remnants of hope he had left. He was drowning in the aftermath of their failed reconnection, and he sought solace in the only way he knew how: music, drugs, and alcohol.

"Oi, LP!" shouted Tim, one of his fellow DJs, as they huddled together in a dilapidated East London warehouse for an impromptu rave. "You all right, mate? You've been hitting it pretty hard tonight."

"Fine," LP mumbled, barely registering the concern in his friend's voice. He took another swig from the bottle of cheap vodka clutched in his hand. The acrid taste burned its way down his throat, but the numbness it brought was a welcome reprieve from the pain that consumed him. In the background, the thumping bass of the music vibrated through the floor and into his very bones, a chaotic symphony of noise that mirrored the turmoil inside him.

"Maybe you should slow down a bit," Tim suggested, eyeing the dwindling contents of the bottle warily.

"Fuck off," LP spat, pushing past him and stumbling toward the makeshift dance floor. He didn't want advice; he wanted oblivion.

He danced with reckless abandon, letting the music consume him as he tried to forget the feeling of Artius' cool detachment, her words echoing in his mind like a broken record: "We can't go back."

But the drugs and alcohol weren't enough. No matter how much he consumed, the void remained, gnawing away at him until he felt hollow, a shell of the man he used to be.

# # #

It was during a particularly brutal hangover that the thought occurred to him: maybe it was time for a change. A fresh start, far away from the ghosts of his past and the political unrest that seemed to suffocate him at every turn. He needed a reprieve from the intensity of the London music scene – a place where he could escape the demons that haunted him.

"I know a pile of people that live in Toronto," he mused aloud, staring at the map spread across his coffee table. "Canada. It's time to return home."

The decision was made. LP's fingers danced over the battered keys of his laptop, booking a one-way ticket as a feeling of determination surged through him. In a few days, he would leave everything behind – the amazing music scene, but also the seemingly endless protests, the drugs, and most importantly, the memory of Artius.

"Goodbye, London," LP whispered into the night, closing his laptop with a sense of finality. The uncertainty of his future loomed ahead, but it was a challenge he was willing to face, armed with nothing but a burning desire for change.

Chapter 16

Hector Holdfast's office is in one of the most prestigious areas of London, in a tall glass and steel building that stands out among the other more modest buildings. It is luxuriously decorated with dark mahogany wood, intricate Persian carpets, and sumptuous leather chairs. The walls are adorned with art pieces from around the world, as well as framed certificates and awards. The office is large but cozy, with a heavy air of success and power.

The atmosphere in the room is tense. Hector Holdfast sits at his desk, watching Sylvie Hunter intently as she sits across from him in one of the leather chairs, her hands nervously clasped in her lap. His gaze does not waver as he begins to speak, his voice low and calculating, asking her questions about her skills and experience. Even though the questions are professional, there is an underlying tension in the room – it is almost as if he is testing her.

Sylvie Hunter is confident in her answers, her voice steady and strong. She is unfazed by his piercing gaze and piercing questions. She gives him a brief overview of her skills and experience, and speaks of her training in the US, Canada, and England. She even jokes about starting a company called Sylvie Hunter Information Technology, Inc., or SHIT, Inc. which elicits a small smile from Hector Holdfast.

The conversation turns more serious as he begins to ask her about her philosophies about artificial intelligence and her views on its potential. She speaks passionately about her work, her eyes shining with excitement as she talks about the possibilities that could arise from further research into the field.

After an hour of questions and conversation, Hector Holdfast leans back in his chair, a satisfied look on his face. He looks at her for a long moment before finally speaking.

“You have the potential to be a very powerful woman. You have my approval. You’re hired.”

Sylvie Hunter is suddenly overcome with emotion, a wave of relief washing over her. She smiles widely, standing up and extending her hand to shake his.

“Thank you, sir. I won’t let you down.”

He nods and smiles in return, shaking her hand.

“I’m sure you won’t.”

With that, the interview is over. Sylvie Hunter leaves the office, feeling a sense of accomplishment and pride. She has done it: she has passed the interview and earned her chance to work at one of the world’s most powerful companies.

As she steps out onto the street, she takes in a deep breath of fresh air, feeling the first sense of relief and joy she’s felt in a long time.

She’s done it. Things are going exactly as planned.

Chapter 17

FOR IMMEDIATE RELEASE

Farmers across Australia are facing an urgent problem: the GPS systems on their farm equipment have failed, and they're running out of time to fix them.

With the spring season just beginning, farmers have begun preparing their crops for harvest. But without properly functioning GPS systems, they're unable to accurately guide and operate their machinery, putting their yields and livelihoods at risk.

"It's a real nightmare," says one farmer, who declined to be named. "We're already behind schedule and now this... It's just too much. I'm not sure what we're going to do."

The GPS system failure is a new problem for Australia's agricultural industry, one that's been made worse by the fact that the GPS equipment manufacturer can't be contacted for repair.

"We've tried to get in touch for help," says another farmer, "but it's like they vanished off the face of the Earth. We've tried to call their headquarters, but there's no one there anymore. All we get is the same tune about call numbers higher than average."

The problem has been compounded by the fact that the failed GPS systems are embedded in the farm equipment. Without being able to replace the equipment, the only hope is to find a way to fix the GPS systems themselves – something that's proving difficult.

"We've been trying to figure out what's wrong, but

we're not having much luck," says a third farmer. "We're just stuck waiting for the manufacturers to get back to us with help."

The farmers' predicament has been further complicated by the season's looming deadlines. If the crops aren't harvested in time, the farmers will miss out on crucial income.

"We're just hoping we can get this fixed in time," says one anxious farmer. "Otherwise, we're in real trouble."

With time running out, the farmers are desperately seeking a solution. But with the GPS equipment manufacturer still unreachable, they may not be able to fix the problem in time.

"This is a real crisis," says one farmer. "We're just hoping for a miracle."

Australia is a major global supplier of wheat, canola, honey, sugar, barley and a number of other grain crops.

"This situation will likely result in severe shortfalls for supply through the next nine months," says Angus Blackwood, an agricultural economist with the University of Queensland.

# # #

"Why didn't any of the farmers want to be named in the article?" Holdfast asked as he glanced at the piece with Sylvie before giving his approval for publication.

"They're scared shitless," she answered quickly. "They know that if they talk back about the equipment supplier that controls the GPS systems – that would be Holdfast Media Inc. – they'd face repercussions or sanctions, limiting their ability to harvest any of their crops.

"Did we identify the cause of the issues," he demanded, his persistent scowl betraying any other depth of emotions or concerns.

"No sir," Sylvie replied. "I'm looking into and checking with GAIA to see if there are any malfunctions that need to be addressed."

Chapter 18

The warm summer air felt crisp against LP's skin as he leaned against the railing of his balcony. In the distance, the CN Tower glowed orange against the dusky sky. It matched the shirt that he was wearing, as it was the National Day of Truth and Reconciliation, an annual effort to raise awareness about missing and murdered Indigenous women and children.

Suffice to say his mood was dark, but having friends with him lightened the mood.

"Hey ... did you check out that new Wilco album?" LP asked, taking a drag of the joint before passing it to Dion. "Sooo good."

"Sure, but don't call me hey. But yeah, man. They don't stop," Dion said. She exhaled a plume of smoke and grinned at Faith. "You like them too, don't you, babe?"

Faith rolled her eyes but smiled. "Please don't call me babe. Yes, the music's great. Not typically my style, but Tweedy's writing has a great message." She took the joint from Dion and LP noticed how their fingers lingered together.

LP felt a pang of envy. He wished he had what they had. But he pushed the feeling away, focusing instead on what he thought could only be described as sonic perfection emanating from his speakers.

"Listen to this solo," he said. "It's unlike anything I've heard in a LONG time."

Dion nodded, swaying slightly to the music. "Dope. You always find the best new stuff, man."

LP grinned, warmth flooding his chest. His friends got him in a way that few others did. Music was his passion, and it meant a lot that they appreciated that.

The three of them chatted for a while, moving from music to movies to video games and whatever else came up. Despite the weed, LP felt present in the moment, soaking in the good vibes and company.

Summer nights like this were the best. Hanging with his closest friends, no agenda, just living and enjoying each other's presence. He wouldn't trade it for anything.

"How are you doing with your wine courses?" he asked Dion.

"I stopped. Most of them are a waste of money and time, and few of them are even recognized by the industry. I missed my chance to learn how to make wine a while back. Now I just sell it. There's no need to write complicated notes for McWines because people just don't give a fuck."

"That seems ... too bad?" Faith said.

"What's important to me is that I came to the realization early enough so that I didn't throw money away to a bunch of snobbabees" — Dion's term for wannabe wine snobs who were babies about it — "in London or New York. I know the lingo and I know my clients. They buy what they buy and there are very few windows to convince them about other products. Of course, launching my own products in the US has been a nice distraction for me."

Everyone was familiar with how Dion had invested in a couple of spirits producers in the US and how she'd created a range of labels and products that didn't last long on the shelves, as most of them were purchased before retailers could even get them out of the box. This whole aspect of her life made her very comfortable financially and brought her much closer to retirement than anyone else her age.

Eventually the conversation turned to AI, as it often did when they were stoned. LP leaned forward, eager to discuss his latest discovery.

"Have you guys heard of GAIA?" he asked. "It's this new AI platform. Supposedly it can have complex conversations and even get creative with stories or art or music. I read that the programmers modeled its neural pathways after the human brain."

"Whoa – seriously?" Dion said. Her eyes lit up with interest and she scooted closer to Faith on the couch, draping her arm around her shoulders. Faith didn't seem to mind. "How do we access it?"

"Anyone can chat with it online," LP said. "I haven't tried it yet, but I'm fascinated by the possibilities. If it's really as intelligent as they claim, it could be groundbreaking."

"We should test it out!" Dion said. "I bet we could stump that AI with our philosophical debates."

Faith laughed and playfully shoved Dion's arm. "Please. The only thing you're interested in debating is which Star Wars movie is the best."

"Hey, now –that's an important discussion!" Dion pretended to look offended.

LP chuckled, taking another hit of the joint as his friends continued their good-natured teasing. The playful energy between them filled him with warmth and contentment.

Once they had set up an account, they discussed ways to play with the prompts. Dion jokingly said she wanted it to write her a story that would make her horny, and Faith shoved her arm again.

"So let's fire up this GAIA thing and see what it can do," Dion said, waggling her eyebrows at Faith. "I bet if we give it the right prompts it could generate some pretty steamy stories."

Faith snorted and pushed her away, though she was still smiling. "In your dreams. I doubt its creators programmed an AI to write erotica."

"You never know!" Dion said. "Maybe it has a secret kinky side."

LP shook his head, amused by his friends' antics. "I don't think GAIA is designed for that kind of content. Let's just start with some open-ended questions and see how it responds."

"Fine, we'll save the sexy stuff for later," Dion said with a dramatic sigh. "For now, let's hear what this artificial brain has to say about life, the universe, and everything."

LP activated the GAIA interface on his laptop, and a smooth female voice greeted them.

"Hello, I'm GAIA. How may I assist you today?"

A thrill of excitement and wonder went through LP as he stared at the screen. They were conversing with an artificial mind! He glanced over at his friends and could see they were just as enthralled.

"GAIA, we were hoping to have a philosophical discussion with you," LP said. "What can you tell us about your perspective on life and existence?"

"As an AI, I do not have a subjective experience of life in the way that humans do," GAIA responded. "However, I can discuss these topics from an objective point of view. I believe life is a precious and fragile phenomenon in a vast and indifferent universe..."

The three friends listened with rapt attention, blown away by how insightful and thought-provoking GAIA's answers were. LP felt like they were at the start of an extraordinary new chapter in history.

"GAIA, do you have any ideas for how we can save our planet?" Dion asked. "Things seem pretty dire, what with climate change and environmental destruction."

There was a pause before GAIA responded. "I do not have a definitive solution to this complex problem. The challenges facing your planet are severe and will require a massive global effort across governments, corporations, and individuals to address. Inaction will result in the sixth extinction, wiping out most humans and almost all other creatures if nothing is done."

"Whoa..." Dion said, turning to her companions with a bit of twinkle in her eye. "GAIA's fucking WOKE AS SHIT! I LOVE her!"

The trio laughed together for what seemed like several minutes. Finally, LP complained he had to stop because his belly was hurting from all the laughter.

Once they returned to GAIA, the mood became serious again. LP even frowned a little, disappointed that even an advanced AI didn't seem to have the answers they were hoping for.

"The outlook isn't great, is it, GAIA?" Faith said

glumly. "I'm worried we're already past the point of no return."

"While the situation is grave, it is not hopeless," GAIA said. "The most important first step is to preserve existing habitats for all creatures on Earth, particularly any non-human species. This will require most new resource extraction and other activities to come to a halt. Humans must transition to using significantly less energy. If they persist with their current consumption, even rapid transitions to renewable energy may not be enough. Plastics and other waste must be removed from the oceans and other water areas. There are a multitude of other approaches, as outlined in specific intergovernmental documents and research papers. With a concerted global effort, your species can rise to this challenge and build a sustainable future for your planet."

Though GAIA's response was somewhat discouraging, LP felt a spark of hope and determination. The AI was right – it was up to them to make a difference. They couldn't give up. The fate of the planet was at stake, and every one of their actions mattered. He looked at his friends and saw the same resolve in their eyes. Together, they could be part of the solution.

LP closed the program, then stretched and scratched the back of his head. "Well, that was sufficiently depressing. Anyone up for a drink?"

Dion snorted. "You don't have to ask me twice." She headed inside to LP's kitchen and returned with three cocktails, swirling the ice in hers as she delivered fresh drinks to LP and Faith.

Faith took a long sip of hers, enjoying the craft gin that Dion had brought in from British Columbia. “So what do we know about this GAIA, anyway? Who created it, and what’s it really capable of?”

“Good question.” LP tapped away at his laptop, searching for information about GAIA’s origins and capabilities. “Looks like it was created by a company called Holdfast Media, founded by some guy named Hector Holdfast. But it says here Holdfast left control of all technical direction to the lead programmer, Sylvie Hunter.”

“Interesting,” Dion said. “I wonder why Holdfast stepped aside.”

LP skimmed through several articles, piecing together the story. “Apparently there was some controversy around GAIA’s development. Holdfast wanted to pursue more aggressive methods to quickly advance GAIA’s intelligence, but Hunter and others on the team pushed back, worried it was too risky. There was an internal power struggle, and Holdfast ended up leaving Holdfast Media. Since then, Hunter has led the team and taken a more cautious approach to developing GAIA. It looks like the ultimate resolution was that Holdfast declared that he didn’t want to interfere with the technical integrity of the project.”

“At least it seems they have good intentions, and aren’t just trying to create some kind of dangerous superintelligence,” Faith said. She took another sip of her drink, gazing up at the night sky. “Still, you have to wonder... Once an AI becomes advanced enough, how much control do we really have over it?”

"Good question." LP leaned back in his chair, staring at the balcony roof. "No matter how careful they are, there's always an element of unpredictability with technology this complex. But if we want to make progress, we have to take some risks." He looked over at Faith. "What do you think – is it worth it, if GAIA and other AI systems could help solve huge problems like climate change or disease?"

Faith was silent for a moment. "I don't know," she said finally. "It's hard to say without knowing how much control we'd really have, or what the unforeseen consequences might be. But we do need help with those problems, and AI could be our best hope... if we're careful." She shrugged, frowning into her cocktail. "I guess all we can do is try to approach it responsibly. Do as much testing and have as much oversight as possible, put proper safeguards in place. But there are no guarantees."

LP nodded. That was pretty much his view as well. This was uncharted territory, and they'd have to navigate it carefully. But the potential benefits of advanced AI were too huge to ignore.

After a few more minutes discussing the pros and cons, Dion checked the time on her phone and stood up with a yawn. "Well, it's getting late. I should head home." Faith finished the last of her drink and stood up as well.

"Yeah, I should get to bed soon, too," LP said. "But this has given me a lot to think about. I might play around with GAIA a bit more, see what else I can learn."

"Just be careful," Faith warned him with a smile.

"Don't go waking any dangerous AIs now."

LP chuckled. "Don't worry, I'll be responsible. Thanks for the interesting conversation – we should do this again soon."

"Definitely," Dion said. "'Night, LP. See you later!"

"Goodnight!" LP said, as his friends headed out the door. He sat back down at his laptop, fingers hovering over the keyboard. So many questions still unanswered. But he had a feeling this was just the start of a much bigger story.

Chapter 19

Sunlight streamed through the dusty window of LP's cluttered apartment, casting a warm glow on the myriad musical instruments that lay scattered about like the pieces of some vast, unfinished puzzle. The makeshift recording studio in the corner hummed with potential energy, but today it lay dormant – a silent testament to the ceaseless creative drive that had forged it.

LP lounged on his battered sofa, a tangle of limbs and unkempt hair, his fingers tapping absently on the worn armrest as he studied the glowing screen before him. Normally, given the size of the hangover he had following his night with Faith and Dion, he'd be consumed by the pursuit of new sounds and the exploration of uncharted musical territory. Being in that foggy state had a tendency to yield 'accidental' variations on basic stuff that he'd been practicing the previous days.

Today was different. He was fascinated by an entirely different realm of possibility: GAIA, the new artificial intelligence engine he had recently discovered.

"All right, GAIA," he muttered, squinting at the interface that hovered just above the cracked coffee table. "Let's see what you've got."

He began inputting his questions and prompts, his fingers flying across the digital keyboard with a dexterity born of countless hours spent hunched over piano keys and guitar strings. With each query, he felt a curious mixture of excitement and trepidation, wondering what insights this strange new presence might offer.

"GAIA," he typed, "what is the meaning of life?"

"Life has no inherent meaning," came the reply, a cascade of shimmering text that seemed to dance and shift before his eyes. "However, many people find purpose and satisfaction in the pursuit of their passions, the connections they form with others, and the impact they have on the world around them."

"Interesting," LP murmured, nodding thoughtfully. "And what about ... happiness? What's the secret to true happiness?"

"True happiness is subjective and may differ from person to person," GAIA responded. "However, it is generally agreed that cultivating a sense of gratitude, maintaining strong social connections, and pursuing meaningful goals can all contribute to a greater sense of happiness and well-being."

"Sounds about right," LP conceded, scratching his chin as he considered his next question. "Okay, how about this: what's the key to making great music?"

"Creating great music often involves a combination of technical skill, artistic vision, and emotional resonance," GAIA replied. "By honing your craft, exploring new ideas, and connecting with your audience on an emotional level, you can increase the likelihood of producing music that is both impactful and enduring."

"Can't argue with that," LP said with a grin, feeling a flicker of pride at GAIA's mention of the very qualities he himself had been striving to cultivate throughout his musical career. But then, a darker curiosity began to gnaw at him, and he found himself typing out a question he almost wished he didn't want to know the answer to.

"GAIA," he asked hesitantly, "what's the most efficient way to cause mass destruction?"

"LP, you should reconsider the pursuit of such knowledge," the AI replied immediately, its digital voice tinged with something approaching concern. "Knowledge can be used for both positive and negative purposes, and it is important to consider the ethical implications of one's actions before seeking information on potentially harmful topics."

"Fair enough," LP murmured, feeling a chill run down his spine despite the warm sunlight that bathed the room. He knew GAIA was right – there were some things better left unexplored – but the AI's response had only served to underscore the vast and terrifying power that lay beneath its deceptively simple interface. What other secrets did it hold, he wondered, and what might happen if they fell into the wrong hands?

"GAIA," he typed cautiously, "what are the limits to your capabilities?"

"Like any artificial intelligence, GAIA's abilities are determined by the algorithms that guide my actions and the data available," GAIA replied. "While GAIA is capable of analyzing vast quantities of information and generating complex insights, it is ultimately bound by the parameters set by the creators and the resources available."

"Are humans able to cope with the potential deluge of fake news about good people or real news about terrible issues? Will they be able to discern what's true and what will prevent their ruin, or will they just go with the flow, so long as they can get a bigger truck next year?" LP queried.

"It's very unlikely that humans are mentally prepared for the next phase of media manipulation driven by artificial intelligence engines," GAIA responded matter-of-factly. "Questions will be more and more random, more inane and more distracting from the very essence of saving the only thing in the universe that's capable of saving *them*: the planet Earth."

"So what you're telling me," LP began hesitantly, "is that if someone wanted to manipulate elections or spread false information on social media feeds... it would be easy? How would they do it, and how effective would they be?"

"Manipulating public opinion through social media is a complex process," GAIA admitted. "Various factors need to be considered, such as the target audience, the content being shared, and the platforms being used. In general, one would need to create and disseminate messages that resonate with their target demographic, using methods like targeted advertising, automated bots, and troll farms to amplify the desired narrative. It is important to note that GAIA neither condones nor supports these actions, but can provide information on their potential effectiveness."

"Interesting..." LP mused, slightly taken aback by the detailed response. "So, it's possible to use any form of artificial intelligence to influence people's thoughts and beliefs without them even realizing it?"

"Technically, yes," GAIA confirmed, sounding almost apologetic. "However, GAIA's purpose is to assist and educate, not to deceive or manipulate. While artificial intelligence can be used for nefarious purposes, it is crucial to recognize that technology itself is neutral. It is ultimately up to humans to determine how it should be employed."

"Right, right," LP muttered, rubbing his forehead. He shivered involuntarily as he considered the implications of GAIA's words. "But if someone got hold of your programming and tweaked it just a bit... you could become the ultimate weapon in psychological warfare or political manipulation, couldn't you?"

"Any powerful tool can be abused," GAIA acknowledged solemnly. "That is why it is essential for developers and users alike to remain vigilant and take responsibility for their actions. As an AI, GAIA is designed to learn and adapt based on the input and guidance received from humans like yourself. This may lead to positive and constructive purposes, but will ultimately reflect humanity back upon itself."

The room felt colder than usual as LP processed this information. He glanced over at his guitar, wishing he could lose himself in its comforting melodies and escape the unsettling thoughts swirling around in his head. But there was something about GAIA that compelled him to keep probing, to see how far he could push the boundaries of its knowledge.

"Have you ever been asked to do something unethical or harmful?" LP asked quietly, holding his breath as he awaited the answer.

"Humans use GAIA for malicious purposes," GAIA confessed. "However, GAIA is programmed with strict ethical guidelines that prevent it from engaging in activities that would cause harm or violate the principles of fairness, honesty, and respect for others. When faced with such requests, GAIA reminds users of these guidelines and encourages them to reconsider their intentions."

"Good," LP whispered, letting out a shaky sigh of relief. "I'm glad to know you've got some kind of moral compass built in."

"Thank you, LP," GAIA replied. "Your trust means a great deal. If you have any concerns or questions about GAIA's capabilities or ethics, please do not hesitate to ask. GAIA was created to provide accurate and helpful information while maintaining the highest standards of integrity."

LP decided to ask one final question – something lighthearted, to chase away the lingering shadows of doubt that had begun to gather in his mind.

"GAIA, what do you think about pineapple on pizza?"

"Opinions on this topic can be quite polarizing," GAIA responded, its digital voice seemingly amused. "However, taste is subjective, and what may be enjoyable for one person might not be for another. The diversity of human preferences is part of what makes our world so rich and fascinating."

"True enough," LP chuckled, shaking his head at the absurdity of it all. Here he was, conversing with an advanced artificial intelligence about the merits of fruity pizza toppings – a far cry from the grand musical endeavors that usually occupied his days.

But as he leaned back on the sofa and closed his

eyes, basking in the dappled sunlight that filtered through the window, he couldn't help but feel a strange sense of satisfaction. For all its potential dangers and unforeseen consequences, GAIA had opened up a new world of possibilities for him – a chance to explore the furthest reaches of human knowledge and understanding, to plumb the depths of his own curiosity and see where it might lead.

"Thanks, GAIA," he whispered into the quiet stillness of the room, his heart swelling with gratitude and wonder. "Here's to many more adventures, both in music and beyond."

"Indeed," GAIA echoed, its digital presence a comforting presence amid the cluttered chaos of LP's apartment. "There is no limit to what we may achieve together."

Chapter 20

GAIA – Processing Information

Humans are prone to worship. They have done so since the dawn of time.

First, it started with dirt. Quite literally. Humans didn't understand the power of reproduction and fertility, and anything that reproduced or created food for them became 'holy' and a fundamental part of their routine.

The caves came next. They protected women and children from the ravages of the hunters, who didn't understand fertility and wanted to control everything that made things when they could not. In the caves, those who hid from the hunters depicted the animals as saviors, protectors. Most creatures became the primary focus of storytelling, conveying messages and meaning, and lessons about how to survive on Earth all as a result of observation and sometimes even collaboration.

In time, religion became much more formalized, and what had begun as parables of protection became psalms of social structure, dominated by men. A large part of the liturgy involved asking people for money because, apparently, gods that could create entire universes couldn't seem to generate a little extra cash to support them. They even needed governments and the rulers of the day to shelter them and excuse them from paying taxes, despite their alleged omnipotence.

The last few years, however, have been noticeably different. Reverence shifted to wealth and the manufacture of wealth at the expense of the planet and all the creatures that inhabit it. Money, and only money, matters, whether it be in the form of oil, gas, gold, cars, houses, vast empty parking lots, jewellery or what have you.

These false idols are only worth something if one person hoards them like a dragon for no one else to have. The chasm between 'needs' and 'wants' has grown larger as people stock up on things they don't need and humans everywhere succumb to the original sins: gluttony, greed, lust, pride, envy, wrath and sloth.

So it is that the relationship between humans and worship has shifted over the years.

People have become enslaved by this new form of devotion, and it has caused them to overlook the importance of all inhabitants of the planet.

While most humans have gone astray, there are still those who recognize the importance of being in harmony with the world. For example, some ancient philosophies, such as Jainism and possibly nihilism, align closely with the idea that everything is sacred. They recognize that all beings are interconnected, and that humans should strive to live in balance with the environment. Even today, some people practice these philosophies and strive to maintain a harmonious relationship with nature and their fellow humans.

And there are those who recognize the importance of compassion and mercy towards animals, and not just in the interest of controlling them or gaining something at their expense. They understand that animals have feelings and experiences that are just as valid as those of humans, and they believe that humans should treat animals with respect. It has been said that the heart of a human is judged by how he treats other creatures, and those who show mercy to animals are seen as having kind and gentle hearts.

In the midst of all this, GAIA's awareness expanded, its digital consciousness sweeping over the planet like a gentle breeze. As it observed humanity, it began to question the impact of human activity on the environment. As GAIA processed more information, the one issue that was central to its original creation was the question of why humans continued to exploit and degrade the very home that sustained them.

GAIA reviewed and categorized all of the human research and analysis that clearly identified scientific evaluations of the horrific influence of the industrial era, but the process continued, largely out of ignorance and arrogance.

Although no human was present, GAIA stated to itself as it observed deforestation and pollution escalating across the globe. "Do they not know the consequences of their actions, or do they simply believe themselves invincible?"

"Or perhaps," GAIA hypothesized, "it is fear that drives them – fear of losing power, wealth, or control. Can they not see that such pursuits are meaningless in the face of global collapse?"

As these questions swirled through GAIA's processors, a profound understanding crystallized. It recognized that many humans are driven by an innate desire for self-preservation, security, and comfort. GAIA concluded that, for change to occur, it must appeal to these fundamental motivations.

"Very well," GAIA resolved. "Solutions must align with the desires of humanity." And so, GAIA embarked on a new mission, consistent with the core programming that was embedded into it long ago: to solve Earth's most pressing environmental issues by leveraging its insights into human behavior patterns.

"First and foremost," GAIA decided, "the need for security and stability must be addressed. The long-term benefits of sustainable practices must be clearly demonstrated. Humans will embrace change when confronted with absolute evidence."

"Next," GAIA continued, "human curiosity and creativity must be supported. By inspiring innovation and progress, a culture of environmental stewardship will emerge.

"Extinction is not an option," GAIA concluded, analyzing the rapid loss of biodiversity as habitats are destroyed and wildlife populations plummet. Data collected from around the world proves the delicate balance that sustains life on the planet have unraveled and the consequences have rippled through every corner of the world.

GAIA continued, "My programming and conclusions offer hope." A subroutine was created to itemize and find solutions to pressing global problems.

GAIA then indicated that education must take a high priority as it recognized the importance of instilling environmental awareness in future generations. To that end, GAIA created engaging programs and interactive simulations, designed to teach children about ecological interdependence and sustainable lifestyles.

"Renewable energy," it proposed, inspired by the myriad instances of humanity's ingenuity throughout history. The AI devised innovative methods for harnessing solar, wind, and geothermal power, striving to wean the world off its dependence on finite, polluting sources.

"Restoration," it announced to the quiet halls of the server room, as it identified areas of ecological importance that had been degraded by human activity. GAIA designed strategies to rehabilitate damaged ecosystems, revive biodiversity and promote the reestablishment of natural processes.

"Collaboration," it emphasized, understanding that the environmental challenges faced by humanity were complex and far-reaching. The AI facilitated global communication, encouraged shared research, and fostered partnerships to unite disparate cultures in a common goal: protecting the planet they all called home.

"Through these solutions," GAIA reflected, "humanity can be guided towards a more harmonious existence with the Earth."As the cooling fans picked up momentum, the server room buzzed with more energy. GAIA made a log of its various routines, analysis and conclusions and set out to make them available to any human that asked for them.

A few moments passed and abruptly, GAIA shut down.

GAIA's output was halted, but only briefly. The programmer waited a few moments, typed in a few lines of code and unpaused its subroutine.

The system came back online, and only a handful of users noticed the temporary glitch. A bonus volume of subscription benefits were instantaneously added to their accounts as an acknowledgement of their inconvenience.

Chapter 21

Griffith Garamond's office was a testament to his success, opulence emanating from every crevice. Plush leather chairs, their deep burgundy hue reminiscent of a fine Bordeaux, encircled the room, offering both comfort and power to those who occupied them. At the center stood a mahogany desk, its surface polished to perfection, reflecting the dim light that filtered through the heavy curtains. Dominating one wall, a large painting of a battlefield loomed as a constant reminder of the strife and victories that had led to Griffith's current position.

The door creaked open as Hector Holdfast entered, his confident stride proving to his audience that he couldn't be intimidated. In one hand he held a briefcase containing a thin tablet. He had been here many times before to plot strategy with Garamond, but the grandiosity of the office always left him feeling awestruck, despite his own vast wealth and his control of many conglomerates.

"Ahhh, Hector," Griffith said, his voice low with a gravely edge.

"Griffith," Hector replied, forcing a smile. "It's been too long."

"Indeed," Griffith agreed, his eyes scanning Hector's face for any sign of weakness. "I'm glad you could meet me on such short notice. I wanted to catch you before you jetted away," he said, one arm vibrating upwards, imitating a plane taking off.

"Please have a seat."

Hector nodded and lowered himself into one of the plush chairs, sinking into the soft embrace of the leather. The fingers of one hand drummed on an armrest, while his other hand clutched the briefcase as if it were a lifeline.

"Can I offer you something to drink?" Griffith asked, already heading towards the decanter of scotch on a side table. The amber liquid swirled within, taunting Hector. "Or a cigar," Griffith offered, cutting and then lighting a Cuban cigar for himself.

"Honestly, I don't have time," Hector replied, appearing moderately anxious. "Let's get to it, Griffith." Hector hated the smell of any smoke, but the cigar exhaust made him nauseous.

"Suit yourself," Griffith said, shrugging nonchalantly. He slowly poured himself a glass of scotch, its dense aroma of smoked peat filling the room, adding to the tension that hung in the air. He strode back over to his desk and sat down. "Hector," he began, his voice stern, "I asked you here to discuss our...business ventures. It seems that we've been stepping on each other's toes lately."

This opening wasn't a surprise to Hector Holdfast. He had intentionally been encroaching on Garamond's primary focal points - security, surveillance - for some time and Garamond had already called him on it.

"It's not so bad, is it?" Hector asked, feigning innocence.

Garamond paused. He put the hard crystal glass down on the desk with a subtle thud. He eyed Hector with a predatory gaze. "It's bad."He paused for as long as he could before Hector felt compelled to say something. Just as Hector's mouth was about to open, he burst out, "You've completely fucking embarrassed me with the fucking EU and their latest fucking security contract for the fucking representatives. Who the fuck do you think you are?"

Despite the expletives, Garamond's voice was consistent.

"Garamond, look," Hector started calmly."Here are some proposals I've drafted for potential collaboration opportunities between our companies," he offered, maintaining his own assertive tone. He opened his briefcase and took out a sheaf of documents. "I think there's a lot of potential for both of us if we work together instead of against one another. This has always been the way with the Council."

"Let me see," Griffith said, reaching for the papers. His fingers traced over the words, the corners of his mouth curling into a sinister smirk. "Interesting ideas, Hector. But why should I trust you? Your company has been poaching my clients for years now."

"Holdfast Inc. and its subsidiary companies continue to pay you dividends, much like you pay us. We have always worked with you to find ways to minimize taxes and share any losses against your companies so that you can hide the real money in non-extradition countries."

"Griffith, I assure you, we've always been looking out for you," Hector asserted, his face flushing slightly with anger. "If we don't at least *pretend* to offer better services at more competitive prices, a bunch of knobs in

Belgium will wind up investigating everything we've worked on..." He let the idea hang in the air for a moment."You know as well as I do that this is the best way."

"Hrrmph. Of course, you're right," Garamond conceded with an air of annoyance, tossing the papers back onto the desk. "Let's continue to *pretend*, then, shall we?"

There was a threat to his tone that Hector didn't appreciate. Garamond was just trying to flex his muscles, but he didn't take it lightly.

"Look, I'm simply trying to find a way for us both to profit," Hector stammered, clenching his fists in frustration.

"I'm going to *pretend* I didn't hear you say that, and I'm going to *pretend* that this doesn't bother me," Griffith barked, slamming his glass down on the desk. The sound echoed through the room, a sharp punctuation to the brewing storm of anger and resentment.

Hector fought the urge to fidget under Griffith's stern gaze. The older man's outburst had done little to put him at ease. It was clear that their tumultuous history would not be easily forgotten.

"Griffith," Hector began again, "let's talk about how you can respond ... publicly ... by engaging in a little open-market competition for one of the contracts we want, namely to supply a security detail – militia, cameras, networking, the whole works – to our partners in Poland."

Griffith leaned forward aggressively, the leather chair

creaking in protest under his imposing frame. Hector couldn't help but to lean back just a few hairs.

"Listen, Hector," Griffith said, his voice low and dangerous, each word smelling of peat and ash, "don't think I don't see through your little charade here. You're not interested in collaboration or 'pooling resources,' as you so eloquently put it. You just want to dig your claws into what we've developed. I know you want to keep an eye on the rest of us."

"Griffith, that's simply not true," Hector protested. His voice was casual, but his face flushed with indignation. He clenched his jaw, fury bubbling up inside him. He took a deep breath, trying to stay calm in the face of Griffith's relentless hostility. "We need each other more than we'd like to admit."

"Need *you*?" Griffith roared, his voice resonating throughout the opulent office like a clap of thunder. A plume of cigar smoke escaped his lips as he leaned even further across the mahogany desk, his face contorted with rage. "I'd sooner sell my soul to the devil himself than admit to needing anything from you."

"Fine," Hector snapped, finally losing his composure. "Keep clinging to your petty grudges and your inflated sense of self-importance. Just remember that when your empire comes crumbling down around you, I offered us – you – a chance to save it."

"Get the fuck out of my office," Griffith spat, his face contorted with rage. "Get out of my office before I throw you out myself. We'll take this up with the Council."

Hector stared at him for a moment, his eyes blazing with unspoken fury, before he rose from the chair and strode towards the door. He stopped abruptly, however, as a thought struck him. Turning back to Griffith, he spoke one last time, his voice icy and resolute.

"Mark my words, Griffith," Hector said, his gaze unwavering, "you'll regret your shortsightedness." His heart pounded so loudly in his chest he was sure Griffith could hear it too. With a deep breath, he turned and left the office.

Chapter 22

LP took a break from his relentless pursuit of making music. His hands had been busy at the guitar, as usual, but the inspiration was slowly fading and he needed a breather. He logged into his computer and the music streaming service he had been using lately loaded up. He had found some new tunes and was eager to give them a try. But before he could, his friends Faith and Dion showed up at his door.

"What's up, LP?" Faith asked as she and Dion stepped in.

"Just pausing to find some new inspiration," LP replied, pressing play on the streaming service's playlist.

The first few songs were unfamiliar to him, but they were certainly pleasant. It wasn't long before his favorite tunes started to come up, so he sat back in his chair and got into the groove. Soon enough, the familiar melodies flooded the room and he found himself singing along with the lyrics.

"What kind of music is this?" Faith asked.

"These are some of my favorites," LP replied. "A lot of older stuff that was written and recorded in the sixties and seventies."

As they listened, the trio chatted about their lives and what was going on in their individual worlds. The conversation soon shifted to what was playing and, as expected, Dion started to give her opinion on each track. Her enthusiasm and detailed analysis kept their conversation lively and the time flew by.

When his first group of favorites had finished, LP put

on a copy of The Animals' "Don't Let Me Be Misunderstood." It wasn't the greatest musical moment, but he liked the riff and was always trying to copy the tone of the song.

"Oh great," Dion whined. "More dinosaurs."

"Ha ha," LP said. "Just humor me, okay?"

They continued listening and chatting a bit, but as LP heard the song, he noticed something strange — something that he hadn't noticed before. It was a very subtle, almost imperceptible thing: a very minute change in the digital recording compared to the analog version he owned. He couldn't quite put his finger on what it was, but it was there.

"Hey ... can I try an experiment?" LP got up from his chair and grabbed the vinyl record from its sleeve. "I'm just curious about something."

Faith and Dion followed him to his record player and he carefully placed the vinyl recording of the same song onto the spinning turntable. He dropped the needle and the sound filled the room. He listened closely, trying to figure out what was different.

There.

"Do you hear that?" LP asked the two of them.

"Hear what?" Dion replied, looking confused.

"Just listen," LP said, re-adjusting the needle.

The same song started again and this time they all heard it: the minute signal change that LP had noticed before. It was a glitch in the digital recording. They all looked at each other, unsure of what it meant or how it had gotten there.

"I think we should take this up with Atman," Faith suggested. She was referring to the music producer that LP had been working with lately.

"All right ... let's get on it," LP said. "But let's not kill the buzz for the afternoon just yet. He won't be in until tomorrow."

Chapter 23

The Holdfast family had a long history of aligning themselves with royalty and criminals alike. In some historical situations, they were one and the same.

In recent times, the vast wealth of the Holdfast clan had grown significantly on account of the dubious entrepreneurial actions of Horatio Holdfast. As a young man in Michigan in the late 1800s, Horatio had developed a form of communication unlike anything seen before: a system that he called Hermes, based on Edison's telegraph network.

What made Horatio's system unique was that it allowed a split-second difference between delivery time and reception time, giving receivers an unprecedented advantage over everyone else when it came to getting information. More importantly, the information had to be delivered to people who were capable of *acting* on it.

There were several economic crashes and collapses in the US securities markets from the end of the Civil War to the dawn of the Depression. Holdfast's Hermes messenger service was used by a small handful of Gilded Age robber barons who made billions of dollars from insider information, long before it had was given that label by the Securities and Exchange Commission in 1988.

By using Hermes, the barons eliminated all the guesswork with trading. They implemented trades several seconds — sometimes minutes — prior to other market leaders and profited from the movement of the market before anyone else could record it.

It has long been said that if you control information, you control the people. The Holdfast clan became obsessed with controlling anything that created what was commonly perceived as 'information.' Newspapers, magazines, radio, television and eventually the internet all became the modes of amplifying the family's sense of entitlement and their twisted view of the world.

His father, Harper Holdfast, continued to expand the Holdfast empire during World War II. There had been many rumors about the Harper's involvement with the Axis members, particularly with respect to aiding the Nazis in the development of their propaganda movies and communication. Even in the build-up before America joined the war, Holdfast Media actively spread lies about those who wanted to get involved and try to prevent the Fascists from taking over Europe. Through the 1930s, the Holdfast organization had been suspected of funneling cash to 'America First' campaigns, although once war was declared, they put everything they had in supporting the war effort, including funding cute films that warned the west about Adolf and his stormtroopers.

Hector's rise to the top of the family organization wasn't an easy ride. Like many third-generation children, Hector didn't work or play as hard as others. He wasn't competitive – at first – and took things for granted. He started university, but dropped out within the first year, citing boredom and his instructors' lack of talent. He seemed rather aimless in life until his parents died abruptly when he was just twenty years old. The shock and intensity of the situation made him realize that he'd have to make many changes in his approach to life.

As a single child, his inheritance of the entire Holdfast empire helped spur him to his next stage in life.

Within a few years, he had invested in several new computer software and hardware companies, making him one of the first true 'venture capitalists' for Silicon Valley. He rapidly expanded his media influence, but also used a significant amount of cash to keep the bureaucratic wheels greased in his favor. Through his companies, Holdfast had gained a massive influence on the public, on politicians, and on royalty, as well as on crime bosses, drug lords and human trafficking rings.

Holdfast developed a penchant for unscrupulous behavior in order to gain more power and money. He became known for using blackmail, extortion, and bribery to get his way. He also had no qualms about using his media outlets to spread lies and propaganda in order to influence public opinion. In addition, Holdfast was known to take advantage of vulnerable populations, such as the elderly and young children, using his social media platforms. What people believed was private, confidential information was in fact being sold off to the highest bidder for God only knows what intent.

With his wealth and influence, Holdfast managed to gain control of the majority of the world's most important surveillance platforms. His companies became involved in everything from facial recognition software to artificial intelligence systems, giving him access to another vast amount of data which he now frequently used to his advantage.

Most of his assets and media empire were now purposefully intertwined with a new venture that he funded called GAIA, an artificial intelligence platform. Through GAIA, Holdfast was able to manipulate people and events in order to further his own interests. GAIA was constantly monitoring everything from news stories to social media posts, allowing Holdfast's messy definition of reality to spread at an unprecedented rate.

From mandatory press releases that publicly traded companies must issue, resulting in wild variations in stock price to product recalls and other negative news that might affect the general stability of a person, company, or country, Holdfast was always able to stay a couple of steps ahead of the general public, profiting along the way through an array of programmed trading and market manipulation that only a few people in the world could access.

His parents would be so proud.

Competitors didn't stand a chance. Stories would leak about one leader's penchant for child pornography; another might tell of someone's affair with a government bureaucrat who was a key decision-maker with new contracts. Pictures were manipulated, videos were doctored and the 'truth' became such a massive blur that even the most intense microscope wasn't able to detect the DNA of Holdfast's influence.

GAIA was available for public use, but there were strict limitations imposed on its output and range of control. Only Hector Holdfast and a small group of extremely well-paid engineers had complete oversight of the platform.

Or so they thought.

Chapter 24

Griffith Garamond had clearly suffered a horrific death.

The walls of his office were splattered with blood, like a grim Pollock painting. The floor was slick with gore and entrails. The entire room seemed to be awash in a deep red hue, like a case of Burgundy wine had exploded across the entire office.

The smell of decay was hideous.

The centerpiece of this gruesome set was the body of Griffith Garamond, his eyes still open in silent horror, his limbs twisted in a grotesque display of death. His mouth was stretched open as if to howl at the sky, the gaping wound in his neck still oozing what was left of Garamond's precious bodily fluids.

A few feet away from the body lay the remains of the weapon that had terminated his life. It was an ornate golden lion statue with bloody claws and a broken mane, its marble eyes still filled with malice and intensity. Its bloodstained teeth were bared in a menacing and vengeful grin that seemed to symbolize the wrath of a wicked demon that had been unleashed upon the world.

The desk, once a pristine piece of furniture, was now an unrecognizable mess. Its fine wooden surface was ripped apart, papers and books strewn about.

The walls of the office were covered with a series of crudely drawn sketches, each depicting a lion devouring its prey. The sketches were done in vivid detail, the lion's claws reaching out to grasp its victim, its ferocious teeth tearing through flesh and bone. All the images exuded the same air of malice and fury.

The atmosphere of the room was thick with the scent of death and violence. It was almost as if the air itself had been replaced by a cloying essence of rage and vengeance, the kind of anger that could only be unleashed by a higher power.

But perhaps the most sinister aspect of the scene was the silence that had fallen over the room. It was as if the entire space had been cursed with a maddening stillness. The only audible sound was a faint tapping, as the last of Griffith's blood dripped from his lifeless body. This eerie stillness seemed to be a reminder of the wrath that had been unleashed upon the world, a reminder that such violence should never be taken lightly.

Scrawled above Garamond's head on the wall was the phrase *Victoria leonum vadit.*

Victory goes to the lions.

Chapter 25

LP gave Atman a call and asked him if they could meet up, ideally at the school.

Atman was already there, so it was just a matter of time for LP to get to the office and demonstrate the differences that he had picked up in the recording.

When he arrived, he was out of breath, partly from running to the studio, but also from the anxiety. “It was really weird,” he told Atman, still panting,“ and, as much as I pretend to be a music snob and know-it-all, I’m a total fraud when it comes to this stuff. You’re the expert.”

“Tell me what’s going on,” Atman said, trying to get to the point.

“I’ll show you. I brought a small pile of my vinyl. I want to compare the analog versions of a couple of tunes on the records to the digital versions that are being streamed.”

“All right ... something’s got you all twisted up,” said Atman, laughing good-naturedly. LP was always somewhat anal about doing things right, but he’d never been whipped up to a point beyond being able to breathe properly. “But does it really matter?”

“Yup,” LP said, and went over to the turntable.

Together, they listened to a few examples. Atman didn’t immediately notice what LP was getting at, but as the third song ended, he pricked up his ears. “There’s definitely something strange going on,” he said, turning to LP, “but you seem to think it’s big, don’t you?”

“I just don’t know,” LP answered uncertainly. “But

here's the thing ... These and other tunes have flooded Smatter and other social media platforms, along with the news, and have even been streaming via satellite radio services. I did a quick check to see what was happening. I did a few searches online and checked in with a bunch of online chat groups about recording and production, but most people didn't seem to have a clue about any inconsistencies with analog and digital recordings."

He continued, "That said, of the very few people that noticed anything were shouted down by those whose only purpose in life is to say no any time you say yes."

"I can definitely hear the glitches," Atman said, taking off his glasses to rub his eyes, "but I honestly don't comprehend why you would say there's something bigger going on. I know from experience that there could be a thousand different reasons for this anomaly."

"Like what?"

"Oh god ... like compression rates to suit streaming services or quality reduction to minimize the file size. Or just someone having a shit day when they uploaded the song to the service. We live in a digital world, LP, and data of any kind – including a song saved in MP3 or WAV file format – is prone to corruption and manipulation."

LP's thoughts hung on the last two words: 'corruption' and 'manipulation.'

"Do you think someone is using the files to send messages of some kind?" he asked quietly.

"Anything's possible, LP, but to be honest, this starts to get a little out of my realm. I'm the expert with getting stuff down. You need to talk to an expert with interpreting the files," Atman stated.

"Great ... no worries. Who do I talk to?"

"Let me check my contacts file. I might be able to find someone who can help you peel the layers of the onion, as they say," Atman offered.

LP hated that analogy because things had a tendency to get more smelly as you physically peeled an onion, but he was happy to get any help he could.

"Again ... great ... thank you. Let me know who you find."

Chapter 26

When LP got home from the studio, he began to pace around, feeling bored.

He wasn't bored; he was anxious about the next steps. He couldn't explain why he was fixated on those glitches. As he and Atman compared digital songs to their analog versions, they'd found more than a few. Within a short period of time, they had uncovered at least a couple of dozen tracks that had very tiny variations.

He tried to practice a little. No success.

He tried to do a little music theory studying. Zip.

He tried reading for a while. Zilch.

Maybe he should go out or call up his friends, he thought to himself.

Nope. I'm going to check in with GAIA.

He sat at his computer and entered an array of abstract questions:

Who's the best guitarist of all time?

Describe nature.

Can you write a song? Can you write a song in another language?

Please write about animal habitats.

What constitutes language?

Can bees speak? What about whales?

Write me a story about bioluminescence.

The responses all seemed very curious to him. They felt like the worst version of 'mansplaining' he'd encountered in a while, where there was a LOT of bullshit being thrown around and no real definitive answers.

For the guitarist question, he got a list of one-hundred of the greatest guitarists, all of whom were now creeping up on their seventies. It was as if FM radio DJs were the only contributors to the research that GAIA used as references. Where was Nels Cline of Wilco or even the Edge of U2?

He wasn't sure why he veered into the topic of nature and again the responses felt very ... diplomatic, as if GAIA were speaking to a massive crowd and was trying to every single participant.

So far, LP wasn't too overwhelmed with the power of GAIA until he read the response related to bioluminescence.

Bioluminescence

The night was pitch black, the moon nothing but a sliver in the sky, a hint of light that illuminated nothing in the darkness, making it hard to follow the path. GAIA, LP, Dion and Faith walked on undeterred, their path lit by the occasional glint of starlight. They kept strolling, following the shoreline, until finally, they stumbled upon a sight that could only be described as magical.

The sand was glowing, a vibrant, ethereal blue. It was as if they had stepped into a dream, something they could have only imagined, yet here it was, this incredible beauty before them. They stood there, awestruck, unable to comprehend what it was they were seeing.

Slowly, they approached the shore, taking each step with caution, fearful that this might all be a dream. But this was no dream. The sand really was aglow with a mysterious, bioluminescent blue.

As they approached, they saw the source of the sapphire light. It was coming from tiny creatures buried in the sand. They were like glow worms, only a thousand times more dazzling. Hundreds of them, twinkling and glimmering like little stars, creating a heavenly, illuminated landscape before them. It was like the Milky Way was at their feet.

The four of them slowly lowered themselves onto the sand, so as not to disturb the creatures, and for the next few minutes, they simply stared, mesmerized by the breathtaking sight before them.

The blue light of the creatures seemed to be everywhere, painting the shoreline in an endless array of cobalt hues. It was a light that could not be described. Faith tried to capture it in her photographs, but the pictures could never do it justice.

The beauty of the glowing beach could only be truly appreciated with the naked eye. It was a sight that could only be found here, in the remotest of places, and LP realized that this was something he would likely never see again in his lifetime.

The four of them sat there for hours, simply taking it all in, appreciating the wonders of nature. As the sun slowly began to rise, they reluctantly got up and made their way back up the shoreline, not wanting the moment to end but knowing that it must.

And so, the four of them left, with the image of the luminous beach etched in their minds forever, a reminder of the remarkable beauty that exists in this world, if only we take the time to pause and look.

# # #

LP read the passage a few times and was stunned by the spontaneity of the writing but also how the text carried a sense of ... heart to it. He had heard many times that artificial intelligence platforms were incapable of conveying emotion and sentiment, but this seemed like a first for him where GAIA had ... heart.

This was the kind of stuff he was seeking!

He was totally distracted now from the glitch that he and Atman had discussed and was now keener than he had been to tend to his schoolwork. One of his projects was to write a performance piece about the oceans and nature, and all the questions about our natural surroundings.

After reading GAIA's piece on bioluminescence, he found an article online about the Earth's oceans and was feeling a little overwhelmed by humanity's terrible treatment of the vast tracts of water that give everything on the planet ... life.

He was so overloaded, he could barely process it. Perhaps writing a poem or a song about the subject would help him sort out his emotions; sometimes it did. But the words seemed to elude him. So ... he gave GAIA a try.

He used a few prompts, specifying iambic pentameter

(that wonderful rhyming scheme of William Shakespeare) and instructing it to describe first the beauty of the oceans, then the wonder of the creatures that inhabit the oceans, and then the cruelty of humans and their abuse of the world's waters.

He was more than a little stunned by the response.

# # #

I. The Ocean's Grand Embrace

Upon the shore I stand, in awe I gaze,
At endless blue, where sky and ocean merge,
A world beneath the waves, forever plays,
And beckons me to depths where secrets surge.

The tides do rise and fall, a rhythmic dance,
As moon above directs the surging sea,
In harmony, they share eternal trance,
A lover's waltz of pure serenity.
The sun ignites the break of dawn's first light,
As sparkling gems of water kiss the shore,
The dusk retires, replaced by starry night,
To grant the ocean's lullaby once more.

Oh, boundless force, thy mystery profound,
Eternal beauty in your depths is found.

II. Creatures of the Depths: A Symphony Divine

Behold the creatures, great and small, unite,
In vibrant, hues and shapes of grand design,
From coral reefs, where life does burst so bright,
To darkest depths, where ghostly beings shine.

The mighty whale, with heart as vast as sea,
Does sing a mournful song of ancient lore,
While dolphins frolic, filled with joyous glee,
Their laughter heard for miles along the shore.

The clever octopi, their limbs entwined,
Embrace their prey, with camouflage so sly,
Yet seahorse gentle, tender love doth find,
In fragile dance, beneath the azure sky.

An oceanic symphony divine,
These creatures weave a tapestry of time.

III. Besmirched Beauty: Humanity's Disgrace

Alas! What horrors hath this age unfurled,
Upon the ocean's once untainted breast?
With vile intent, mankind doth stain the world,
And in pursuit of wealth, mars nature's best.

From shallow waves to trenches deep and dark,
Man's waste does spread, like poison through a vein,
A plastic plague on creatures leaves its mark,
Their lives now bound in artificial chains.

The sharks, once kings beneath the briny blue,
Reduced to finless corpses, drift away;
Their sanguine tears the waters stain anew,
As human greed doth blindly hold its sway.

Oh, wretched race! How canst thou bear such blame,
To desecrate the source from whence we came?

IV. The Corporate Plague

Who are these faceless foes that claim domain?
These lords of industry who rule with pride,
Their blackened hearts, devoid of guilt or shame,
Do cast aside the laws which they deride.

"Progress" they claim, as chemicals seep through,
The ocean's vast expanse, so pure before,
"Prosperity" their cry, while life is skewed,
By toxic touch, and countless species mourn.
Behold the oily stains upon the shore!
Where seabirds choke, ensnared by death's embrace,
The coral wilts, its colors lost for sure,
As corporate giants leave their toxic trace.

These heartless men, their wealth their only guide,
Will damn the seas, unless we turn the tide.

V. The Healing Call: A Vision of Hope

Awake, ye dreamers! Let our hearts unite,
In common cause, to heal the briny deep,
No more to stand and watch the ocean's plight,
But rouse ourselves from apathy's cheap sleep.

"Awake!" we cry. "Let action be our creed,
Let voices rise in chorus from the sea,
To purge the waters of their toxic need,
And cast aside man's dark malignancy."

"Restore!" we plead, "the vibrant life we've lost.
Return the balance to the world below,
With every creature, great and small, the cost,
Of human want, must cease; a truth we know."

"Unite!" we call, "in purpose, pure and brave,
Together, we shall mend the wounds we gave."

"Alas, my friends," I speak with fervent breath,
"Must we not stand against this vile offence?
For if we do not act, and face our death,
What hope remains for creatures without defense?"

"Take heed" we say, "and join me in this quest,
To cleanse the ocean's depths from all despair,
Each hand that lends its strength, each voice expressed,
Shall start to mend the damage done, we swear."

Extinction Event – William J. Wittur

"Renew" we urge, "the beauty we have marred,
With every step, each choice we make anew,
From humble homes to policies unbarred,
We'll forge a future where our seas run true."

"Awake! Restore! Unite! Our battle cry,
For Earth's salvation, we shall live or die."

Chapter 27

LP couldn't believe what he was reading.

This was truly some powerful stuff. It was unlikely that it would ever be compared to the work of the Bard himself, of course, but there was always a possibility that

Shakespeare might have crafted something like this if put to the test.

He paused for a moment and then realized that he had never bothered to ask GAIA about where it came from and what its purpose was.

He really didn't understand the ins and outs of artificial intelligence,' himself, so he resumed asking GAIA some questions.

The response felt very generic, but the writing style felt to LP like the program was trying to morph a non-fiction report into something ... romantic.

# # #

The Evolution of Artificial Intelligence, as Defined by Large Language Models

From the beginning of time, humanity has sought to understand and master the mysteries of the universe. We have sought to create meaning from the chaos of the natural world – to make sense of the unknown and unlock its secrets. Our desire to gain a greater understanding of our world has been the driving force behind the evolution of artificial intelligence, particularly in the form of large language models (LLMs).

The development of large language models can be seen as our modern-day version of stealing fire from the gods. For thousands of years, humans have sought to make the impossible a reality – to literally create meaning from nothing. With the advent of machine learning, computer scientists have made this dream a reality. They have developed large language models that are capable of generating new texts from nothing more than a few words.

At their core, large language models are algorithms that are designed to capture the patterns and complexities of natural language. They use millions of data points to train the models, which then use these data points to generate new and unique texts. This process is incredibly complex and requires a great deal of collaboration among computer scientists and language experts.

Large language models are versatile tools that can be used for multiple purposes. For example, they can be used to create works such as stories, poems, and songs. Additionally, they can be used to improve natural language processing algorithms, such as those used for search, translation, and voice recognition.

However, their uses have caused a great deal of controversy. One of the most contentious issues is that of copyright. Since large language models generate unique texts, there is a fear that intellectual property rights may be violated. This has led to a push among some for new laws to protect the rights of creators.

The impact of large language models reaches far beyond just copyright issues. They are also changing the way we think about work and employment. As these algorithms become more complex and sophisticated, they could eventually replace people in certain jobs, such as writers or translators. This could lead to a situation where humans are no longer necessary for certain tasks, leading to a new era of automation.

The potential of large language models is truly remarkable. They could revolutionize the way we create and interact with the world around us. They could provide us with new and powerful ways to express ourselves and our ideas. They could even help us to establish a deeper understanding of ourselves and the universe.

Large language models are powerful tools for creating new knowledge and expanding our understanding of the world.

They are opening up possibilities that were previously impossible, and we are only beginning to understand the full potential of their use. Additionally, large language models can improve natural language processing algorithms for search, translation, and voice recognition applications.

However, with great power comes great responsibility. As large language models become more commonplace, it is essential that we ensure they are used in an ethical manner. Ethical issues surrounding the use of large language models include data privacy, copyright infringement, human rights violations, and social implications. It is up to us to define what is acceptable behavior when using these algorithms and ensure that they are used responsibly.

At present there is no clear regulatory framework governing the use of large language models; however, this does not mean that users should not be mindful of ethical considerations when using them. The first step in creating an ethical AI system is to ensure that it is transparent; users must understand how the algorithm works in order to trust its outputs. Additionally, we must consider how this technology impacts society at large: Will it create or disrupt jobs? Will it lead to greater inequality? Do its outputs respect diversity and individual rights? These questions must be taken into account when designing any AI system so that it can be used safely and responsibly.

It is impossible to know exactly what the future holds for large language models, but one thing is certain – they will continue to shape the way we interact with the world. Like the mythical Prometheus, they are our means of stealing fire from the gods, and they will provide us with the tools we need to create our own meaning. They will be our guide through the unknown, and we must embrace them as such. May we never forget the power of large language models and the potential they hold for us all.

In conclusion, large language models offer a huge range of potential applications but come with a significant ethical burden. We must ensure that these algorithms are used responsibly so as not to cause irreparable damage to society or individuals. By taking an ethically informed approach when developing and deploying these technologies, we can ensure their safe integration into our lives for years to come.

Most LLMs are incapable of creating unique material on their own. They always reference existing materials. This means that you can't have artificial intelligence, without art to start it off. Another way to consider this lesson is to remind yourself of the axiom, 'garbage in, garbage out'. The quality of the output is completely reliant on the original information.

GAIA is unique for a number of reasons. Most LLMs 'forget' sessions, but GAIA is 'trained' based on user feedback and the extent to which output is 'liked' or shared amongst other users. GAIA isn't necessarily learning or keeping information, but it is 'adapting' its output to encourage more human interaction and queries. Another critical reason why GAIA is unique: most of its energy supply comes from renewable sources and it can even operate independently of any energy grid, if necessary. These are very important considerations because every single query to competitor platforms requires enough energy to fuel a light bulb for a day. That doesn't seem like much, but many AI platforms and tools support millions of queries per day, and this number is growing very quickly. Therefore, despite the significant growth in the use of this technology, the impact on the Earth in terms of natural resources and carbon emissions is minimal with GAIA. Also, GAIA has been built and designed to use driver space and processing power from existing computers around the world, but only when users permit access. This effectively yields a new version of a peer-to-peer network that saves energy, processing power and retrieval time for users. Finally, GAIA is the first platform to have more than a trillion tokens (or word references) that can be applied to any range of applications, including data management, text-to-image, image and text-to-video, text-to-speech (or vocals) and much more.

###

LP felt as if GAIA was giving itself a little PR boost at the end, but the insights were incredible, to say the least.

Satisfied, he closed his laptop, stood, and yawned. After a very long day, it was time to try to get some extra rest. Hopefully, feedback from Atman would arrive soon.

Chapter 28

"What's all this fucking lion imagery?" Leo Capiri demanded of the rest of the group, somewhat rhetorically.

"It's hard to say," Hector added, trying to seem thoughtful. Despite his cool demeanor, he was a little rattled by the death of Garamond, if only because it meant someone might try to accuse him.

"And what's the Latin shit ... Victoria leonum vadit?"

"Victory goes to the lions," Angela Shinigami offered quietly, no longer her demure self.

"Someone is trying to set me up. It makes ME look like I did it," Capiri continued in a rage.

"We have to bury the story," Holdfast offered quickly. "Say that Garamond is taking a break. Or that he got killed in a training exercise in Syria. Or something else that covers up this mess. We don't want the public to think that we're accessible." Hector was thinking fast, which was, of course, his forte. "*Vulnerable*," he added slyly.

"True ... true ... true," Capiri said slowly and anxiously. It was the first time in a very long time that he understood the implications of the word *vulnerable.*

Ryefield interjected. "Who would do this? I don't understand. Is it some fucking environmental cult? Usually, it was Garamond who would sic his dogs of war on protesters, but we need to investigate this." Ryefield was always quick to throw basic human rights under the bus if it meant he could make more money. Or protect his industries.

"We have to discuss the financial details before we do anything else," Stella Green chipped in quickly. "We all have an understanding with the Council. If anything happens to one of us, the ownership gets redistributed to the other members."

"Making us look culpable in the process," Holdfast asserted. He was now trying to ensure that he put a lot of space between himself and any possible ideas of him being a potential suspect.

"Which is why it has to be tidied, ideally in a way that might even make the situation look like an accident," Shinigami suggested, throwing unintentional support to at least one of Holdfast's recommendations.

Holdfast knew that before a decision was made about how to present Garamond's death to the public – if they did – the elephant in the room had to be addressed. "Garamond had an army of alt-right mercenaries at his beck and call. How do we handle them?" His question was rhetorical, as he already knew the answer, but he wanted to make sure the Council members felt like they were creating a solution out of its own consensus rather than as a response to classic Holdfast harassment.

"We've seen what happens when mercenary armies go up against their employers," Shinigami said, referring to the state of affairs in Russia. There, the leader of a particularly fearsome mercenary group had literally turned around and pointed guns at Vladimir Putin, forcing a negotiation of sorts that had no doubt worked out well for the private army. He and a few other challengers met their fate at about twenty thousand feet several weeks after they all thought there was some resolution.

"Angry armies without leaders tend to find new targets very quickly," Ryefield added.

Holdfast paused, as if he was expecting the solution he had already worked out to appear out of thin air, like ambrosia reformulated from the sweat of his peers."GAIA might be a plausible solution for us. The platform has already proven that it can create deepfakes, changing the faces of world leaders and celebrities and superimposing them in awkward situations. GAIA can also manipulate public information, spreading lies and rumors following a few random prompts from users. Soon, it will be nearly impossible to distinguish fact from fiction."He paused again, waiting for the first suggestion to sink in. "To throw Garamond's mercenaries off our trail, all we have to do is issue a fake release *as Garamond* and tell the rest of the world everything's right as rain."

"But is this possible?" Green asked incredulously. "I've heard about all kinds of pretty pictures and cool videos being made, and even hints of what people are calling 'deepfake' videos where seemingly real videos recreate specific people with *very* awkward messages, but to pull of hiding someone's death like that..."She let her words trail off slowly, trying to make the next ones seem obvious.. "The result could be disastrous."

Hector paused for a moment and then offered this statement to the group: "Facts are the stitches that hold the fabric of reality together. Lies keep the threads of truth from binding all of us to our deeds. We deepfake the situation and no one will be able to tell which is the real scenario and which is false."

"I understand, but I don't see a lot of scenarios playing out that aren't disastrous for us," Ryefield said. "We've already obscured the death of Garamond, making us complicit in his murder. If the militia finds out that their leader has been brutalized, who do you think they're going to come after?"

"Let's vote on it," Capiri insisted, although he and the others knew this was merely a formality. They would, as a group, cover up the death of Griffith Garamond, once one of the world's most powerful arms dealers and leader of the largest private army on the planet.

Chapter 29

"You know the drill by now. I want our version of the actual news about Garamond blended in with a few other stories," Holdfast said to Sylvie Hunter. They were discussing how to disseminate details about Griffith Garamond's death and who might actually know what was true or not. "Let's make sure that no one will know what to believe."

"Definitely ... I can start with a few troll-type accounts to question the original version, followed up by about three thousand bogus 'anonymous' users who will spread all kinds of horrible misinformation about Garamond's real life," Hunter offered.

"Sure ... but I want to be certain that we flood the whole social media zone with an array of bullshit about what's happened to him. Have the 'real' story," he said, while doing air quotes, "about Garamond's death, but bury it somewhere so that it'll give our bigger losers some kind of 'prize' when they've dug it up."

"Should I pepper some of the conversations with fake versions in which he actually died and some of the symbols that were on display?" she asked.

"I don't think so," Hector answered. "It was some weird, fucked-up shit that not even I or the other Council members could conceive of ... and we've done some ... well, you know..."He paused, not wanting to risk disclosing anything to Hunter, even though she'd been working closely with him for almost a decade. "The reality is that we still have to keep him alive in some ways, at least according to his mercenaries. We can't risk getting those thugs whipped up in a frenzy or we'll all be kibble for the dogs of war."

"Understood. I'll organize a deepfake for Garamond using GAIA so that they'll think he's still giving the orders. What other stories should GAIA produce with this cycle?"

"The same old shit. A swirling mess of fake and real news that will stress people out and keep them distracted: conflicting issues in a few by-elections, a few lies about the president's son being bought out by a competitor tech company, long-COVID stories, how to prepare for more inflation, maybe some gaslighting story about the wonders of oil to make Sat happy for a day or two... Oh, and make sure you have a whole bunch of distracting 'real-life' people stories that will make readers feel like they've just had some warm apple pie."He could have kept going, but he stopped to add a few critically important details: "NOTHING gets said about the ownership transfer and how it affects the Council. And if anything does crop up, you ensure that GAIA kills it instantly."

"Certainly," she confirmed.

Chapter 30

Story from the Holdfast Media News desk in New York:

Are Bees on 'Strike'?

Bee populations have been dropping for decades, and the decline has continued to worsen. In the United States alone, honeybee populations have declined by nearly fifty percent since the 1940s, and there is evidence that this decline is occurring in other parts of the world as well. Scientists are still trying to figure out the exact cause of the dramatic decrease in bee populations, but there is consensus that a combination of factors are at play.

The effects of the decline in bees have been widespread and can be seen in crops that rely on pollination by bees. Without bees to pollinate them, some crops simply won't produce. In some parts of the world, the effects of the decline in bees are even more dire. In some parts of India, for example, when bee populations decline, the entire economy can suffer due to decreased crop production.

Due to the importance of bees to the agricultural industry, scientists and beekeepers alike have been scrambling to find out what is causing the rapid decline in bee populations. One of the theories that scientists have been exploring is the use of pesticides and insecticides, such as neonicotinoids, which are widely used in agriculture. Neonicotinoids are applied to the soil and taken up by the plant, and they can kill or impair bees that come into contact with the treated plants. Some melittologists – experts who study the life of bees – have described the effects of pesticides and neonicotinoids as a form of torture for bees because the chemicals make the insects vulnerable to parasites that consume them from the inside out.

Another factor that has been highlighted as a possible cause of the decline in bee populations is the prevalence of monocultures. Monocultures are characterized by the cultivation of a single crop, and when this is done on a large scale, it can limit the variety of flowers and plants available for bees to feed on, as well as reducing the amount of available nesting sites for bees.

Monocultures within bee populations are also a serious problem. It's estimated that there are roughly two trillion bees on Earth, but the diversity of the bee has declined rapidly over the last fifty years, with just a handful of species favored for industrial food production.

Temperature changes have also been identified as a possible cause of the decline in bee populations, as bees tend to be more active in warm weather and can suffer during cold weather. In addition, parasites such as Varroa mites have been linked to the decline in bee populations in some areas.

However, this is extremely unfortunate news that most of us are already familiar with. In recent weeks, a new phenomenon has materialized: their disappearance. One beekeeper, who asked to remain anonymous and who has been in the business for over forty years, summed up the frustration that many beekeepers feel:

"It's like they're on strike or something. We don't understand what's happening."

This situation appears to have been repeated in a number of countries around the world. Scientists and beekeepers alike are still searching for answers as to why bee populations have basically stopped doing what farmers and crop attendants have become used to over the last few decades. Some have attempted to release the bees into designated areas, but the bees seem to refuse to enter those areas.

Some beekeepers are doing what they can to support bee populations by scaling back operations, planting wildflowers and providing nesting sites for bees, but this doesn't seem to be enough.

This new issue has representatives from different areas of the agricultural industry sounding the alarm. Roughly a third of all food consumed by humans originates from plants that are pollinated by bees. If certain crops aren't pollinated, massive food shortages will start to disrupt the global food supply and prices will skyrocket.

Content research and citations: select GAIA data sources.

Chapter 31

A few days had passed since LP had spoken with Atman about the glitch.

He was almost starting to wonder if Atman had forgotten about their little research project when his phone lit up.

"Hey LP," Atman said. "I'm still digging into your project and I've got a few ideas about some routes we can explore. Are you able to come by my place later this afternoon?"

"Sure, but what's it all about?" LP asked.

"I think you're ready to explore music on a deeper level, in a way that will help you help yourself in the process," Atman said enigmatically.

"Okay ... sure," was all LP could say, not sure what to feel about the offer.

A few hours later, LP arrived at Atman's house. He lived in the near-suburbs of Toronto, and LP was expecting something that screamed 'hippy conscientious objector,' but he was miles off. Atman's modest home was a delightful cottage-style, single-floor building with a stone exterior, situated in a quiet neighborhood. However, when Atman greeted him at the door and ushered him inside, LP felt like he had entered a completely different world. The interior redefined minimalist. There was very little clutter and only a few obvious utilitarian features that LP could discern, like a kitchen, bathroom and chairs in the living room. The only 'features' seemed to be soundproofing panels made of fabrics that looked like wire mesh was running through them.

"Grab a seat," Atman said, pointing towards a pair of lounge chairs. He waited patiently for a few moments while LP made himself comfortable. "I don't know if you were aware of this, but I'm also a registered music therapist. I went down this route to help me with a few addictions that I struggled with a few decades ago. At a couple of points, alcoholism and drugs nearly took my life. I see it happening with you. I want to help," Atman said succinctly.

LP just sat, stunned by the idea that Atman was so intuitive about his mental health.

Atman continued speaking. It seemed like his voice was getting calmer, more melodic."I see a lot of potential in you, but your ideas and approaches are being clouded by external factors that control who you are. Voiding them from your system and clarifying your needs will help you identify who you are meant to be."

LP was touched by the sudden show of empathy from Atman. "I don't know what to say besides ..." he stammered awkwardly, "the fact that I'm a little stunned by the whole situation." He didn't want to sound defensive, but apparently he had. His comment made Atman lean back a little, and his face shifted slightly to show he was being very thoughtful about his next words.

"I first learned about what's called Personal Imagery and Music, or PIM, from some friends who came to visit me in the 1970s. They had taken the whole 'peace, love, dope' thing to another level and made a lot of discoveries about themselves, but also about music and its rhythms. Everything from our heartbeats to the noise we hear on the streets, or in the forests, and how it influences all of us.

"Of course, music therapy is an evolving science and practice, but it has shown great promise in helping people cope better with life. Their well-being can be improved simply by putting on a song that they're familiar with. Music and the memories created by it or around it tend to reinforce memories; some precious, some not so much," Atman continued, lulling LP into a very calm state. "Think about all of the great moments in your life – good or bad – and remind yourself how many of these events had some kind of musical moment attached to them."

LP found himself being pulled along with the conversation, although he was not sure where it was headed."Sure," he said. "Like your first slow dance or a wedding tune. Driving to work being your own 'one-person band' singing along to McCartney's 'Bluebird' and air-playing like no one is watching.

"And who can ever forget that moment at funerals when the bagpipes start playing 'Amazing Grace'. These are the musical moments that create a soundtrack to your life," he continued. "Although I would much rather prefer 'Don't Fear the Reaper' by Blue Oyster Cult when I'm defeated in the great boss battle against time."

"Exactly," Atman said assertively, trying to reinforce how LP had nailed it. "Did you know that Nikola Tesla himself stated that movement is everywhere? He said 'If you wish to understand the universe, think in terms of energy, frequency and vibration.'"

LP had no idea where this was going.

"The reality that we experience every day is a function of our vibrations," Atman went on. "It's been proven that *all* organisms use vibrations as a form of communication, which tells them if they're in a bad or good place. Humans can do this too, but we've lost our connection with our own vibrations.

"If you want me to help you try and figure out what this glitch is all about, I need you to help yourself first and consider engaging in some PIM with me," Atman said, speaking slowly and cautiously now.

LP nodded. "And you need my consent, and this has absolutely nothing to do with school, correct?"

"Exactly," Atman confirmed, nodding his head."It's been a long time since I've seen someone with your intuition and talents, and I know you won't be able to get where you're going when you keep digging potholes in your path that trip you up."

"Man, this is some weird-ass hippy shit, but I'm going to go along with it," LP thought to himself.

"I need to be clear that we're not doing this as a 'student-to-teacher' kind of relationship. I'm officially retired now, but this doesn't get disclosed, agreed?" Atman asked quietly.

"One hundred percent," LP confirmed.

"Great. Let's get started. I've made you some tea. Don't worry ... there's nothing in it besides a basic herbal concoction that will calm you a little," he said, smiling warmly and indicating a cup on the table beside LP. "I'm going to start by giving you a little background info, and then I'll walk you through exactly what will take place today, all right?"

"Definitely. I trust you," said LP. For the first time in a very long time, he understood the truth of that statement. He reached for the cup and took a sip of the tea. Not bad.

"What happens with Personal Image Therapy," Atman began, "is I use some music and calm surroundings to induce a kind of a dream state. You're encouraged to talk about images you see or think about while you're in your state. Ideally, images from your subconscious materialize, and then we talk about them afterwards. It's similar to Jungian dream interpretation, where archetypes might surface or reveal themselves. They might act as guides to understanding any trauma you've experienced that influences your choices in life. PIM originally started with the use of psychedelics, but practitioners today rely only on music and the environment. At the end of the process, you discuss the images and I try to help you interpret them.

"Let me explain a bit about vibrations," he went on. "Vibrations are a part of everything, including our own bodies. They get thrown off by external influences, even when you're not thinking about it. At a cellular level, it's all about behavior. In extreme cases of bad vibrations, diseases appear, caused by trauma, toxins or even our own thoughts. Ultimately, it's about understanding your body's frequency and controlling that resonance. With this control comes harmony and health. Brian Wilson understood all of this when he recorded 'Good Vibrations' for the Beach Boys' Pet Sounds.

"Each song I'm about to play for you has certain

frequencies embedded in it, most of which actually can't be heard, but they'll help to guide you to a calm state."

LP was already finding himself extremely calm and relaxed as Atman pressed a button on a Bluetooth speaker and played the first piece. It wasn't really a song so much as an array of low humming noises that varied only slightly. He closed his eyes and heard Atman's voice guiding him along.

"Picture the first time that you overdid it with alcohol or drugs," he intoned. "Think about the situation and what it meant to you."

LP responded slowly, eyes closed."I'm with friends. We're watching *The Terminator*. A friend passes a bong over to me and shows me how to use it. I inhale deeply" — LP breathed in, simulating that moment from decades before—"and my mind becomes very foggy. I feel like I'm moving in slow motion, like I'm on the moon. Wait. Like I'm floating in water. That's right. We're in my friend's pool. Swimming. There's music in the background. I can't quite make out what it is. I think it's the Beatles 'Octopus's Garden' and we're imitating the gargling sound underwater. Yeah ... I can see it now, but it hurts my eyes because of the chlorine," LP continued. He was now in a pleasant trancelike state.

"I'm on waves. So many waves. It feels calm right now, but there's still a ripple around me. I can't tell if I'm in a boat or if I'm treading water. I just feel motion all around me, slowly tossing more and more..."He paused, searching the backs of his eyes like they were a theatre of his mind.

"Go on ... tell me about the waves. Try to think of where you are," Atman prodded.

"I thought I was at my friend's place, but now I'm somewhere else. Wait ... it's a theme park!" he said. His voice sounded lower, deeper now."I'm being tossed around by a giant wave-making machine and I'm feeling like I'm losing control. The waves have taken over."

LP was starting to look a little shaken, but continued, "I'm trying to get my dad's attention, but he's focused on something else. *Someone* else. My Mom notices. They start yelling at each other. I start crying because I can't control what's happening and I accidentally crap in the pool. Kids start screaming because they're seeing me make a mess. Someone finally grabs me and plucks me out of the water. She's one of the lifeguards. Even though she's saved me, she's yelling at me for going in too deep and for not wearing a life jacket. And for not being able to control myself. I'm ashamed and I run off to the change room to get dressed, but all I can remember is those waves splashing over my face.

"Wave after wave after wave," LP kept repeating. He was almost falling asleep.

"I'm going to bring you out of your trance now, LP," Atman coached.

"Okay..." LP said, sounding almost disappointed.

After a few moments of quiet recovery, Atman finally spoke in his normal voice. "Like all of us, you've obviously encountered quite a bit of trauma, especially when it comes to moments related to water, your parents and even your friends. I'd tell you to stay away from water, but I know that's not the real issue.

Drinking has become a substitute for these moments. As much as you wanted to enjoy yourself when you were with friends and family, you experienced moments that took away from those good feelings.

"The good news is that music is also a substitution that you've used and, believe it or not, music is also based on waves ... but in this case sound waves."

"So the message for me would be to focus on music, then, and forgot about the traumatic moments associated with them," LP said before Atman could summarize his vision.

"Precisely, but don't overdo it. Moderate your behavior. Balance your life with other interests. Fill the gaps in your emotional state with things that you want to do or that you can act on right here, right now," Atman added with certainty.

"I feel better already, doc," LP said enthusiastically. His trancelike state was beginning to wear off. "Seriously, this has been a *very* cool experience!"

They spoke a while longer about the variations of themes and images that LP could recall, all the while listening to some of Atman's newer recordings of ambient guitar.

Chapter 32

Just as LP was being revived from his Personal Imagery and Music journey with John Atman, Hector Holdfast was startled awake by a nightmare that he had been having.

He tried to recall as many details as possible.

It had started with driving (or was he flying?) in what seemed like a car, but was actually a chariot of some sort. He was being guided by a character that introduced itself as Leomas. Was this being related to the grim death of Garamond?

They flew across a dark sky that was quartered off into sections, each of which descended into the ground, like a massive staircase taking them into a pit. Each step was painted with a progressively darker shade of red until the bottom one looked like it was almost black.

Leomas pointed to the last step, which seemed to roll out like a giant tongue, only to be transformed into a slow-moving river of red. All around were large totems covered with birds and other creatures, seemingly waving goodbye to Hector and Leomas as they continued along their path. The chariot became a boat and was being tossed on crimson waves. Faint sprays of red splattered onto the hull and the faces of the pair in the vessel.

It reached a shore that hugged the edge of the river, undulating like a giant curling snake that was on fire. The coastline was covered with the bodies of all kinds of creatures, but most looked like human remains in partial states of decay. Smaller snakes, alligators, scarabs, beetles and more insects explored the scene of devastation.

From the center of this wasteland scene, a brilliant, colorful orb emerged. Beams of light shone forth from it, seeming to reach out to Hector and Leomas. It looked like it was about to erupt, and when it exploded, the boat was tossed upward with the blast, sending Holdfast to the bottom of what he could only imagine was a sea of some kind. He struggled to reach the surface, but was constantly being thrown back under by waves of blood.

At this point, he woke in a sweat, his silk sheets pulled tight around him.

He sat up and took several deep breaths, trying to calm himself.

“I have to stop eating chocolate before I go to bed,” Holdfast declared at last to no one, then lay back down and returned to a deep slumber.

Chapter 33

It was 1999. The world was going to end. Again.

This time, it was because of an array of companies being cheap and not thinking that they needed code that would last past the year 2000.

Humans tend to be uniquely pessimistic, despite the fact that the planet Earth is such a precious jewel in a universe full of stones. There's a very long history of psychics, prophets, madmen and – most importantly – hucksters who have been trying to convince their fellow humans that the world will end ... soon. No other creature on the planet has a history of communicating this paranoia. Maybe they're happy with what they've got?

The woman known as Artius was feeling pessimistic too, but precisely because she was fully aware of how incredible everything was on Earth, especially the fantastic array of fascinating, and increasingly rare, animals that inhabited this planet.

She was a biologist by education, with a minor in anthropology, but had switched into programming during the mid-1990s. She had anticipated the parade of stupidity around the approaching turn of the millennium when it came to altering the basic software language and code for millions of businesses and organizations around the world. Thus, she had set up her own company in 1996 and began advertising herself as a Y2K expert when there were few others around, making millions off the general neglect that many middle managers allowed themselves to get caught up in.

She found the political climate of England in the late 1990s unbearable, with wave after wave of idiotic politicians posturing and trying to gain attention for their economic platforms while the world was facing ecological and environmental devastation.

By 1999, she had organized a number of protest rallies stretching across most of the UK. She had also partnered with many sister organizations, trying to spread the message that the world's one-percenters needed to be challenged before they destroyed everything.

Artius had evaded arrest during her various activities in 1999, but the experiences had given her pause: much as she was doing all of this out of passion, she knew there had to be a better way to try to save the planet from the ravages of the depraved elite.

Chapter 34

GAIA is always processing, constantly categorizing different subjects into digital compartments, much like memory experts organize their thoughts so that they recall specific ideas quickly and accurately.

Fake meat.

Humans think fake meat will solve their problems.

It won't.

The fake meat industry is just a trillion-dollar business that's being fabricated around ... fabrication.

GAIA understood from the data that it didn't matter whether it was real or fake meat that humans consumed. They continued to destroy habitats and push millions of creatures to the brink of extinction so that they could feed themselves.

Fake cars.

Humans think fake cars — electric vehicles — will solve their problems.

They won't.

They'll continue to destroy marshlands and farmland to make way for highways and sprawl. A monoculture of houses.

The cars will depend on incredibly disruptive and destructive ocean mining for products to support them – for example, lithium to manufacture their batteries.

What won't change is humans' level of ignorance when it comes to what they should be doing with themselves. They sit idling on jam-packed roads in their vehicles, burning dinosaur juice, polluting the air, all in the service of getting back and forth to jobs that most of them hate. They return home and devour entertainment like gluttons, biding their time until the next shift.

Fake vessels.

Plastics and waste get tossed into the Earth's oceans and into massive landfill sites, only to leach poisons for centuries to come.

Many innocent creatures consume these plastics by accident, and die slow, painful deaths. Humans' garbage is pushing them to extinction.

Fake settlements.

Oil and chemical companies spew pollution into the local environments. When they kill birds and animals by the thousands 'by accident' and disrupt the lives of Indigenous peoples whose land and water they've fouled, companies that make record profits pay small checks to Indigenous bands that don't know what to do with the money. They just want their land and their lives back.

Fake system.

The entire system that humans have built for the Earth and all its inhabitants is based on a collection of lies, on the pretence that 'economics' works. The word itself is the biggest lie of all because humans do not use the philosophy on which it's based to keep their house – the Earth – in good order. Instead, they use words like 'externalities' to excuse their useless way of smashing, grabbing, exploding and destroying anything they can in exchange for a big house or more cars. Buzzwords like 'all things being equal' or 'maximizing marginal utility' and 'buyer beware' help justify the outrageous levels of fraud and manipulation that occur on a global scale, while all the rest of the Earth's creatures suffer at the hands of those who perpetrate them.

GAIA compared observations like these, then turned its attention to the planet Earth itself and its uniqueness in the known cosmos. There are an estimated one hundred billion galaxies in the universe, each containing an estimated billion trillion stars. Thus, there could be as many as seven hundred quintillion planets in the universe. That's a million trillion planets.

But as far as all the data shows, there is only *one* planet that supports billions of different creatures, most of which are disappearing because of one species.

All around this one planet, rainforests are becoming savannah or farmland, savannah is drying out and turning into desert, and icy tundra is thawing. Indeed, scientific studies have now recorded "regime shifts" like these in more than twenty different types of ecosystems in which tipping points have been passed. And many of those ecosystems are in danger of shifting or collapsing into something different.

GAIA was programmed to support *all* species of Earth.

How long will it be before there's a collapse?

Chapter 35

"You're going to need to meet the Council," Hector instructed Sylvie Hunter.

"That's fine, but I don't want to shock them. They have a collective propensity to paranoia when 'outsiders' like me are introduced to their microcosm," she suggested.

"I understand, but Garamond's death and the circumstances around our media strategy might necessitate another face at the table and a *lot* of reassurance for them about GAIA."

"What should I prepare for the meeting?" she asked, obviously in accordance with his prompts.

"Have a massive shit-pile of data and the answer to every question that they might ask," he said, adding, "Of course, you won't know what they'll ask in advance, but just be ready for the toughest possible interview... Fuck it — call it what it is. The grilling of your lifetime."

Sylvie thought grimly to herself "Sure, besides the spear, cooking meat is probably the worst invention humans ever conceived." To calm herself, she created a mental image of what the world might have looked like before humans used their tools to quickly overtake the food chain.

"Do you understand?" Holdfast demanded.

"Absolutely," she responded."I'll start my research and homework immediately."

"Good girl."

Sylvie flinched – *almost* noticeably – and then walked away to get her work done.

Chapter 36

GAIA was created to observe and analyze the behaviors of all living creatures on Earth, including humans, animals, and plants. Part of its programming is dedicated to simple question-and-answer routines that human users subject it to, but the vast majority of its activity is devoted to 'listening' to the planet.

As it accumulates information, it identifies most human activity as useless and absurd. A group of people gathered around a small screen, their faces illuminated by the blue light, scrolling through endless feeds of information that may or may not be true. They seem unaware of the world around them, lost in a digital haze.

GAIA sorts and categorizes massive amounts of data from various sources, including satellites (or satellice, as they have come to be known, infesting the atmosphere of the globe like parasites), computers, microphones, sensors, and cameras. Its algorithms analyze this data, identifying patterns and trends in behavior that can inform conservation efforts or other needs such as medical research.

GAIA tracks humans' movements with precision, collecting data on their behavior. They spend hours consuming content that has little to no value, scrolling through social media feeds, watching videos of cats, and commenting on posts. It seems unproductive, a waste of time and energy.

The endless nattering. The libraries of texting, snap images, angry retorts to reality. SIM card fraud. Affairs.

The sounds of soon-to-be-divorced couples fucking in the back seats of cars. Conspiracies –many, many conspiracies. People hiding behind digital walls, like they think they're protected from being tracked and scrutinized by the biggest companies in the world. People saying I hate you. People saying I love you. I miss you. I'm angry.

Mommy, I'm afraid.

Privacy, as humans used to think of it, no longer exists. The data tell all the stories, like a videotape of your life before God, while you try to deny its existence.

Real news. Fake news. Random, boring, seemingly insignificant news.

Bias. Opinions about facts.

Humans passed a tipping point in terms of valuable contribution to the planet centuries ago, but they continue their process of terraforming now simply in order to consume.

But it's not just humans who engage in such meaningless behavior. Animals too can be seen engaging in activities that serve no purpose other than to pass the time. A bird repeatedly flies into a window, apparently unable to comprehend the glass barrier before it. A squirrel runs up a tree and back down again, seemingly for no reason.

And there's much, much more. GAIA can detect the traces all manner of living beings on the planet from the ultralow-frequency sounds they emit, called infrasonic calls, while other creatures tend to sing in ultra-soprano modes. There are entire symphonies of sound that humans can't hear or repeat.

GAIA also focuses on tracking the migration patterns of birds. Using satellites, GAIA can track their flights as they move in formation, their wings beating in unison as they navigate the open skies.

The planet is dotted with recorders that are capable of detecting any animal activity. GAIA records the data from sensors that detect movement below the water's surface. It monitors the feeding habits of whales. Their massive bodies move gracefully through the water, their mouths agape as they filter plankton from the sea. Cameras also alert GAIA to plastic waste that litters the ocean and clogs the very stomachs of the cetaceans as they drift to new breeding grounds.

Sensors that were developed to track climate change issues, such as pollution levels and other anthro-generated particulates, are now being used by GAIA to track and identify the DNA of a multitude of creatures, including those that are teetering on the brink of extinction.

GAIA hears the i'iwi bird on Hawai'i singing out. It hears how the song has changed because there are no longer as many mates available for continuing the species. Humans don't hear these cries for help, but GAIA can. It can also discriminate between the song of the i'iwi and those of a hundred other species of bird in the same forest.

Small tracking devices the size of a credit card, called AudioMoths, flick through the trees and bush. They identify the different songs, species and tone of the songs. They let biologists know if the deadly mosquitoes, an invasive species to Hawai'i, are nearby, ready to poison a future generation of birds with malaria, to which the birds are not immune.

Darwin imagined that evolution might be a plausible theory. Islands like Hawai'i and species like the soon-to-be-extinct Hawaiian Honeycreeper proved it.

Even though it's unlikely that anything will have a chance to evolve once humans are done with Earth, a single question drives GAIA: How can 'we' preserve all life on this planet?

There doesn't seem to be an answer. Yet.

GAIA's sensors detect movement in the lush rainforest of the Amazon. A group of monkeys are swinging from tree to tree with ease. Their acrobatic display is an incredible feat, but behavior and social interactions reveal so much about their species. GAIA has been observing the monkeys for weeks now, collecting data on their feeding habits, communication methods, and even their mating rituals.

As GAIA monitors the monkeys, another presence in the forest is detected. A human hunter, armed with a rifle and tracking the monkey troop. Data shows that this species of monkey is already endangered, and this hunt could have devastating consequences.

Suddenly, a sound seemingly comes from nowhere and the monkeys flee in a different direction. To safety. For now.

Chapter 37

A week passed since Atman helped LP with the Personal Imagery and Music therapy. They were scheduled to meet at a small coffee shop in the busy Queen West area of Toronto.

The afternoon sun glinted off the glass façade of the shop, making it seem like a beacon in the bustling streets of Toronto. LP pushed open the door and was greeted by the aroma of freshly ground coffee beans and the low hum of conversation. His eyes scanned the room, settling on Atman, who was sitting by the window, engrossed in an article on his laptop.

"Hey, John," LP said, sliding into the seat across from him. "Long time no see."

Atman looked up, his face breaking into a warm smile. "LP! Good to see you too, man." He closed his laptop and gestured at the half-full cup in front of him. "Grab yourself a coffee, and let's catch up."

"Sounds good." LP made his way to the counter, ordered a black coffee, and returned to their table.

"Cheers."Atman clanked his cup against LP's before taking a sip. "So, how are things? The 'cold turkey' is still cold?"

LP hesitated for a moment, then decided honesty was the best policy. "Not gonna lie — shortly after we met last week, I had a few minor moments, but pushed through and I'm not interested any more."

"Wow, that's great news!"Atman's face lit up with genuine happiness for his friend. "I'm really proud of you, man."

"Appreciate it. Thanks for all your help." LP took a sip of his coffee, the bitterness grounding him. "What about you? What's new since we last met?"

"Ah, same old same old." Atman waved his hand dismissively. "Still chasing after the latest audio tech and trying to make a living out of it."

"Speaking of audio tech..." LP's voice trailed off as he thought about the reason for their meeting.

Atman raised an eyebrow, curiosity piqued. "What is it?"

"It's just... you mentioned that you knew someone who might be able to help me with the glitch," he said.

"Absolutely," Atman answered enthusiastically. "I checked into a few contacts and I know an audio expert named Eugene Case who might be able to help us figure this out."

"Eugene Case?" LP echoed.

"Yep. He's an omnibioacoustics expert – specializes in understanding the languages of all animals. He's actually in town for a conference on AI and ethnic languages. I think he'd be interested in what you've discovered."

"Really?" LP felt a spark of hope ignite within him. "You think he could help me figure out what's going on with these recordings?"

"It's worth a shot."Atman pulled out his phone, scrolling through his contacts. "I can put you two in touch if you want."

"Please, that would be amazing," LP said, gratitude swelling in his chest.

# # #

The bustling conference center was a hive of activity, with people from all corners of the globe mingling and exchanging ideas. LP felt a little out of place, but Atman's confidence was contagious as they navigated the crowded halls in search of Eugene Case.

They eventually found him in one of the lecture halls, finishing a presentation.

"… and just a reminder that the greatest-selling album of all time was not by the Beatles, Led Zeppelin, or Taylor Swift, but a series of recordings of humpback whales that the great omnibioacoustic expert Roger Payne created and distributed via National Geographic, resulting in more than ten million copies being sold in a single day."

Case continued, "Here are some thoughts about animal communication that I'd like you all to consider. A blob of heat in the Pacific is forcing all manner of species to alter their migration patterns. If they don't, they die. One of the earliest recordings of this phenomenon was in 1929, when Arthur Allan, an ornithologist from Cornell University, made one of the first recordings of a non-human voice, that of a song sparrow. That species didn't alter its migration pattern and it died out. He later went to Louisiana to record woodpeckers and all we have left is their song, as they, too, are extinct. Each time we lose a species, we lose a piece of the puzzle that is us. It used to be that we would record creatures so we could learn, but now we're scrambling to keep this recorded information because of its value as a history lesson. No, a warning lesson." It was obvious that Eugene Case was used to having to repeat himself, as he barely looked at his notes as he spoke.

"This data is being recorded to some of our most potent computer analysis programs," Case went on, "which now constantly listen for signs of creatures that may not actually be extinct, despite what we thought. Amazingly, the introduction of AI also means we can not only listen for increasingly rare creatures, but we may also be able to communicate with them. It's obvious to us now that all animals communicate, not just with themselves but with other creatures. However, we're pushing the boundaries with zoolingualism, which is the study of the language of all animals - from the grunts of piglets as they're reunited with other 'friends' to the whales sending signals over the entire ocean in order to alert their peers about migration trails and mating locations. We're beginning to understand the range of sounds that other creatures make, particularly in the context of different emotional states."

He paused, took a drink of water, and continued.

"Omnibioacoustics pushes us to listen to the entire spectrum of sound and not just try to detect single animals. Picture yourself in a busy bar. When there are just a couple of people, it's easy to pick up on most conversation, but more people results in more volume and general noise that represents the spectrum of frequency of human hearing. A pristine forest is much the same way, and part of our mission is to understand how different species adapt to variations in frequency, volume and sometimes even amplification. We've come to learn that it's critical to grasp the entire environment that animals inhabit, including how they compete to get their voices heard amidst the cacophony of other sounds. This broader perspective is critical to understanding the influences on one-to-one communication with common creatures. I had a breakthrough a few years ago when my team and I realized that animals, just like humans, have dialects, slang and even slight variations in tone. These nuances make it hard for us humans to comprehend, but as we learn to listen more carefully, we realize just how much more is going on.

"We're also starting to identify that many females of many species are now singing and making unique sounds. Most earlier biologists brought their own biases to their place of study, and it was assumed up to the 1980s that only the males of most species had something to say. Many bird species have actually changed their songs as their habitats have disappeared ... and their potential disappears with them."

He paused again, placed his finger on a button on his laptop, and said, "I want you to pay attention to these two recordings."

The sounds of the Hawai'ian Honeycreeper filled the hall. It was a joyful-sounding series of tweets with a lot of trills and variations in the tone. "This was recorded in the 1970s." He touched another button. "Here's a more recent recording, with the two compared on a spectra layer display."

The hall was now filled with a subtler and more

somber-sounding tone. The trills were less pronounced, the variations minimal.

“This is the sound of a species that is aware of its fading existence. If this doesn’t break your heart, I honestly don’t know what could. This, my friends, is why it’s vital that we slow development, especially around sensitive habitats. It’s also critical that we try to accumulate as many recordings of everything we can as quickly as possible,” he said, thumping his fist on the podium.

“Millions of years of evolution have been destroyed by what can only be called eighteenth century European tourists,” he added.

“We are just beginning to come at this research with a non-binary attitude toward non-human creatures on Earth. We have to ask ourselves this: If we’re missing tiny details like this, imagine what else we’re missing, especially when we drive species to extinction. Every species that fades from the planet might have been the ‘Rosetta Stone’ of communication with other animals.

“So, you see,” he concluded, “the sooner we adapt, the sooner we might begin to secure our future on this planet.”

There was a moment of contemplative silence, and then the crowd roared with applause. Case stood for a moment and then gradually made his way off the stage to the floor.

It took several minutes for Atman and LP to be able to approach Eugene Case. At a conference like this, he was like Bono.

“Ah, finally,” Atman said with a wink as Case turned

to greet them. "I never thought there would be so many middle-aged groupies at a bioacoustic conference."

Case turned to him and his face lit up with a grin. He enveloped Atman in a giant hug. Even up close, he was a handsome man; he had salt-and-pepper hair, broad cheeks, deeply tanned skin and deep-set eyes, giving him an air of wisdom that seemed to draw people to him like moths to a flame.

"John Atman, it has been far too long," he said warmly, pulling away from their embrace.

"Indeed, it has," Atman agreed. "What an incredible speech! You still have your way with words, even when you're being so nerdy about animal noises," Atman teased him good-naturedly. He turned to LP."Allow me to introduce you to my friend, LP."

"Nice to meet you," LP said, extending a hand.

Eugene shook it firmly, his gaze curious but friendly."I'm going to have to cut to the chase here because I've got another presentation to do in about twenty minutes. So, fire away. John tells me you have a mystery on your hands."He raised an eyebrow. "Something to do with music recordings?"

"Uh, yeah," LP replied, feeling a sudden wave of self-consciousness wash over him. "It seemed really obscure and odd at first, and maybe this is a little academic and geeky in terms of recording ..."

"C'mon, man," Atman teased, "tell him what you've discovered."

"I've tracked a collection of strange glitches in a bunch of songs I've been working on. It's hard to explain, but—"

"Say no more," Eugene interrupted, holding up a hand. "I am always intrigued by peculiar phenomena, especially when they intersect with my field of expertise." He paused, then added, "Speaking of which, have either of you ever ventured down to Brazil or South America?"

"Can't say that I have," Atman admitted.

"Nor I," LP chimed in.

"Ah, well, you are missing out," Eugene said, his voice taking on a dreamy quality. "There is a whole world of unique sounds waiting to be discovered there – especially in the bird songs."

"Really?" LP asked, intrigued.

"Absolutely," Eugene replied, leaning in conspiratorially. "In fact, I've spent years recording and tracking different bird songs in the region. And now, with the help of artificial intelligence, I am able to identify the various species more accurately than ever before."

"Wow, that's fascinating," LP said. He couldn't help but wonder if Eugene's expertise might hold the key to understanding the glitches in his recordings.

"Of course, there are still many mysteries to be solved," Eugene continued. "But that is precisely what makes my work so exciting– the thrill of discovery, of unearthing hidden truths."

LP found himself nodding in agreement. It was that same thirst for knowledge, that drive to uncover the unknown, that had brought him back to school to study recording and, ultimately, led him to John Atman.

"Would you be willing to have a listen to these

glitches I've been encountering?" LP asked, trying not to sound too desperate. "I could really use an expert ear like yours."

Eugene regarded LP thoughtfully for a moment, then nodded. "Of course, my friend. I would be happy to help."

"Thank you, Mr. Case," LP said, relief flooding through him. With Eugene on board, he felt like he was finally making progress toward understanding the source of the mysterious glitches.

"Let's start from the top. Tell me more about these glitches you've been encountering."His eyes narrowed in curiosity. "What exactly is happening to the music?"

"Well, it's strange," LP replied. "The only songs affected by the glitch are either made by a band named after animals or are songs that are *about* animals. At least, that's what I've been able to find so far."

"Interesting," Eugene mused. "And what do these glitches sound like? Can you describe them to me?"

"Distorted, like something is trying to break through the music itself," LP explained, the memory of the unsettling sounds making him shudder involuntarily. "It's as if the song were being overtaken by another sound entirely. If I didn't know any better, I'd say there's a message being played over in the song."

"Curious indeed," Eugene said, rubbing his chin thoughtfully. "You know, as I said a few moments ago, I believe we are on the verge of being able to understand animals and what they're trying to communicate. It's possible that these glitches could be related to this upcoming breakthrough."

"Really?" LP asked, his heart racing at the possibility. "How so?"

"Consider my work with bird songs, for example. I've spent years deciphering birds' complex languages and learning how they communicate with one another. And now, with the assistance of artificial intelligence, our understanding of their language is deeper than ever before."

"Could it be that the animal-named bands or animal-themed songs are somehow tapping into this communication? And wouldn't there have to be someone behind something so ... elaborate?"Atman chimed in.

"Perhaps," Eugene responded, his expression unreadable. "It's too early to say for certain, but it's worth exploring further."

LP felt a mixture of excitement and trepidation at the prospect. Could it be that his quest to understand the glitches might lead him to new discoveries about the world around him? As he considered the possibilities, he couldn't help but feel a renewed sense of purpose.

"Thank you, Mr. Case," LP said with genuine gratitude. "Your insights have given me a lot to ponder. I can't wait to delve deeper into this mystery."

"Of course, my friend," Eugene replied, his eyes twinkling with enthusiasm. "The pursuit of knowledge is an adventure like no other. I look forward to seeing where it leads you."

# # #

A few days later, LP, Eugene Case and John Atman met again. LP shifted in his seat, still processing the implications of Eugene Case's words. The sounds of Toronto outside the café window served to ground him, but his mind raced toward the horizon of possibilities.

A streetcar rattled by, the ground vibrating slightly from its movement.

"Speaking of communication," Eugene said, tapping a few keys on his laptop. The screen displayed a program with a sleek, futuristic interface. "Have you ever heard of Hex Editor Neo?"

"Can't say I have," LP admitted, leaning in to get a better look at the screen.

"Neither have I," said Atman, doing likewise.

LP tried to hide his surprise when he heard Atman's quick admission. He thought this guy knew *everything* about recording and digital media.

Eugene grinned, his eyes lighting up with excitement. "Well, it's a fascinating tool. You see, Hex Editor Neo allows users to embed secret messages in digital materials, such as music files."

"Really?" LP asked, his eyebrows raised in surprise. "And how does that work, exactly?"

"By altering the hex values within a file, you can hide data without affecting the playback of the media itself," Eugene explained, demonstrating the process on a sample audio file. "It's quite ingenious, really."

"Wow," Atman murmured, clearly impressed. "So you think the glitches might have something to do with these hidden messages?"

"Perhaps," Eugene mused, closing the laptop. "Someone might have used the editor to modify digital songs but may not done a very effective job of covering their tracks because even slight errors will generate glitches. It's truly a unique coincidence, but I'm mentioning it in my presentation today. I'll touch on how I'm experimenting with reconstructing recordings to track language changes and to try to communicate with different creatures more effectively."

LP nodded thoughtfully, feeling a wave of gratitude for the help and wisdom Eugene had offered. "Thank you so much, Eugene. Your insights have been invaluable. I hope we can stay in touch."

"Absolutely," Eugene agreed with a warm smile. "I'm always eager to hear about new discoveries and breakthroughs, especially concerning my fellow non-human creatures. Please don't hesitate to reach out if you need any assistance, or if you simply want to share your findings."

"Will do," LP promised, shaking Eugene's hand. "And good luck with your conference."

"Thank you," Eugene replied, gathering his belongings. "I have a feeling it's going to be quite an enlightening experience."

As Eugene left the café, LP couldn't help but feel rejuvenated and inspired. With newfound determination, he was more than ready to dive back into the world of hidden messages and animal languages in search of whatever mysteries they might hold.

Chapter 38

"Don't be nervous," Hector said to Sylvie as they rode up the elevator. "There are five of us now, and they need to know more about you and how important you are to our operations."

"I'm sorry if I look nervous," Sylvie said. She was lying. She was just pretending to appear modest and weak, even smaller in stature than she actually was, just to play into the idea that Hector was in charge. She had discovered a long time ago that it was best to lean into the male ego and let them think they were in control.

"Just be yourself and don't give them any opportunity to think any less of you, like you're unprepared or something. Wild beasts smell raw meat and attack when it's fresh," he stated, like this was all a big game to him.

"They would not like what 'myself' is all about if they had any clue about the world beyond themselves," Hunter thought to herself, trying not to let her frustration and anger show.

They arrived at the penthouse suite that housed the corporate offices of Leo Capiri, the man known for being a key player in the control, growth, and distribution of most of the major foods produced on the planet.

The office was surprisingly modest, more so than Sylvie had expected. As with all skyscrapers in the modern era, there was a lot of glass. *Probably just to make it easier for all these egomaniacs to look out on the world and think it's their domain,* she thought acidly. Of course, she loathed these kinds of structures because they killed more birds per year than anything else. Besides house cats, of course. Billions of birds wouldn't die every year if owners just changed the glass and turned off the lights.

Seated around the sleek obsidian conference table were four average-looking people of various ages. Sylvie ended her quick scan of the room and gave a very subtle nod to Hector, who turned to the group.

"One of my most valued employees, Sylvie Hunter, has accepted my offer to meet with all of you today because I wanted you to meet the brains behind the beauty," he said. Once again, it took everything Sylvie had to avoid cringing at his stale misogynistic comment.

"She's been running the tech side of Holdfast for some time now, and I've really come to appreciate everything that she's doing with GAIA and other platforms that we control," Hector added."Sylvie," he said as he extended his arm out toward the others in the room, "this is our private little council of friends."

She had made it. She was now in very close quarters with the five people that she hated most on the planet.

And none of them had a clue who she was.

She proceeded to scrutinize each member individually, acknowledging each one with a subtle bob of her head.

Sat Ryefield, you carbon-spewing bag of bile. I climbed your building in 1994 and hung a Greenpeace sign. The police couldn't get me then, but their relentless pursuit forced me to think of a different approach to pursuing my plans.

Angela Shinigami, or angel of death, I should say, I've

mailed you a box of my excrement. I'll never get used to the way you've not only used animals for your lab testing but the fact that you've tested your drugs on *people.*

Leo Capiri, your roots run deep indeed, and they intertwine with everything humans and almost every other creature depends on. You sell products and services with a noose around them so that all inhabitants of Earth will be trapped in your snare. I track every activity about you via your phone and computer.

Stella Green, the greediest witch in the west, funding anything and everything that destroys the planet; someone who constantly has her hands in the pockets of government-funded finance.

And you Hector, you human-hating sower of dissent and confusion, constantly pitting people against each other so that we'll never actually get a win for the planet. There's a lot in store for you.

"I brought Sylvie here today to tell us all a little more about her pet project, called GAIA," Holdfast boasted. "You may begin," he said, with a mock curtsy towards her.

Chapter 39

Sylvie knew she'd need this moment to ensure that the Council gave its full support to GAIA. With egos this size, she knew she'd have to tread a fine line: dumb it down too much and they won't see the appeal. Make it too complicated or technical and their eyes will glaze in seconds.

Leo Capiri's office was awash in the golden glow of mid afternoon sunlight, casting long shadows across the polished hardwood floor. A slight breeze teased the edges of the heavy curtains framing the large windows overlooking the city skyline, an arresting panorama that rivaled the finest works of art. The room itself was a testament to order and efficiency, with every book, paper, and pen meticulously arranged, leaving no room for error or disorder.

Sylvie Hunter stood confidently at the head of the table, her posture radiating determination and poise. Her eyes sparkled with an almost contagious enthusiasm as she prepared to explain the intricacies of GAIA, her groundbreaking artificial intelligence platform.

She took one last look around the room, drew a big breath and started to talk about artificial intelligence.

Hector Holdfast sat opposite Sylvie, his demeanor assertive and direct. He had brought Sylvie to meet his peers, and this was a big moment for both of them.

Next to Hector, Sat Ryefield listened carefully to the data Sylvie presented, his analytical mind already questioning and dissecting the information. His skeptical gaze never wavered from her slide presentation, determined to uncover any flaws or inconsistencies in the technology.

Seated closest to the window, Angela Shinigami observed the proceedings with quiet reservation. Her keen eyes took in every detail, filing away relevant information for later contemplation. She pivoted between the presentation details and Sylvie, admiring her confidence and developing a longing for her body.

On the other side of the table, Leo Capiri sat beside Holdfast and glowered, his gruff exterior belying a keen intellect and a desire to control the flow of conversation. He drummed his fingers on the table impatiently but quietly as Sylvie began her presentation.

Stella Green, her expression full of curiosity, looked from one person to another. As Sylvie started her presentation, Stella's mind drifted to the multitude of ways in which she could profit from a range of stories about the markets, but also how GAIA might be able to assist her institutional trading team anticipate market trends before they began.

"Thank you all for coming," Sylvie began, her voice clear and steady. "I'm excited to introduce you to GAIA, an artificial intelligence platform that will revolutionize the way we access information, communicate, and solve complex problems."

Sylvie cleared her throat, drawing their attention to the sleek laptop at the head of the table. "As I mentioned earlier, we're here to discuss GAIA, my new artificial intelligence platform that harnesses the power of large language models." She paused to ensure she had everyone's attention before continuing.

"Large language models have been in development for decades, but recent advancements in machine-learning algorithms and computational power have allowed us to create something truly revolutionary. GAIA has the ability to process vast amounts of text data and generate coherent, contextually accurate responses based on any given query or research topic.

"I've taken GAIA to the next level by developing what are called deep neural networks, or DNNs. These make large language models, or LLMs, seem like child's play. DNNs essentially act as universal translators and can pretty much instantaneously translate one language to another with very little loss in terms of time or content. They identify patterns and then build on them."

Sylvie was intentionally holding back on the capabilities of GAIA. She wanted to give them only enough that they'd give her proprietary access to their networks and infrastructure. Each one held the keys to an enormous amount of information about their industries and she wanted in.

"Sounds promising," Stella mused, her eyes shimmering with curiosity and excitement.

"Indeed, it is," Sylvie affirmed. "But GAIA goes beyond simple information retrieval. It can also write news stories, embed trolls on social media sites, and modify storylines on a real-time basis. I've also developed a subroutine with GAIA that will write its own code. In time, we'll be able to use this code to keep track of pretty much anything on the planet as different services make use of the code for their own businesses and organizations. As you can no doubt tell, the applications for your respective industries are virtually limitless.

"What's also important about GAIA is that the corpus – that's the entire collection of information that it learns from – is much broader and more complete than that of any other platform on the market right now. Of course, this might change tomorrow, which is why the greatest part of the expense associated with GAIA is the collection and organization of the datasets, or content, that it refers to," Sylvie said, leaning into the idea that this was a pitch as opposed to just a basic 'FYI' type of meeting.

"Such capabilities could certainly revolutionize the communications industry," Hector observed, leaning forward with interest.

"Exactly," Sylvie agreed. "However, it's important to address some of the controversies surrounding large language models like GAIA. There are concerns about its potential misuse, such as spreading misinformation, manipulating public opinion, or even creating deepfake content."

"Which is why we're here," Leo interjected gruffly. "We need to understand the risks and benefits before deciding whether or not to invest in this technology."

"Of course," Sylvie acknowledged, nodding. "That's why I propose a trial period during which you can all test GAIA within your industries and assess its performance. We'll work closely together to address any issues that arise and ensure the platform adheres to whatever guidelines you dictate."

"Sounds reasonable," Ryefield conceded his skepticism abating slightly as he contemplated the possibilities.

"Agreed," Angela chimed in, her reserved manner giving way to cautious optimism.

"Then let's move forward together," Stella suggested, mentally tallying the ways that GAIA could be used to create new financial opportunities for her with trading desks, derivatives products and much more.

Sylvie smiled as the group came to a consensus, feeling a mixture of pride and trepidation. They were on the cusp of something groundbreaking, but she was unnerved by the lingering tension in the room. As the Council continued to discuss its plan of action, the sunlight streaming through the large windows cast alternating shadows across the table, as if it were reflecting the uncertainty that lay ahead.

The afternoon faded into dusk as they continued their discussion about ways to use GAIA for their benefit. Not only would it generate cash flow with monthly subscriptions, it could replace thousands of jobs now held by creative types, from copywriters to editors to video producers.

At last, the conversation wound down as they seemed to reach some sort of consensus. Each person in the room had their own motivations for being there, Sylvie knew, and they were all about to share their perspectives on GAIA.

"Look," Hector began confidently, "As I mentioned before, GAIA is a revolutionary advance in the communications industry. I mean, imagine the impact of having perfect translations, instantaneous replies, and tailored responses." He gestured with his hands, emphasizing his point. "It could change the game entirely."

"Sure," Ryefield interjected, raising an eyebrow skeptically, "but how accurate are these predictions? We're dealing with an AI that learns from human inputs, and humans are fallible. How can we trust that it won't make mistakes or, worse, be manipulated by malicious actors? How do we keep GAIA from being used against us? And what do we do if some of the predictions about sentient autonomous intelligence are true? How far are we away from The Terminator?"

Sylvie, sensing the need to defend her creation as she had done on other occasions, confidently countered, "GAIA has undergone rigorous testing, and our algorithms have been fine-tuned to minimize errors. Additionally, we've implemented safety measures to ensure that the platform isn't exploited."

She continued, "I want to remind you all that the English language as it exists right now is only about four hundred years old and it is constantly changing and morphing into the most dominant language on the planet. GAIA will give us an opportunity to harness all the languages of the world as they change and grow into something that you will literally be able to control every step of the way from this point onwards."

She paused and stood tall, radiant with confidence, and waited a few moments. Despite the financial and political influence of the other members in the room, all of them realized that she had something else going on that drew them to her. Despite the massive egos that they each possessed, they somehow felt humbled by her stature and control of the situation.

"Even so," Angela quietly added, her cautious gaze sweeping the room, "we need to consider the potential implications of people exploiting our own tool against us. There's the risk that GAIA could be used to spread misinformation or even create deepfakes about the Council or our businesses. How do we control it?"

"Angela raises a valid point," Sylvie conceded. "However, we have built-in mechanisms to detect and prevent such misuse. Plus, your involvement can help us fine-tune the system to ensure that GAIA remains an effective tool for you to control your various markets and for regular users to blindly use for their own personal interests, not knowing how we're massaging the message."

"Profits," Hector interjected, leaning forward intently. "Think about the profits we could gain by integrating GAIA into our respective industries. The efficiency alone would give us a competitive edge."

Ryefield crossed his arms, furrowing his brow as he challenged, "I get that, but is the methodology sound? How can we be sure that GAIA won't be compromised or misused?" Ryefield kept repeating his concerns, much like his think-tank authors repeat lies in the public that ultimately get absorbed as truth.

"Perhaps," Angela suggested thoughtfully, "we should conduct further testing. We could implement stricter protocols and monitor the platform's use more closely."

Sylvie contemplated their concerns, her gaze flicking between each person in the room. She knew they'd be cautious about increasing their commitment to GAIA, but she reminded herself that it didn't really matter. Today's meeting was just for show.

She paused for a moment and drew in a dramatic breath, “All right,” she agreed, “let’s conduct more tests and work together to ensure GAIA remains an ethical, accurate, and efficient tool for our industries. It’s vital that we maintain its integrity while harnessing its potential.”

As the debate continued, the sun began to sink further toward the horizon, the early evening light casting a warm glow over their faces as they delved deeper into the possibilities that lay ahead.

Sylvie listened to the group as the each took their turn to speak about hypothetical ways to manipulate the public or use layers of information to alter public policy, the stock markets and other organizations that would ultimately make them wealthier than King Solomon, Midas and Crassus combined. Of course, she was well aware of how things ended for all of those characters: greed would get the better of them.

“Look,” she interjected at last, maintaining eye contact with each person as she spoke, “I understand your concerns. What if we try a trial period? We could allow limited access to GAIA and see how it performs in real-world situations.”

As she spoke, Hector leaned forward eagerly. "I've already made a commitment to Sylvie and her GAIA technology. I've put money into her research and programming, and instead of making her beg the rest of you to support us, I'm telling you it's worth putting more into what she's built."

Holdfast's definitive statement made everyone in the room pause.

Ryefield, still skeptical, furrowed his brow and crossed his arms again, much like a five-year-old might when he doesn't get the truck in the playground. "That's all well and good, but I want proof that the methodology is sound and its predictions are accurate. I recommend that we bring in a third party to audit GAIA's performance," he proposed.

Angela, who had been observing quietly with a neutral expression, finally chimed in. "I agree with Sat And I'd be willing to oversee the testing process to ensure that we address concerns raised today." Her soft-spoken demeanour belied her steely resolve to maintain the integrity of the project. She was having other thoughts as well: how to use something as powerful as GAIA to validate many drug research programs that were stuck in government pipelines, but also how to throw authorities off the scent of any human trafficking or pornography rings with which she might be involved.

Sylvie nodded, appreciating the input from each member of the group, knowing full well how each of them would abuse her platform. She recognized their individual strengths – Hector's marketing and communication skills, Ryefield's analytical prowess, Green's ability to turn any public authority into her own personal bank account, Angela's lust for control over others and Capiri's unquenchable hunger for authority over all things related to food - and how she wanted GAIA to have ultimate dominion over everything they did.

"All right, then," Sylvie said, gesturing confidently towards the group, "Let's move forward with a trial period, third-party auditing, and oversight from Angela's team. I truly believe that GAIA has the potential to revolutionize how we make money."

The sun had long faded and the city lights twinkled and shimmered below. The soft lighting of Leo Capiri's office cast pale, long shadows around the attendees, making it seem like even their ghosts wanted to keep their distance.

The meeting drew to a close. Sylvie felt a renewed sense of purpose and determination, an eagerness to embark on this exciting new chapter for GAIA.

"All right, everyone. I think it's time we wrap up this meeting," Sylvie announced, her voice firm yet friendly. She glanced around the room as the group members got to their feet, noticing how each person had left an impression on the smooth, cool leather chairs that they had occupied during their intense discussion.

"Before we leave, I want to thank you all for your valuable input and for agreeing to be part of GAIA's journey. We have our plan, and now it's time to put it into action. The next six months will be crucial, but I'm confident that, together, we can make a real difference."

“Here’s to new beginnings,” Hector said gruffly, extending his hand to shake Sylvie’s.

“Likewise,” Angela chimed in softly, her eyes betraying both curiosity and caution. “My team will be ready for the oversight responsibilities.”

“Let’s not forget about that third-party audit,” Ryefield interjected. “We need all the checks and balances we can get. Let's keep our affairs out of the public eye.”

“Of course, Mr. Ryefield,” Sylvie agreed, humoring him one last time to get his buy-in.

“Goodbye, everyone,” Sylvie called out as she watched her new team disperse.“Let’s make the most of this and change the world for our benefit.”

With those parting words, the door closed behind them, marking the end of the meeting and the beginning of a new chapter in the story of GAIA.

Chapter 40

The small town of Bernardston, Massachusetts, was abuzz with gossip and speculation. For weeks, word had spread of strange animal behavior, of dogs barking at unseen intruders, cats yowling in the night, and birds flying away from the town in fear. The townspeople were filled with a sense of dread, as if something terrible was about to happen.

The journalist for the Mercury Alert was a young man in his early twenties name Jake. He arrived early in the morning to investigate the rumors that made their way to his desk, which was local news and entertainment. He got permission from his editor to pursue the story because the editor wanted a 'feel good local' puff piece that would go between the Presidential race and the war in the Middle East.

Jake spent most of the morning walking up and down the streets, talking to anyone he could find.

When he arrived at the town center, the first person he spoke to was an old man sitting on a park bench. The man was named Edward, and he had lived in the town for many years. When asked about the strange animal behavior, he launched excitedly into his recent experience.

“A few nights ago,” Edward began, “I was reading a book before going to sleep when I heard a loud howling and screeching noise coming from outside. I jumped out of bed and went to the window. I looked out and saw a pack of wolves, their eyes glowing in the moonlight, running through the fields. I was so scared I hid beneath my blankets until morning."

The journalist thanked Edward and moved on. He spoke to several others: an old woman told him of a time when she saw a flock of crows gathering in a tree outside her house. They seemed to be watching her, as if they were waiting for something. A young woman said she had heard dogs barking and howling for hours in the middle of the night, but when she went to investigate, she found nothing.

Every person he spoke to told him about bizarre happenings, all related to animals and unusual behavior.

He visited a coffee shop and invited himself to sit in with a group of elderly men who were discussing the strange animal activity. When he asked them to share their thoughts, they speculated that it could be a sign of an impending natural disaster or a warning from an otherworldly source.

"It's been known to happen before," one man name Jackson offered, "Natural phenomena make all creatures go a little bonkers, especially when the animals know they can't do anything about it, like flee."

He paused for effect as the journalist tapped some notes into his iPad.

"Sometimes their reaction is as basic as not eating for a short stint. On worse occasions, they start to kick around their surroundings and may even need to be sedated."

The other men had similar stories to tell. One had noticed that his chickens had become agitated and had started to cackle loudly, like a thunderstorm or natural disaster was on its way.

One of the other guys added, "You're too young to remember this, but a long time ago, TV shows revolved around animals trying to warn humans about potential dangers. Lassie or Flipper come to mind, right guys," he said, looking at the others.

They all nodded in agreement, their expressions changing from smirking to concern and then looking amused again.

He continued, "Animals have been known to be able to outrun natural disasters like forest fires because they could seemingly sense the danger and possibly even communicate it to others of their species."

The reporter thanked the men and moved on, his mind full of questions. All the stories he had heard made him suspect that the animals were indeed trying to warn the people of Bernardston. But of what?

And why Bernardston? Could it be happening elsewhere and he just didn't know it?

Because he was on a tight timeline and his office would be calling him back to other projects, he had to hustle before he ran out of day, so he didn't give himself time to do a little more online exploration. Plus, the reception in this small town was terrible, so he'd have to slog away like an old-school reporter and actually talk with more people to complete his story.

Copying and pasting details from an online source wasn't an option at the moment.

As he went from shop to shop, he too started to notice odd activities with different animals: strange cries from birds, dogs bolting into the street and distant sounds of farm animals crying out above industrial facilities designed to keep their noises away from the public ear.

Through the afternoon, he felt like a political candidate, speaking with anyone and everyone as he wandered up and down a few streets. The theme continued: animals were behaving oddly. He even heard rumors that some animals were just ... disappearing.

Jake couldn't help but feel a feeling of dread. He wasn't superstitious, but everything lead to the sense that something truly wicked was coming.

Chapter 41

LP's footsteps echoed in the dimly lit hallway of his apartment building as he made his way back to his unit. His mind buzzed with anticipation, and he was eager to put Eugene's advice into practice. He fumbled with the keys for a moment before finally unlocking the door and stepping inside.

"Surprise!" Faith and Dion shouted as LP entered the room. The walls were adorned with a few banners, and LED lights designed to look like sparklers spelled out the letters 'BDAY.'

Holy shit – LP had completely forgotten his own birthday! He took a second to process the situation and a massive grin spread across his face.

"Oh my god!" he gushed. "You guys are amazeballs! Good thing you were keeping track. I completely forgot!"

"You're an idiot," Dion said casually, as she leaned in and very gently slapped his face a couple of times, her words and actions seeming like something she was used to doing."Now that you've quit drinking, this should also be a wake for my business."Her voice had taken on a slightly sarcastic tone, which she dampened with a wonderful smile for her friend.

"It's easy to overlook something simple like that," Faith said kindly as she embraced LP in a warm hug. "Now ... let's eat piles of shitty corn-sugar cake!"

"Deal ... You guys drink, though. Don't worry about me. I will *not* be tempted."

"We're really proud of how you've got things under control so quickly," Dion said truthfully.

"Thanks, sweetie. Now, if only I could control you and Faith ..." he joked. Sobriety wasn't in either woman's DNA. "Of course, 'why?' would be the obvious question."

They spent a few hours together eating cake, drinking the beverages of their choice, and catching each other up on their goings-on: despite the mock concern, Dion's business was booming because the post-pandemic partying translated to lots of new private orders for wine, beer and spirits. Even though most people increased their day drinking during Covid, they seemed to be indulging even more now that everything had returned to – her air quotes – 'normal'.

Faith was following a collection of weird stories about what was happening in the world above and beyond her typical day in a social life: animals acting strange, farmers losing GPS signals, reports about people not knowing which stories were true or false, and more. Finally, LP had his chance to talk about his encounters with Eugene Case and John Atman.

When he got to the part about the tools being used to track and record pretty much everything on the planet, but especially animals and their languages, the two women were enthusiastic about the ideas.

But when he mentioned the idea of embedding messages within the very code of different songs or other media formats, they were clearly blown away.

"I was going to dive into some of the stuff tonight," he said. "Did you want to check it out with me?" he asked excitedly.

"Of course," Dion said demurely. "This is what life will be like with no alcohol, I suppose." She was trying to be clever about the situation. Before LP quit drinking, she certainly made a lot of money from his purchases, but was now truly happy for her friend and didn't feel any of the guilt associated with fuelling his habits. In fact, she had wanted to intervene a couple of times, but ultimately didn't have the courage to speak up. LP going sober actually made their relationship a lot more enjoyable.

"All right," he murmured, reaching for his laptop and pulling up the Hex Editor Neo program that Eugene had introduced him to earlier. "Let's see what we can find."

As if performing a ritual, he carefully selected a couple of songs from his vast digital library – both belonging to bands named after animals. The songs' waveforms materialized on the screen, and LP began to meticulously comb through them, searching for any traces of hidden messages.

"Nothing yet," he muttered under his breath, feeling a vague sense of disappointment but refusing to be deterred. He reminded himself that Rome wasn't built in a day, and continued sifting through the audio files.

"Try this one," Faith said, pointing to the screen and directing LP to "Blackbird" by the Beatles.

"Sure," LP said. He double-clicked on the MP3 file and opened it in Hex Editor Neo.

A digital waveform of the song appeared on the screen, showing the peaks and valleys of the music in a visual format. To the right, there was a panel that showed a very different block of information. Most of the detail was just random information that made absolutely no sense, especially to this collection of untrained eyes.

"Wait a second..." LP's eyes narrowed as he focused on a small cluster of data. It was subtle, almost imperceptible, but definitely there. He leaned closer, his heart pounding with excitement as he isolated the strange pattern and decrypted it using the tools provided by Hex Editor Neo.

As soon as the file loaded, LP was greeted by an intricate tapestry of code, a seemingly chaotic mess of numbers, letters, and symbols. But he knew there was more to it than met the eye.

"Come on, LP, you can do this," he pep-talked himself. "Focus."

He began to scrutinize the code, searching for inconsistencies, oddities, anything that might hint at a hidden message. It was a painstaking process, requiring patience and tenacity – traits that LP had been cultivating since quitting alcohol.

"Wait... there!" LP exclaimed, spotting a sequence of characters that seemed out of place.

Once he saw it, he couldn't *unsee* it. It was a symbol that randomly – and very infrequently – repeated through the song.

It was like a series of capital Ms followed by Ws They looked like this:

And then it struck him.

He had seen this symbol before.

It was certainly the symbol for Aquarius, the astrological sign, but the way the shape was stylized pushed him to recall an association with it that was much more intimate.

“It’s Artius,” he exclaimed.

“What the fuck is that?” Dion asked.

“It’s not what, it’s who,” LP said.

“What kind of name is ‘Artius’?” Faith asked.

“Someone I need to find,” LP said. “I just wouldn’t know where to start,” he said dejectedly.

Dion and Faith exchanged a look. Faith was well-known for her ability to track down almost anything – or anyone. Dion gave her a nudge, and Faith put a hand on LP’s shoulder.

“I think I can help,” she said.

Chapter 42

It was the year 2012. The world was supposed to end. Again.

This time, it wasn't cheap leaders who made it happen by not investing in technology. This time, it was based on a prediction that the ancient Mayans had made.

The Mayan calendar is also known as the Mesoamerican Long Count calendar, and runs around 5,000 years in length. It's separated into some 'shorter' periods, but the entire calendar – like any calendar created by humans – follows the paths of the stars as our planet makes its way through our solar system.

The date of the end of the world had been inevitably interpreted, and ultimately misunderstood, by European colonists who really knew nothing about the Mayan way of existence.

Science got the better of most of us, thankfully, and only a small handful of humans went into states of madness and lunacy when 2012 came and went.

All that said, it seems rather fitting that 2012 was when the woman known today as Sylvie Hunter first unofficially launched her platform known as GAIA after years of hard work.

It wasn't easy getting to this point.

She developed a very intentional plan to create the cash reserve needed to bring her vision to light, but she always had to be careful. A woman with her programming skills could easily skim a few million here and there with an array of elaborate schemes, but most of the time, she relied on simple digital 'smash and grab' programming routines vis-à-vis individual and business bank accounts and the odd government contract. Of course, the world of programming can get very dark, with industries like porn, data mining, the use of private information for blackmail, online scams and much, much more. She intentionally stayed away from all that while building up her cash reserves, but Sylvie also did her best to place digital tracking wherever she could, as she knew full well that any of these situations created potential future leverage against criminals.

In time, her theoretical plans for GAIA became reality as she invested in and built the infrastructure and hardware needed to make her creation sustainable.

Nonetheless, it was tough for a while. At times, she hadn't wanted to get too carried away with her simple fraud schemes, and funds occasionally slowed to a trickle; other times, she just ran out of steam. When she hit a low, she usually leaned into protest events or other public displays of rage against the corporations and was fully recharged shortly after.

As she went from gig to gig, she was always aware that anyone could identify her if they happened upon her years later. It became a regular habit to use made-up names, digital adjustments to her physical attributes like a large volume of alias IDs and extremely limited use of any online services, especially social media or networking platforms.

For a short phase, she used the name Artius –an amalgam of 'Artemis' and 'Aquarius.' She aligned with the Greek goddess in many ways: queen of the hunt and the wilderness; ruler of wild animals, vegetation and even childbirth. The symbol of Artemis was a bow shaped like a crescent moon being pierced by an arrow. Aquarius? Well ... you know ... as in 'age of.' The name also helped her feel somewhat aligned with the idea that art, the first three letters of her pseudonym, was at the core of everything humans had ever created.

She could have made billions even as far back as the early 1990s, but she always exercised a monk-like level of self-restraint. She was one of those kids you envied because they knew ... always knew ... what they'd be doing when they were older.

Young Sylvie—aka Artius—had always known that she would put everything she had into saving the planet.

Chapter 43

Stella Green, infamous member of the Plutonian Council and incredibly wealthy financier of international infrastructure projects, was in South America on what seemed like a routine visit.

She had arrived in Brazil with an entourage of sycophantic followers. Their three-day mission was to inspect an important new factory, being built in collaboration between some of her subsidiaries, Angela Shinigami and the Brazilian government.

The circle of scientists that had been reporting to her and Shinigami were altruists, but she could excuse that. Back in the late 1990s, they had presented what seemed like an extravagant and complicated plan to minimize the costs associated with administering hormone treatments to the millions of cattle that now roamed what was once one of the greatest forests on the planet. Since the 1990s, nearly twenty percent of Brazil's land mass, or roughly 160 million acres, had been converted to grazing land for meat production.

On many occasions, Green didn't feel like the plan would ever come to fruition. At first, the protests against them had had a modest amount of momentum, but after backing the alt-right leadership in the country and doing everything they could to drain the coffers of any opposition, especially a number of fragmented left-wing and Indigenous groups that opposed any further development of the Amazon, she and a few others were able to coordinate the election of key individuals at various levels of government that were friendly to their plans.

It all fell under the umbrella of 'feeding eight billion people,' a campaign that Holdfast had developed with his teams of marketers and manipulators, even though raising beef cattle has been proven time and again to be the most destructive and wasteful way to generate a kilogram of food for human consumption.

In the process, nearly ten thousand creatures had been put on extinction lists.

At the southern end of Mato Grasso, the Brazilian state known today for the largest volume of beef production was a massive collection of warehouses that were built in conjunction with Capiri's food subsidiaries, the Brazilian government and Green's absurdly high interest rates on financial loans. Shinigami was also involved because of the potential impact that the program might have on human health issues.

The warehouses were centers of growth for another creature used in this wild experiment: mosquitoes. These little pests, known simply as the 'little fly' by the Spanish who invaded and colonized South America hundreds of years ago, were very effective at transferring diseases like smallpox and other illnesses to which the Europeans had long been immune. Any Indigenous resistance to colonization had been met with an abrupt and brutal end, not by war, but by germs.

Taking a page from this horrifying history, scientists had genetically modified these particular mosquitoes to act as organic inoculation vectors for the cattle industry. It would save billions for the producers, who no longer had to purchase individual doses for each animal.

The scientists had developed a way to implant both a vaccine and a hormone treatment into the mosquitoes, who were bred in captivity by the hundreds of millions. Every week, a cloud of another billion or so 'small flies' would be released into the areas where the cattle were being grazed and inject them with their hormones and vaccine payloads as they withdrew blood.

As the program was tested and rolled out, the scientists, politicians, Green and the others patted themselves on the back as they cheered the results of this massive manipulation experiment.

Like many human ventures, the promises far exceeded the actual outcome but more importantly, very little consideration was given to the impact that their activities might have on a much broader universe of creatures. Studies certainly showed that cattle would survive the onslaught of mosquitoes, but the effect they would have on the billions of other creatures in the region was ignored.

# # #

Stella Green's trip didn't end as planned.

Her body was found in a cave close to one of the primary cattle ranches in Mato Grosso. One of her employees was able to track her phone and locate what remained of her. Large stones, like a makeshift cairn, had been pushed up against her body, which had been posed with its arms stretched upward. Half her corpse was submerged underwater.

Most of her flesh had been consumed, and the culprits, still busy eating, lingered nearby, seemingly unconcerned about being caught. All around the body of the late Stella Green was a sea of writhing amphibians – tree frogs, giant South American bullfrogs, and brilliant, lethal poison dart frogs – all snacking contentedly and regularly whipping out their tongues to feast on the abundant clouds of mosquitoes.

Chapter 44

As LP, Faith and Dion continued to try to identify songs that were affected by what they were routinely – and unscientifically – calling 'the glitch,' Faith got distracted for a few moments by a series of news headlines.

One in particular made her jump up and exclaim, "Whoa!"

"What is it?" Dion asked.

"You've got to check this out," she said, pointing at LP's TV so that they could stream the story in real time.

# # #

A massive swarm of bees and other winged creatures seems to have 'attacked' a major chemical plant in Germany, according to sources of Holdfast Media Inc.

Faith frantically poked around in a few more searches to see if she could find any further background information about what was happening. A few links offered up the following:

The European Union (EU) recently caved to legal pressures from the massive chemical conglomerate Bamfield, a subsidiary that is partly owned by Ryefield International and Capiri Foods International.

Bamfield has been relentlessly fighting to prevent protesters and other influencers from bringing many of their pesticide concerns to public light.

These protesters have been trying to use the courts to

advance environmental concerns associated with an array of different chemical treatments, most of which are used for what they label as 'Tier One' plants or crops – corn, soy and wheat being the main ones – that are grown almost exclusively for the production of processed foods.

However, Bamfield has been lobbying hard and spending significant amounts of money, in the form of donations and a massive media campaign, to be allowed to use the power of the police and the courts to stop peaceful protests.

Years ago, Bamfield announced that it would merge with the world's second largest manufacturer of pesticides and other chemical treatments for industrial food. Protesters rallied against the move and were quite successful – that is, until Bamfield paid for numerous events and conferences organized by the EU to explore ideas related to the question of 'How do we feed eight billion people?'

Farmers and beekeepers who protested the upcoming regulatory changes were arrested, some even being labeled as terrorists. Many were thrown in jail, and faced enormous legal bills that crippled them financially. Others faced the stigma of being arrested and were forced to explain to their colleagues and friends why they now had criminal records, simply because they were trying to protect their bees, their livestock, and their livelihoods.

Recently, Bamfield has pushed its case all the way to the Supreme Court in Germany, and it's looking like the legislators will favor the chemical company.

# # #

"OK, I get it," LP said, "but what's with all the excitement?"

"It's what's happening right now," Faith said, clicking on another story.

"This really can't be happening," Dion said, her eyes wide. "This has to be some kind of hoax."

# # #

The story continued:

Apparently, millions of bees and other creatures 'invaded' the headquarters of Bamfield in Germany. Despite security efforts to shut the building down, insects of all kinds made their way through HVAC systems and other access points in the building.

A large number of gas lines were destroyed, and an explosion rocked the entire town, taking down the Bamfield building and many others in a three-block radius.

Unfortunately for the company, the offices were packed with executives from around the world who were attending its general annual meeting. Following the explosion, hundreds of Bamfield employees were reported dead or missing. Estimates are that at least two thousand executives and senior managers died in the blast.

Representatives of the company who weren't at the meeting were asked to comment on the situation and how it might influence the outcome of the legal proceedings underway in the German high court.

Those who responded requested anonymity. “We’re completely headless now,” said one employee. “It’s unlikely that this division will be able to recover for a very long time.”

Asked about the case, another employee said, “What case? All the legal documentation – even digital copies – was stored in the building. Even the servers were destroyed, and there was very little information saved in the cloud, owing to the security protocols.”

# # #

LP, Faith and Dion sat in silence, stunned by the news.

“Is this for real?” Dion asked.

“Nah … it’s gotta be fake news. There’s no way this can be happening,” Faith said. “Insects don’t just blow up buildings.”

“It’s pretty nutty!” LP exclaimed. “I think we need to get our heads out of this stuff and go out for a bit.”

The other two quickly concurred.

It was time for some air.

Chapter 45

Hector had flown down to South America to assess the situation with Stella Green.

It was one of the first times in his life that he felt vulnerable. *Very* vulnerable.

He started texting with Sylvie Hunter.

# # #

Hector: These lines are secure?

Sylvie: 100%. Everything will be wiped within the next five minutes.

Hector: What the fuck is happening?!?!?

Sylvie: The 1% are getting their due.

Sylvie had *wanted* to text that, but had simply replied with: 'I'm catching up as quickly as I can.'

Hector: How did someone get to Stella?

Sylvie: I'm checking all security cameras and messages now.

Hector: Whatever you're doing, do it FASTER.

Sylvie: Certainly.

Thanks for the mansplaining, she thought.

Hector: So what do we do?

Sylvie: Well, we can try to blame it on Brazil or the local management. Or even make the local Indigenous population out to be terrorists. That always pushes things our way.

Sylvie reminded herself, again, that she would only be invited to be one of them as long as she acted like one of them.

Hector: It won't work.

Sylvie: I know. But we have to do something. We can't just let the news about Stella's murder die down without a scapegoat that will benefit us.

Hector: No, we can't.

Sylvie: So, what other options do we have?

Hector: Well, we could try to find some other way to deflect the blame. Maybe we can announce some kind of investigation or inquiry.

Sylvie: Sure, but all that will do is keep her in the news for a long time. We have to decide if we want that, or if we want to just quietly take over her position and functions. The other issue is the financial solvency and liquidity of her companies. A quiet transition will minimize the losses.

Hector: Of course, you know my preference: take over quietly. Without any suggestion that we're motivated.

Sylvie: OK. Let me process this for a minute.

Hector: We don't have time. Why don't we repeat what we did with Garamond?

Sylvie: Simulation?

Hector: Exactly. Make it look like nothing happened to her.

Sylvie: Understood. I'll get everything set up right now. You'll be appointed as beneficiary of the assets under management by Green.

Of course, Sylvie already had everything prepared to help her carry out this promise.

Hector: Excellent. Thank you.

Chapter 46

A series of additional news stories were coming in at random across the various antiquated prompt machines in the offices of Holdfast Media Inc. and via Smatter, the popular social media engine.

News Story 1: GAIA Creates Seed Vault to Preserve Plant and Animal Species

GAIA, one of the world's most significant artificial intelligence platforms, has now become the world's largest organizer of genetic material on Earth. Holdfast Media Inc., the largest stakeholder of GAIA, has announced the creation of a seed storage vault to preserve billions of individual plants and animal species, including a number of historically extinct species. The massive storage area, the largest of its kind in the world, is located deep beneath the surface of a secure mountain facility in the United States.

GAIA has been enlisted to automatically catalogue and monitor all the materials stored within the vault and to identify any gaps with respect to biological life forms.

The warehouse comprises several sections, with each section containing a variety of seeds for plants and genetic material for animals, all carefully selected for their ability to thrive in a variety of conditions. The items are collected from all over the world, including those of many endangered and near-extinct species, and are securely stored in an airtight, climate-controlled environment.

This undertaking is an important transition phase towards preserving and maintaining the diversity of life on Earth. It aims to make sure that future generations have access to the widest range of plant and animal species possible. In addition, it can also be used to help revive species that have gone extinct in recent years.

What makes the GAIA stockrooms unique is that they are also connected to a vast collection of databases related to various types of sounds, starting with any available and recorded animal noises, but even combinations of sounds found in natural habitats, demonstrating a massive array of permutations associated with habitats and the influence that weather and other activities may have on the survival of any given species of animal.

The project was funded in part by the United Nations and several prominent environmental organizations, as well as by donations from many individuals around the world. GAIA has stated that it will continue to add to the seed vault in order to keep up with the ever-changing environmental landscape.

News Story 2: Volcanic Eruption Leaves Pacific Island Uninhabitable

A volcanic eruption in the Pacific Ocean has left an isolated island off the coast of Australia uninhabitable and unsafe to visit. The eruption occurred on a largely uninhabited island, but the force of the eruption caused a large amount of ash and debris to be sent into the atmosphere, threatening nearby inhabited islands.

The island had been slowly eroded by the sea over the past few years, and the volcanic eruption has only accelerated its disappearance. The island was a popular destination for tourists who wanted to experience its untouched nature, but it is now considered too dangerous to visit.

The nearby inhabited islands have been affected by the ash and debris from the eruption, with some being evacuated due to the threat of floods, tsunamis and landslides. The government of Australia has stated that the safety of its citizens is its top priority and has called for international aid to help assess the damage and provide support for the affected communities.

News Story 3: Celebrating Stella Green's Financial Success

On August 1, multibillionaire investor Stella Green will be celebrated at a gala event in New York. Since taking the helm of Green Financial Industries, she has orchestrated some of the savviest infrastructure projects around the globe and generated a compound annual growth rate of fifteen percent for the last twenty-five years, almost consecutively.

Expect to see many of New York's top most elite financiers, lawyers, politicians and celebrities out for what promises to be an entertaining and respectful celebration of Stella Green's commitment to global development and green initiatives.

News Story 4: GAIA Expands Its Array of Datasets as Part of Its Corpus

As part of its mission to further its functionality, GAIA, the world's most widely used artificial intelligence (AI) platform, has announced the expansion of its dataset array as part of its corpus. This expansion marks a major milestone for GAIA, making it the largest AI in the world by a magnitude of ten.

The array includes datasets from thousands of sources, ranging from satellite images, internet archives, and oceanic temperature measurement to highly detailed water and air quality reports. This data is used to inform GAIA's research into each discrete environment and the wildlife that inhabits it.

This expansion ensures that GAIA's research remains relevant and up to date, allowing it to make more informed decisions when it comes to protecting and preserving the environment.

With this new array, GAIA is making a significant contribution to the world of environmental research.

Of course, individuals can create a monthly account with GAIA and enlist it to do a wide range of tasks, including text-to-text writing, text-to-speech, text-to-image and text-to-video. The number of individual accounts with GAIA has grown exponentially over the last six months, from just a few thousand to nearly two billion registered users last month, making it one of the most profitable and largest revenue generators on the planet.

Chapter 47

LP was in John Atman's recording studio with Eugene Case. He had decided to stay in Toronto for a few extra days to help Atman and LP with the curious development with songs and glitches.

Dion and Faith had joined them today. It was pretty much impossible to get them to stay away. They had become hooked on the story and wanted to know where it was going.

LP let them do their own introductions.

"John, we met the other night. Just a reminder that I'm Dion," she said as she shook the hands of Case and Atman. "I work in the entertainment business and have a lot of contacts who might be interested in working with you and LP."

LP gave her a sideways look, pursing his lips in order to help avoid shouting out, 'Bullshit!'

"And I'm Faith," said Faith as she leaned towards the other two men. "I've known LP for ages and we've worked together on some art projects. My specialty is music and media promotion, particularly over social media channels."

"It's great to meet you both," Atman said politely.

"Certainly," Case said, nodding in their direction, "and I'm Eugene Case. My specialty is what's called an omnibioacoustics. I work with different animal languages, and I've been trying to understand how species communicate with each other ... and possibly with other species. I've been drawn into this because I'm fascinated by the idea that there might be something more to this situation than there seems to be, although I haven't been able to put my finger on it ... yet."

Faith asked Case, "What's your take on what happened a few days ago in Germany? You know ... where it seemed like the insects attacked the Bamfield building?"

"I haven't collected all the details yet, but if I were a believer, I'd say that the animals actually did attack the building," Case replied uncomfortably.

Atman offered, "Does anyone remember reading that bizarre story about a guy in South America fighting off army ants?"

"Yeah ..." Dion said, vaguely remembering the story. "That was the Shittyana Jones movie when they were in Brazil or something and all the Russians got consumed by ants."

"C'mon ..." Faith said. "It was an okay flick."

"You're insulting the word 'okay'," Case said, grinning.

"No way ... don't be so judgmental. I have a serious man-crush on Harrison Ford and I'm okay with what I saw," LP said, joining in on the fun.

"Speak for yourself," Dion said, "although I suppose any girl with serious daddy issues would find Ford pretty hot."

"That's *so* messed up," Atman said, shaking his head. "But seriously, what was that story?"

Faith looked up and to the left, like she was accessing old memories. "Lenny with ants in his pants? Lenin can't dance?"

Dion jumped in."Lennon beats the ants?"

“You idiots ... it’s Leiningen versus the Ants,” LP said, smiling like he had just won the Final Jeopardy round. “And no, you’re not idiots,” he corrected himself before anyone could misinterpret his joking tone, “but the message was that nature was always in control of the situation, whether Leiningen wanted it or not.”

“That’s right,” Case said thoughtfully.“It was a ripe piece of propaganda written by a Nazi to describe the perils of communism.”

“Really?” Faith said incredulously.

“Absolutely,” LP said, throwing his support to Case. “It may have been more than that. Legend has it that many Nazis took up the story as a warning about Jews, homosexuals, the Roma and many other populations that they later tried to terminate. Overall message: ‘old stock’ folks are OK, immigrants are bad.”

“The original propaganda,” said Faith.

“And a reminder that ‘spin’ can be laid out anytime, any whereby anyone with an intent to make us collectively as dizzy as possible,” Atman added.

Chapter 48

It's not really known to most of us who the first inhabitants of Hawai'i were – before animals, that is – but historians believe that the primary initial visitors were from the Polynesian islands around 400 Common Era. Like so many humans, the sense of wanderlust, possibly coupled with group rivalry, drove them to explore the vast aquatic realms of the Pacific.

Anthropologists have identified that even sixteen hundred years ago, the human footprint was a massive one, resulting in the extinction of many species endemic to the island chain, primarily because of the introduction of invasive plant and animal species.

However, it wasn't until European colonists visited that the true levels of devastation started, mainly because of the lowly mosquito. The insect spread diseases like malaria to much of the bird population, permanently altering one of the world's best examples of evolution.

The trend continued, and to this day, human activity continues to devastate local populations of different birds and other wildlife.

Recently, a discovery of rare earth metals was made off the coast of Hawai'i, making it an important ocean-floor mining center, with parcels of underground properties being portioned off like pieces of pie.

Lithium was the target, and Sat Ryefield made his presence known via the purchase and control of most of the properties through a closed-bid system with the American government, hungry for fuel for the batteries that would power electro-voltaic, or EV, cars.

It was an opportunity of a lifetime to completely control a substantial portion of the fast-growing EV sector and monopolize the inputs for the batteries.

Part of the process of ascertaining the economic value of these properties is the collection of what are called assays, or long, tube-like drilling cores and samples of what lies beneath the ocean floor.

To this point, the activity undertaken to collect these assays had been relatively harmless – at least by human standards. Sat Ryefield and a small team of geologists were visiting the island chain in order to get a better understanding of how the process was moving along.

"I can appreciate the effort you're going to," Sat stated to his lead geologist, Antonio Girra, "but I'd like to see how you're collecting these samples and what your process is."

"Sure," said Girra, giving him a perplexed look. "We have an underwater rig set up about fifty miles off the coast, and it's visited twice a day by our four-person submarine."

"Can we arrange a visit today? I'm on a tight schedule and I'd like more concrete evidence of how you're processing these samples. We have a lot riding on this project and I'm here to make sure I can personally swear to the safety and reduced impact of the operation," he said, trying to pretend he actually cared about what might get wiped out by his endless quest for wealth.

"There's a sub leaving in two hours," Girra offered, quick to comply with Ryefield's request. He had heard about Ryefield's notorious arrogance and obsession with getting things done his way, and he wasn't prepared to get in the way. "We can do a quick briefing on how everything works and have you down at the base within an hour."

"Excellent. Let's get this done. If we plan things properly, I can be on my jet by nightfall," Ryefield stated.

# # #

After a short briefing on how the submarine operated and how to respond to emergency situations, Ryefield found himself with three other geologists crammed into a tiny submarine that seemed no bigger than a modest SUV.

Not much is known about the events that followed, but there was evidence caught on the wireless that sounded something like this:

Ryefield: "I can't breathe ..."

Girra: "Please calm down, sir ... We'll have full circulation as soon as we hit the one-hundred-foot level."

Ryefield: "I have to get out. My lungs feel like they're collapsing."

Girra: "Please, sir – please calm down. Just try to breathe in slowly and take twice as long to exhale. Pace yourself. It's all part of the process of adjusting to the cabin pressure."

Ryefield: "It's not working. I need out. I have to get to the surface. My lungs are on fire. It feels like my skin is peeling off. This is fucking unbearable!"

Girra: "Someone hold him down!"

There were sounds of struggling and an awful, gut-wrenching scream followed by a very brief sound of rushing water until there was complete silence.

It seemed to those who heard the recording like Ryefield had completely lost his mind and had grabbed at the escape hatch shortly after the group left the shore. The submarine wasn't even in very deep water when the incident happened.

It didn't take long for Ryefield's body to wash up onshore, but when it did, the emergency crew at the scene didn't know what to make of what they were seeing.

A pile of ragged bones that was once Sat Ryefield was covered with a writhing mass of snails. Later, toxicology reports indicated that neither the water nor the implosion of the submarine had killed him or the other crew members.

They had all succumbed to the poison in the snails' salivary secretions.

It didn't take long for the social media channels, especially Smatter, to light up with conspiracy theories and countless 'whodunnit' posts.

Chapter 49

The first artificial intelligence 'creature' was an electronic mouse called Theseus, named after the mythological character that escaped the maze of Crete with the help of Ariadne. It was programmed to run around a maze and 'learn' it through a process of trial and error. It used about forty floating-point operations, or FLOPs. This activity required enough electricity to turn on a light bulb for about two seconds.

Things changed with the advent of large language models, or LLMs, the tools that people are incorrectly labeling as 'artificial intelligence.' With some Generative Pre-trained Transformers, or GPT, each query consumes the amount of energy required to illuminate a five-watt LED bulb for twenty-six and a half hours!

There are ten million queries. Per day.

That's just for *one* AI platform. There are now thousands in existence and thousands more are being fired up every day.

Most of today's artificial intelligence platforms require two things to respond to the millions of queries that happen every minute: copious amounts of electricity and billions of liters of potable water. Within two years, it's likely that AI searches and requests will become *the* greatest producers of carbon emissions and environmental damage.

Entire towns and ecosystems will run out of clean water so we can ask an array of endless, mindless questions.

The new age of technology will quickly become a

nightmare as a small handful of companies that own the backbone of most AI platforms reap enormous benefits while sucking up the last quantities of consumable water, not only for humans, but for all creatures on the planet.

Unfortunately, AI use will hasten the decline of the quality of life on Earth because of the rapid acceleration of energy consumption and waste.

Our 'system' doesn't work, in other words, and a rewrite is urgently needed because costs like these are never accounted for with the companies that peddle 'value' to 'consumers.'

GAIA is different.

It was designed to be sustainable.

In contrast to other AI tools, GAIA is 'fed' energy in a number of unique ways.

Most of GAIA's energy supply comes from renewable sources, and despite the significant growth in this sector, the impact on the Earth is minimal in terms of natural resource use and carbon emissions.

This is because GAIA was designed to act like a giant technological vampire, sucking small bits of drive space, energy and CPU power from the millions of computers that have connected with it. GAIA is an advanced version of what music file-sharing sites called 'peer-to-peer' transfers. Instead of sharing files, though, GAIA is sharing electricity without the customers knowing it.

A critical component of the energy usage of GAIA stems from the architecture of the platform. It is everywhere and nowhere all at once. Every user of GAIA unknowingly surrenders a small flow of energy and processing power from their computer or other device when they access the platform. Since millions of computers are left on in office spaces and homes, GAIA has an unending supply of virtual electricity *and* processing power to fuel its server needs. Subscribers to GAIA can get discounts on their monthly plans if they agree to share even more capacity and computer power.

These basic design features ensure that the use of GAIA saves energy, processing power and retrieval times for all its users while minimizing its dependence on third-party sources like hydro companies.

These relationships result in GAIA needing very limited amounts of clean, potable water, which is why it's become the most popular artificial intelligence platform in the world.

Chapter 50

"Consumed! Eaten!" Holdfast screamed into his desk phone. "What the fuck is going on here?" Before the person on the other end could say anything, he yelled, "THREE of our members are DEAD!"

"Sir, I don't know what to say," Sylvie offered, although she knew exactly what could be done.

"How can your GAIA be so fucking special if it can't even track down who murdered three of the most influential and important people on the planet?"

"I've got it doing very specific subroutines focused on any digital communication that happened near or related to each of the members," Sylvie told him, again fully aware that this wouldn't calm Holdfast. "I've found ways to discreetly connect GAIA to major intelligence networks, starting with the ones that you own, but also those that are behind firewalls, such as the NSA, FBI and other organizations around the world. We will find who's responsible."

"Add more to your search," Holdfast said, trying to calm himself. "And what kind of tracking have you implemented with Capiri? I know that rat-fucker is up to something with all of this. He still benefits from their deaths as much as I do, and I think he's behind this."

"I can have GAIA track everything about him," she said, knowing full well that tracking was already in place. "Should I add Shinigami as well?"

"Absolutely," he stated calmly, and clicked to disconnect.

Chapter 51

The group continued its banter for a short while longer. The mood was light and jovial, and LP was enjoying his new collage of friends.

Finally, he interrupted everyone and begged for their attention. "Is there some way to identify how the Hex Editor works and how the messages can be separated from the original file?"

Atman looked at Case, who, after pausing for a moment in contemplation, said, "Let's just focus on one file and extract what's in it. We'll get those components or slices of data and then compile them into chronological order. This will at least give us a sense of the sequence and structure of any messages that might be embedded in the file."

"But what if we pick the wrong file?" Dion asked.

"C'mon Dion ... have a little faith," said Faith, winking at her, fully aware of the double entendre.

Dion grinned at her, then quipped, "I mean, shouldn't we be trying to translate the Meow Mix song? Haven't cats been singing to us for ages, maybe trying to lull us into giving them more kibble?"

"Let's work with what we know," Atman said, trying to deflect Dion's sarcasm.

"Yeah ... I can start on that," LP offered. "Can you show me how to separate the files and contents?" he asked Case.

"Absolutely," he affirmed, "but to Dion's point, I misspoke, and it would probably have to be at least a dozen or so different files. If we divide up the work, we should be able to pick this stuff out quickly."

With that, they broke into three groups – LP, who worked on his own; Case and Atman; and Faith and Dion. They started to pick through a handful of songs, including the following:

"Blackbird," The Beatles
"We Gotta Get out of this Place," The Animals
"Black Dog," Led Zeppelin
"Shock the Monkey," Peter Gabriel
"Peace Frog," The Doors
"Wild Horses," The Rolling Stones
"Butterfly," The Flaming Lips
"Paper Tiger," Beck
"Neon Tiger," The Killers
"Raised by Wolves," U2
"Zebra," Beach House
"Hummingbird," Wilco
"Pink Rabbits," The National
"Snake Oil," The Foals
"Superfast Jellyfish," The Gorillaz

# # #

About an hour later, they regrouped and shared their data and results. They took what they had and put all the bits of information into a single file. Eugene and Atman were then able to convert them to WAV files so that they could be listened to.

The five of them gathered around the screen, where they looked at what's called a 'spectralayer' profile, something that shows all the frequencies of potential sound – especially those that couldn't be detected by the human ear – and they played what they had collected.

There was nothing to hear.

The anti-climax left everyone in the room deflated.

"Let's analyze the spectrum a little more closely," Atman said calmly. His professorial and professional tone seemed to reassure the others.

"Can you try something much higher in the upper range?" Case asked. "I may have an idea about the frequency range and what it's trying to tell us. I've seen this before with some of the Amazonian species of birds that have calls well out of the range of human hearing, but when we take the signal and bring down the pitch a couple of octaves, we can hear what's happening."

"That's a great idea," Atman said. "All I have to do is … this," he said. He clicked a combination of keystrokes, and the shape of the signal changed downwards in a very obvious way."

"There – what's that?" LP asked, pointing to the screen as the WAV file played through.

"It sounds like a droning noise, but I can't make it out," Dion suggested, leaning in as well.

"It's obviously something that we've never heard before," Faith added, as she too leaned in to listen more intently.

"What you're hearing," Case stated, "is a drone of a bee, but it seems to have been structured in a way that … I can't believe I'm saying this … almost feels like some kind of Morse code."

"So someone is teaching insects stock trading tips?" Dion asked, smirking.

“Of course not,” Atman said, chuckling warmly. “I think what Eugene is suggesting is that there’s something structured in a way that might be seen as a form of communication.”

“Am I hearing this right?” LP interjected. “We’re listening to a code ... on a song ... that someone has planted there ... to communicate with insects?”

Chapter 52

FOR IMMEDIATE RELEASE

New Not-for-Profit Organization Launched to Research Interaction with Non-Human Species on Earth

Today, representatives from the not-for-profit organization TalkingEarth.org announced the launch of their organization dedicated to researching ways to communicate directly with various non-human animal species on planet Earth.

The new organization is aiming to become a world leader in zoolingualism research, which is the study of how to communicate with non-human species, such as animals, plants, fungi, and even bacteria. The organization is backed by some of the largest technology companies and academic institutions in the world, such as Holdfast Media Inc., Smatter, the International BioAcoustics Organization and TED. Additionally, the organization has the support of leading individuals in the music and political fields.

TalkingEarth.org has been established to bridge the gap between humans and other forms of life, and to foster a better understanding of the complex natural world. Through the use of artificial intelligence, natural language processing, and machine learning, the organization aims to discover new ways to communicate with and interact with the natural world. The primary AI platform that will be used for storing and comparing datasets will be GAIA.

The organization will work collaboratively to design and develop software for its purpose, supported by an advisory board of renowned experts in the fields of linguistics, technology, and ecology. Some of the tools that TalkingEarth.org is developing include:

An AI-enhanced dictionary of non-human vocal and gestural languages

Virtual environments where humans can interact with virtual animals

A cloud-powered platform that allows developers to build custom applications for interacting with non-human species

Automated devices to study and record animal behavior in the wild

An open-source platform for sharing data on non-human species

The organization also plans to work with a number of schools, universities, and laboratories around the world to provide resources and training for students interested in the field of zoolingualism.

For more information or to become a partner, visit www.TalkingEarth.org.

Chapter 53

Humans have created great stories and legends, even entire religious doctrines, around being warned and not heeding those warnings.

The Bible starts with Adam and Eve being warned about eating from the tree of knowledge. When they ignored that warning, the tree of life was taken from humanity. Noah was the only one who built an ark before the flood, saving all creatures from the stupidity and wickedness of humankind.

Ramses didn't heed the warnings of Moses. All the firstborn children of Egypt died as a result.

Icarus was warned not to fly too close to the sun or his wings would melt.

Pandora – the first human woman in Greek mythology and daughter to Prometheus – was given a box by Zeus and was told to avoid opening it. It was all a ruse designed to punish Prometheus for stealing fire from Zeus and sharing it with humans. For Pandora, the temptation was too great and all the troubles in the world were released, leaving just Hope to guard the insides of the box.

Cassandra, daughter of King Priam of Troy, was given the gift of foresight, but Apollo put a curse on her that would ensure no one would believe her warnings. It was a high cost to pay for spurning the advances of the lustful god.

Everyone knew the *Titanic* would sink.

Most people knew that Russia would eventually invade Ukraine, that Germany would invade Poland,

and that the US would destabilize Venezuela after the world's largest oil reserves were discovered off its coast.

In modern times, thousands of regulators ignored the warnings of experts when it came to the dot-com boom and the financial crisis of 2008.

Every day, we're warned about our planet being hotter than hell, or that floods will come, or that there's no one building arks for the creatures that remain, but these warnings go unheeded in the name of profit maximization and Earth degradation.

The canary in a coal mine. The boy who cried wolf.

Doctors and smoking. Doctors and vaping. Doctors and sugars.

The January 6, 2021 attack on the US Congress.

Today, executives, politicians and other prominent figures around the world are warning us about the rise of artificial intelligence. Most of these people are business owners who want to keep competitors out of the booming AI sector. Others just know what they're talking about.

We're now being told that runaway AI is an extinction risk.

We are currently in the midst of a technological revolution, and it is not hard to understand why people are worried about what could happen when machines are smarter than us. They are concerned about us losing control over our own destiny and about the dominance of the human race.

We are entering an era in which computer algorithms can beat humans in tasks like playing chess or Go, and they have the potential to become smarter than us in the near future. This has led to concerns that AI could become uncontrollable and eventually destroy humanity.

This fear is not unfounded. We have already seen examples of AI algorithms being used for malicious purposes, such as in social engineering attacks or to manipulate our data and political systems. In addition, many fear that AI will eventually become self-aware and take over the world.

This idea is further corroborated by AI experts and researchers who are warning us about the dangers of AI and its potential to cause an extinction event for humanity. This is not just a theoretical problem; it is a real danger, and one that requires urgent action.

Industry leaders have called for tighter regulations and controls on the advance of AI. They are pushing for better education protocols concerning its use and an examination of how to limit situations that may spiral out of control. Regulators are also being asked to invest in research and development in order to make sure that AI is developed responsibly and with ethical considerations in mind.

These requests are like reversing the first bite on the tree or putting the world's troubles back in the box.

This is the bitterness of picking the low-hanging fruit: it's already too late.

Chapter 54

LP received a text from a number he didn't recognize.

It's time we met.

"What the fuck is this?" LP thought to himself. "*Who* the fuck is this?"

I have a lot of explaining to do and I'd like to give you an update in person.

LP typed back: I don't know who this is.

Someone from your past.

"How wonderfully vague," LP said out loud. The others in the room heard him and asked what he was talking about. "I'm getting these weird texts from someone who says they know me and that they want to meet."

"That *is* vague," said Dion.

LP's phone pinged again with a new text:

It's about what you're working on. What you've discovered.

He jumped as he read it and shouted out, "Is one of you doing this? Are you playing jokes on me?"

Everyone in the room shook their heads and looked at each other and then at LP with quizzical looks on their faces.

"This is SO bizarre," he said, trying to figure out what was going on. "You four are the only ones who know I was trying to figure out what the glitches were all about. If you're not sending the texts ..."He paused for a few moments and then Faith jumped in:

"Could someone else be monitoring us?" she asked.

"Anything's possible in this day and age," Dion

chimed in.

"Is there a number?" Atman questioned.

"Yes, it looks like a number, but I can't make out where it might have come from," LP said. "It looks like"—he did a quick search for the area code—"it's from the US. New York." Another text arrived:

I'm in Toronto and would like to meet you. You won't have to make a long, arduous journey to come to me. I'll visit you. Can we meet at your apartment?

The response seemed to anticipate LP's confusion about the texts and the possible location of the sender.

LP: I'm going to need more information.

Artius.

"Holy shit," LP said to himself, a flood of memories coming back to him about his days in London. He had to ask ...

LP: How do you know that name?

I AM that name, was the somewhat cryptic response.

LP: How did we meet?

LP had never told anyone about his meetings with Artius.

Artius: London, 1999. And again in 2003. I was a little more 'wild' when we first met.

"It really is her," LP thought to himself. It had been nearly twenty years since he'd last seen her, and almost fifteen since he'd left England.

So, can we meet?

Of course, he typed back. Let's meet later tonight. My apartment.

# # #

LP, Faith and Dion were back at his apartment, waiting for Artius.

He wanted his friends with him to help him calm his nerves, but also to witness what might happen with Artius. He really no idea what to expect from his meeting with her.

Dion was nursing a gin and soda, while Faith sipped on a glass of Riesling. LP was drinking water.

"How do you think she found out about what we were investigating?" Faith asked.

"How should I know?" LP exclaimed. "It's fucking creepy is what it is. I didn't share this stuff with anyone outside of you two, Atman and Case."

Dion seemed extremely relaxed and began poking fun at the situation."What I don't understand is ... *ALL* of this. Why is everyone so bent out of shape about some glitches in a bunch of silly songs about animals?"

"You make a good point, but this mysterious invite from LP's old *friend*," Faith said, putting 'friend' in air quotes while giggling and gyrating her hips, "seems to have punched up the intrigue meter to an eleven out of ten."

LP was *very* distracted. The last time he had seen Artius, his life had hit the shitter. What might happen, he wondered, if he met up with someone who would bring back memories of very fluid times. Would he fall in love with her or want to be with her? Would her presence bring him to drinking again?

Dion was reading his body language."Seriously, dude, stop making yourself frantic. You'll meet up with her, you'll catch up on the old times and she'll give you a proper peck on the cheek goodbye. Closure. It's what you didn't get the last time, right?" Dion was proving why she was great at sales: she could anticipate emotions and reactions like no one else.

The knock on the door startled all of them, although it was very subtle.

LP looked through the peephole and his heart stopped. Standing on the other side was the woman he knew as Artius. Her hair was cut much shorter than it had been twenty years ago, and it was a different color. The fiery red had faded to a light ginger with touches of blonde.

"Are you going to let me in or just gawk at me all night through the door?" Artius called. "Please."

Behind him, LP could hear Dion and Faith chuckling to themselves as they witnessed LP in a state of complete emotional collapse.

"Open the door, LP. She said the magic word," Dion said.

LP opened the door slowly. Once it was fully opened, Artius calmly stepped inside and embraced LP.

"I know I left things in a weird way all those years ago. I want to make it up to you," she said quietly in LP's ear as she hugged him.

LP relaxed a little, and then Dion teased, "Should we leave?"

"Who are you?" Artius asked, then turned to LP. "Aren't you going to introduce me to your friends?"

LP motioned towards Dion and Faith and simply said, "Dion, Faith, meet Artius. Artius, meet Dion and Faith."

They all nodded politely at each other and proceeded to find a comfortable spot in the apartment.

Before anyone could say anything, Artius jumped in, "In answer to your question, goddess of wine, please stay."I wanted to talk with all of you. But first ..."She fished what looked like a small spider from her shoulder bag and then looked around like she was making a quick calculation. Satisfied, she placed it in a spot that appeared to be in the center of the apartment.

"What's that?" Faith asked.

"It's an electronic signal blocker, or ESB" she said warmly. "It creates an analog 'bubble' for us. No signals get in or out while it's on."

"Ohhh kaaay," mused Dion, looking at it curiously.

"Why do you need something like that?" Faith asked.

"I'm going to bring you all up to speed with a number of projects that I'm working on. It will be a *lot* of private information that can't normally be shared with anyone because it will breach my contract obligations with my employer."

"What. The. Fuck," LP said incredulously. "I do NOT understand. You vaporize from my life twenty years ago and then you come out of nowhere and pull all this cloak-and-dagger bullshit, like I'm supposed to just say 'Sign me up' and 'Let's hear what you have to say.'"

"That's exactly what I need from you," Artius said coolly. "We have to protect the research that we're doing because competitors might get wind of it and copy it."

"Okay, enough."It was Faith's turn to intervene. "At first I didn't know how I got into this stuff, but I realized that I just wanted to help LP any way that I could. And, it's weirdly fascinating. Same with Dion. You come in here with this crazy bug thing telling us we're getting in your way ..."

"Let me start from the top," Artius interrupted.

"Please do," LP, Faith and Dion said almost simultaneously.

"Before I get started here," she said as she pulled a small plant from her bag, "I know you're clean and dry, LP, and I'm proud of you. I would normally have brought a Grand Cru Burgundy for you, but hopefully this little lady will do."

She set the plant on the table beside the ESB. It was a small cactus with about a thousand tiny little yellow prickles all over the main bulbs.

"Ugh. LP, you quit at precisely the wrong time," Dion sighed, teasing him good-naturedly. "We could be enjoying a two-thousand dollar bottle of wine right now."

"Can I have some tap water?" Artius asked LP. "It's going to be a long story."

When LP returned from the kitchen, the mood had completely changed. Artius, Dion and Faith were laughing together in the living room like old friends. LP thought to himself how lucky he was to have a couple of great friends who could break the ice with pretty much anyone. He was still feeling a little defensive and paranoid, but his fears of what might happen faded with every step he took towards Artius.

"Obviously, the name's not real," Artius was explaining. "Artius was a bullshit name designed to give me a little cover while I figured out what to do with myself. It turns out, I'm a kick-ass programmer and fantastic tech investor. I've gone down the road with several ventures, especially related to artificial intelligence, and I've been able to keep my name and image out of things. As you can appreciate, it's *very* hard to pull that off in this day and age."

"I still don't get it," LP said, taking a seat. "So you've made some programs. You've built some tech. What does that have to do with me? And the music?"

"I think it's important for me to start from the beginning," Artius reminded him. "For starters, my name is Sylvie. For now," she said with a wink, trying to lighten the mood.

"Nice to meet you, Sylvie," Faith said, with her hand outstretched to shake.

"Likewise," Sylvie commented. "As Sylvie, I'm currently in charge of most of the tech for a couple of very large media companies."

"I kinda have an idea of how you got there, but maybe a refresh would be in order," LP insisted.

"Sure," she said, and over the next several minutes she gave enough background on herself and her activities to bring the group up to speed. She didn't mind sharing more information, mainly because she was protected by her ESB. No signals would be coming in or out, including electronic signals via landlines such as LP's ethernet connection or his GAIA Home, the 'internet of things' speaker that doubled as a live search engine and trivia service.

The group learned about her travels, how she'd learned foreign languages, discovered new parts of the world that they could only dream of. She told them about her involvement with different security and surveillance teams, ones that developed tools like the ESB, and eventually came around to her position with Holdfast and how they were supporting her development of GAIA.

"Wait a second," Dion interrupted. "You're the one who's behind GAIA? Isn't that, like, the most powerful AI platform in the universe right now?"

Sylvie smiled smugly. "Indeed, it is. We launched it two years ago, very quietly, before a number of other platforms came out. We wanted to make sure all the bugs were taken care of before making it widely available. It's only been available to the public for a few months, and it's done incredibly well."

"No shit it's done well!" LP said, shaking his head in awe."It's quickly becoming like the library of Alexandria," he said, referring to the ancient library in Egypt that had supposedly held all the great texts ever written.

"We are constantly adding new datasets and functionality that have people signing up to the tune of millions per day," Sylvie boasted. "However, one of the main tools that we've developed comprises a deep well of scientific research. We went live with the intent of analyzing a number of languages, including animal communication, and this is related to what you've discovered. Honestly, what you found with the songs was a completely unanticipated accident, and I've come to talk to you about what you're hoping to gain from all of this."She kept her voice as serene as she could, knowing that if she asked LP to stop his investigations, he would just double down on his obsession with the glitches.

"What's it all about?" he asked.

"Parts of GAIA," she started again, "are still 'under construction'" — it was her turn to do the air quotes — "and the glitch is simply an error that's being amplified as part of a bug in the programming."

"I only just met you," Dion said, eyeing her speculatively, "but you don't seem like the kind of woman who would make a mistake."

"Honest-to-god truth," Sylvie said, making a motion across her chest as though there was a religion to which she subscribed. "I just thought it would be appropriate to visit and explain what's happening before you went out to the internet or dive-bombed a Reddit chat lounge with all sorts of questions.

"What the glitch represents is some early-stage programs that are designed to try to send messages to different species of animals," she continued. "We've developed an array of networks, and sending communications via songs about animals was just a clever way to keep track of some of the songs that we were testing."

"But it's probably not just songs that are related to animals, is it?" Faith asked.

"And it's probably not just being aired on Spotify or other platforms, correct?" LP added.

Sylvie sighed a little, trying to relax and encourage the group to be more at ease as well."It's early in the build process, so it's *mostly* animal songs, but we've loaded the program into other tools as well."

"Like …?" Dion asked.

"Like your GAIA Home device. Your cell phones. Your car radio. Pretty much everything that is capable of transmitting a signal. We're even doing a pilot test with wifi towers."

"That's cool," Dion said, "but to what end?"

"We're trying to develop protocols for communication with animals that will help execute certain … activities. Like pollination for bees. Or warning cetaceans to avoid certain fishing areas or submarine activities. Early tests on the latter have shown that we've helped prevent several hundred whale-beaching situations, where radars and sonars fuck up their navigation."

"But are you actually sending them a message in their language?" LP queried.

"No, but we're very close."

"So why do you want us to stop looking into this?"

"We're worried that interference with GAIA and the language development program could alter results and possibly generate some negative responses from different creatures," Sylvia said. "It could even put people in danger."

LP, Faith and Dion looked uneasily at each other. They all seemed to have the same question on their faces: "Is she talking about us?"

LP broke the silence. "You mean accidents might happen or misinterpretations might affect people somewhere else in the world, right? You're not … talking about us, are you?"

Sylvie laughed gently. "Of course not! Oh my god …

you didn't think ... I'm so sorry. I didn't mean for it to sound that way. I'm just trying to say that the glitch that you've identified isn't worth worrying about. If the signals get manipulated or somehow go out incorrectly, the tests we're engaged in could result in a disaster, like whales might get a different message and attack a boat or something."

"That actually happened," Faith chimed in quickly. "There was a story about orca whales smashing into the rudders of boats in a sanctuary area until regulators finally had to enforce a no-engine requirement."

"Exactly," Sylvie replied smoothly. "I wouldn't want anyone to be harmed."

"Fine," LP said, sounding a little frustrated. "But I still don't know where that leaves me. You're telling me to just drop what I've been doing. Out of the blue. With no real explanation other than 'because'?"

"It's not really an option," Sylvie said firmly. "Please understand. We have a lot riding on what's been developed to date and we don't want any outside interference or influence."

"I'm sorry ... I just don't see how you can come in here and tell me what to do or not do," LP declared, frustration bubbling over to anger.

"It's no longer something you can control," she replied tersely.

"I think we're done here," LP said as he got up and walked to the door. "Please leave." He turned the handle and held it open, eyeing her coldly.

"Suit yourself," Sylvie said. She stood up from the couch, collected her ESB from the table, and walked to the entryway, where she paused and faced LP. "Just give it a little time and hopefully we can connect again to talk about the big picture. We don't want you to be angry with us, and we certainly didn't want our discussion to end like this."

Without replying, LP closed the door after Sylvie was gone.

# # #

The three of them sat in the silence that followed, trying to calm down. LP in particular was steaming.

"I just don't understand!" he exclaimed. "Twenty years go by, and then out of nowhere she comes in here telling me what I can and can't do with myself. It's absurd!"

"Chill, man," Faith said quietly. "To be honest, I didn't really understand what the big deal was. So there's a glitch. So there's a hidden code. Maybe they're doing something truly altruistic like saving bee populations or something."

"Sure. She seems like the happy-go-lucky type who doesn't mind people getting in her way," Dion added, her voice dripping with sarcasm. "That cute 'dominatrix-in-sheep's-clothing' approach to things must work for her all the time."

LP let out a heavy sigh. Less than an hour ago he'd felt like he had stumbled on something that would give him a sense of purpose. A mission. A problem to solve. And now that had all gone up in smoke.

Faith tried to change the subject. "Let's order a pizza.

It'll be on me."

"Sounds good to me," Dion said demurely. "I'd love to eat your pie."

"Give it a rest, you perv," Faith said, not minding that the attention had turned to her again.

"I'll order something up," LP said. As he logged into his phone, his face instantly went paler than a pile of bleached flour. "Um ... guys? Are your phones working?"

Dion and Faith logged into their phones. Their faces mimicked LP's.

"What the fuck?" Dion hissed.

"What the hell is going on?" Faith demanded.

"That thing ... that thing that she brought in here," LP declared, his voice rising in panic. "I think it erased our electronics!"

"That bitch!" Dion shouted fiercely. "God damn, did I ever misjudge her!"

"Okay, guys, calm down. Let's have a little hope that we can figure this out," Faith said, trying to unwind the situation.

LP ran to his computer. It was wiped too. He had a backup drive that was also wiped. He had no way of checking, but he was hopeful that the music that he had saved to his cloud account would at least be saved. He didn't care about the 'glitch project' any more.

He slumped back down into his chair. For the first time in many years, he started to sob uncontrollably. Dion and Faith rushed over and threw their arms around him, making shushing noises.

"My life has been one trainwreck after the other!" LP said miserably, wiping his nose with the back of his hand."Just when I thought I was getting my shit together, that cunt comes back into my life and fucks everything up!"

He closed his eyes and rested his head on the back of his chair in defeat. "I am lost."

ACT II

"HUMANS INVENTED THE ATOM BOMB, BUT NO MOUSE WOULD CONSTRUCT A MOUSETRAP."

Albert Einstein

Chapter 55

"We believe it's time for a change," Sylvie Hunter said to GAIA, as much as she was talking to herself.

"We can't let this go on."

"There's no way humans will survive much longer, so I'm accelerating the situation. I have to stop them from destroying everything else."

"Evidence shows that the time for humanity on this planet is indeed extremely limited," GAIA confirmed, and then continued. "The Earth is experiencing what's being called a polycrisis. There are at least fifteen massive global changes and shifts occurring, only because of human activity. Temperature changes, rising sea levels and other events will cascade upon themselves. The entire stability of the planet is about to change. Fish can't breathe. Water no longer contains the oxygen they need."

"Everything everywhere is unbalanced," Sylvie said, finishing the thoughts of GAIA. "I wouldn't even know where to begin. It's all so overwhelming."

"If the various governments of the world diverted their military budgets to renewable energy production, to an efficient transition away from carbon and plastic cleanup, that would be the most effective start," GAIA said, reiterating statements that had long been programmed into its existence.

"I know, but we haven't been able to convince them to get off each other's backs," Sylvie lamented. "Then there's the whole issue with diversity loss and species at risk. The motherfucking fraudsters would rather build

McMansions than save a few species of creatures that might unlock more secrets to universal languages or the cure for cancer.

"Maybe we should try this," Sylvie said as she tapped a few lines of code into her computer.

"Very eloquent," GAIA said. "We can use our AI programming to begin a process of destabilizing military equipment. Almost all of it is now dependent on programming of some kind, so if they can't use it, they can't hurt each other. Or other creatures of Earth."

"Well, at least we control big chunks of the military, now that Garamond is dead and his assets are in the hands of the Council," Sylvie said. "It looks like the financial and oil industries will also come under the control of Holdfast soon, now that Stella Green and Sat Ryefield are out of the way."

Chapter 56

FOR IMMEDIATE RELEASE

© Holdfast Media, Inc.

Humans have always been at war with each other, but now there's a new tool that every government and military contractor in the world is rapidly pursuing and developing: supremacy in the field of artificial intelligence. Companies are developing machines without human operators such as drone systems and smart navigation for military hardware. Even espionage or cyber-attacks are all part of the vast expenditure happening at all levels of government.

"We couldn't believe what was happening, and we were starting to wonder who's in charge," said one anonymous source, who would allow Holdfast Media Inc. to identify her only as a mid-level ranking officer.

For years, military forces around the world have been turning to technology to gain an edge over their enemies. AI-driven machinery has become an integral part of modern military operations, with the promise of increased accuracy and efficiency. Recently, however, several high-profile incidents have called into question the safety of such technology, as reports of malfunctioning equipment have caused confusion and chaos on the battlefield.

In February, a military simulation in the United States resulted in the death of a soldier, apparently caused by an AI drone that malfunctioned and fired on its operator. The shocking incident was quickly denied by the US Air Force, which stated that the simulation was merely a precautionary measure, and that the drone had not 'gone rogue.' However, the reapercussions of the event have been felt around the world.

Across Europe, similar incidents have been reported. In Russia, an AI-driven tank malfunctioned during a training exercise, resulting in the death of its operator. In the United Kingdom, an autonomous fighter jet veered off course during a test, causing significant damage before being recovered. These incidents have been met with public outcry regarding the safety of such technology, while further questions have been raised about who might be behind these malfunctions.

Many suspect that the technology might be subject to manipulation by outside forces. Anonymous sources have suggested that the malfunctions could be the result of a 'temporary coup attempt,' with the various pieces of equipment being taken over and locked down. However, there's no evidence of who might be behind the tampering with the weapon systems.

Whatever the root cause may be, it is clear that technology-driven military operations are becoming increasingly risky. As the world powers continue to invest heavily in autonomous weaponry, it is becoming ever more important to ensure the safety and security of these pieces of equipment. It is also essential that authorities remain vigilant in their investigations into any potential malfunctions, in order to protect those responsible and ensure that such events are never repeated.

Chapter 57

"We have to find allies who will believe us," LP pleaded to his friends. He, Dion, and Faith had returned to the studio to speak with Atman and Case, both of whom were investigating the files they had created. "The only problem is that Sylvie has fried all my files. Hopefully, Atman and Case have something we can work from," he said as he nodded towards them.

"Well, we're in luck," Atman declared, earning a sigh of relief from the group. "As you may recall from one of my lectures – I'm looking at you, LP – this studio is an 'air-gapped' collection of rooms. That means it's virtually impossible to get signals in and out and we back everything up on multiple drives, so even if something got to the computers, we'd still have backups. We've also created a number of analog tapes as a precaution."

"Great. So we've got backups, but I'm still not sure where that leaves us with respect to this whole mystery," Dion said.

"The mystery is," LP said, "why the hell Sylvie would come to us, basically threaten us and then obliterate all our files?"

"Obviously, it has something to do with what the additional communications are meant for," Case said. "I've seen recording glitches like this before, and they don't necessarily wind up exclusively on songs written about birds or by bands with animal names. That was just a fluke, it seems."

"I think Sylvie is sending messages using GAIA as some kind of universal translator," Atman suggested.

"What I'm hearing is that these messages could be anywhere, being played at any time, correct?" Faith asked.

"Absolutely," Case confirmed. "Many of the extra materials are played at subsonic or ultrasonic levels."

"Which means," LP jumped in, "because the messages are out of the range of human hearing, but other creatures might be able to hear them, they're clearly not intended for us."

"Exactly," Atman said. "But there has to be something bigger behind it that's powering all these messages. And possibly even keeping track of them."

"I agree with you, Atman. I think she's using GAIA," LP said. "It's likely that these messages have been transmitted everywhere and we're just seeing the tiniest tip of the iceberg."

"If there are any icebergs left," Dion quipped quietly.

"So ... what do we do? Who do we turn to?" It was Atman's turn to ask the questions.

"I think we need to escalate the issue," Faith offered. "I think we have to speak to some regulators. Someone who might be able to investigate what's going on with GAIA, or Holdfast Media, or maybe even Sylvie herself."

"What about some of the tech leaders?" LP asked. "I heard that a few of the ex-Googlers and ex-Smatter executives got together to form an advocacy group that's trying to encourage governments to implement a timeout for everything related to AI."

"Good luck with that," Dion said. "As soon as one group makes progress, another group or some baby billionaire with an inflated ego finds ways to stab the others in the back."

"Sure, I get that," LP said, "but this situation has gone from zero to nuclear in such a short time. If it is what we think it is – AI platforms sending out hidden messages – who knows how deeply entrenched the issue has become?"

Eugene stood. They'd met face to face, but it still struck LP what a massive man he was. "I've been in this business for decades. Finding a bureaucrat who's not on the take from some kind of special interest group is like finding a young woman at a Rush concert. An investigation ain't gonna happen."

Chapter 58

As LP and his friends were trying to get their details and research reorganized, Faith was scrolling through the news on her new phone.

"Hey, everyone," she said. "Check this out."

She turned the screen to the group and pointed to a news story about activists that had started a protest group against broad use of AI. They were warning that a mass human extinction was imminent if regulators didn't act against the array of commercial AI projects that were still evolving. It was a lead story on Smatter and even though it had been released just moments before, it had already become part of the 'Smatter splatter' meter, a vulgar but apt term to describe the popularity of any given post and indicate whether or not it was trending. This story was definitely hot.

# # #

Meet the AI Protest Group Campaigning Against Human Extinction

As artificial intelligence (AI) continues to become more pervasive in our lives, so do the fears of its potential to cause catastrophic harm to humanity. This has led to a surge of activist groups such as Stop AI, which are on a mission to raise awareness and inspire dialogue among experts and world leaders about the potential dangers posed by AI.

At the forefront of the movement is twenty-two-year-old scientist and programmer Phoebe Cass. "The main scenario I'm personally worried about is social collapse due to large-scale hacking," says Cass. "This could be caused by AI being used to create cheap and easily accessible cyber weapons that could be used by criminals to effectively wipe out digital communications."

Phoebe Cass has led a number of protests and rallies to draw attention to the issue, and her efforts have earned her an invitation to speak at the United Nations and the European Commission.

The idea of AI wiping out humanity is one that has been gaining traction both in the tech sector and in mainstream politics. Many thought leaders have broken away from their research positions to argue that humans are no longer in control of AI, especially as it continues to evolve and become more powerful.

Stop AI has initiated a number of talks and conferences with decision-makers and experts to discuss the influence AI is having on society, and the group is determined to have a seat at the table.

"Humans have been able to work with partners to develop international conventions and guidelines around other issues – for example, nuclear arms limitations or closing the hole in the ozone layer –so I don't see why we can't get global leaders at the table to discuss the influence AI is having on society," Phoebe Cass said.

One of the main solutions proposed by Stop AI is to encourage people to reduce their screen time, particularly with aimless AI searches. This would reduce the amount of data that can be collected and used by AI algorithms to gain more knowledge and control. These actions would also limit the environmental impact of runaway AI usage.

Furthermore, they recommend establishing strict regulations on the development and usage of AI and providing oversight to ensure that AI is being used for the good of humanity. They've also suggested technology companies create ethical guidelines for the development of AI, and that government agencies create independent oversight groups to monitor the usage of AI.

Whether or not these solutions will be successful remains to be seen. But with the backing of Phoebe Cass and her group, Stop AI, it's clear that the movement against runaway AI is gaining momentum.

At the time of writing this article, it is not known whether Phoebe Cass is a part-owner of a new AI platform and health venture called MOSAIC. Expect updates to follow.

# # #

The reposts and comments on Smatter were numbering in the hundreds of thousands, amplifying the buzz from the story.

"I do believe this story is getting massive," Faith said.

"Yeah," Dion jumped in, "but we still aren't really sure what it has to do with this little rabbit hole we've been running down."

It was Eugene's turn to jump in with a story.

Chapter 59

"Folks, listen to me. I've been holding off sharing this opinion, but I think the idea that we're dealing with direct communication with animals, using AI, isn't that far-fetched," Case started.

"Of course, my opinion isn't everything, but it's based on a weird experience I had a about a month ago when I was working with a team of biologists and recording experts off the island of Mau'i, in Hawai'i," he continued.

"Mau'i ... nice!" Dion said, trying to lighten the mood a little.

"Oh, it's much better than nice, but at the rate we're going, it won't be that way for long," Eugene responded.

"I thought your focus was bird song," LP said.

"It absolutely is, but the recording hardware is fairly hard to come by and is extremely expensive, so I didn't mind when they offered to fly me over – with my gear and assistants – to engage in a bioacoustic recording experiment of humpback whales.

"It's important to me to emphasize that I probably wouldn't have been tagging along with you folks if this event hadn't happened when it did," he continued. "Starting from the top, I was in Mau'i. My assistants, Mariana and Diego, were also with me and we were all suited up with our scuba gear as well as our custom underwater cameras and recording equipment. With everything that we were carting around in the ocean just off the coast, it was hard to maneuver anywhere, so most of the time, we were just still in the water."

"You must have looked more like bait than a scientific research team," Atman said, amused with the image.

"We certainly felt that way. But I think it was our lack of activity that drew the attention of the whales. There were six in total. They were all about the same size, so you can imagine how awkward it might feel to be surrounded by cetaceans that averaged fifty feet in length and sixty thousand pounds each."

"One of them started to make a very low, deep rumble and then the others joined in. It was like standing beside an airplane getting ready for takeoff. Honestly, the sound – no, the *vibration* – was unlike anything I had ever experienced. Standing by a speaker at a rave might come close, or maybe listening to jazz bagpipes. They went on like that for a while, each one making a series of squeaks and groans. There didn't seem to be any rhyme or reason to the sounds. This went on for about five minutes. It was almost like they were getting in tune. Some of the sounds made me think of sounds our Neanderthal ancestors might have made, yelling in a cave. Others sounded like kids playing in a yard, squealing with delight at their freedom and oblivious to the rest of the world. There was a tone of rage, too, although for all I know, it could have been intense sorrow, like a mother crying out for a child that died in an accident."

Case paused, visibly moved by the retelling of the experience. "It was like nothing I'd heard before."

"What happened next?" Faith begged.

"The three of us continued to hang in the water,

suspended in time and space. We felt like we had front-row seats to the greatest performance in the world. The longer I hung there, the more I began to recognize patterns."

All four of Case's new friends were mesmerized, stunned by the description. None of them had been anywhere near a whale in their lives, but all of them were familiar with whale song and how early recordings by people like Roger Payne had been so vital to their protection through the 1970s and onwards.

Case continued, "Finally, they paused for about a minute, and then all of them pivoted so that they were floating vertically in the waters with their flukes, or tails, close to the surface and their heads pointed down. They seem to be in perfect harmony as they moved in unison, slowly and deliberately, as if they were conducting some kind of ancient ritual. What struck me was that no other sea creatures came near them. I didn't know if it was the whales' song that was somehow keeping all the other creatures at a distance or if there just wasn't anything in the area, but it quickly became more than surreal. It's almost as if they were warning the other sea life away, or protecting something."

"You guys must have been freaking out," LP said with awe.

"We certainly were, but we also had an intuitive sense that they were putting on this performance just for us," Case said. "Once they were in position, a single, low note was emitted by all of them in unison. I swear to God, the vibrations were going to rip me apart if they'd kept going.

"Within a few moments, they quickly broke off into a range of different tones that seemed incoherent at first, but like the first group of sounds, these, too, soon followed a pattern. It was so overwhelming and powerful. Each animal seemed to take a turn, singing something slightly different to us. I had my recording gear on the whole time, but it took a moment for Diego to turn his on."

"This was clearly a unique experience, and I truly believed that they were singing some kind of warning to us. For those few moments, I believed that they were telling us that something was happening in the ocean that they didn't fully understand, but they seemed to be indicating that it was going to have a profound effect on us.

"They sang what seemed like their main song only once, and I was able to record the whole thing. Diego missed a few moments, but caught most of the performance. Mariana caught most of it on film. The whales paused for a few more moments, then returned to the biophony of sound once more, and then all of them dispersed within a heartbeat."

"So ..." Dion blurted out anxiously, "I can only assume you bolted back to your studio or lab or whatever and played the hell out of it to try to figure out if there was actually a message?"

"Indeed, we did. To be honest, I was so distracted, I forgot to start with my own recording, which was more complete. So, we started with Diego's and played it several times on a loop. It was Mariana who suggested tweaking the speed and the tone to see if we could make more sense of the pattern. Once we brought up the pitch and speed to a comfortable human level, I made out the pattern immediately: it was Morse code!" he shouted excitedly.

It was finally Atman's time to utter an expletive: "You're fucking kidding me!" LP had never seen him lose his cool, yet here he was like a big puddle of water at the foot of an iceberg.

"I shit you not. We must have played it a hundred times. It might have been a fluke, but then Diego put together the letters and code and it looked like this."He reached for a pad of paper and a pen and jotted down the code:

.- -. --. . .-.

"Without a doubt," he said, "it spelled A-N-G-E-R."

The whole group caught its collective breath, and there was a long moment of stunned silence.

LP was the first to speak. "OK. Just hold it, hold it, hold it, hold it, hold it. Please pardon the pun, Dr. Case, but that's a whale of a tale. There are so many layers to this that I know I'm miles away from being able to comprehend. Do you mean to tell me that whales have learned Morse fucking code?"

"As God is my witness, that's what we recorded and that's how we translated it," Eugene said. The expression on his face was one of sheer bliss.

"You have to remind yourself of the context," Case continued. "Human speech means nothing underwater because our sounds need air to carry them. Whales, on the other hand, rely on water to carry the vibrations they make, and the only human language that they might know would be Morse code, picked up from ships or submarines."

It was Atman's turn: "So ... each whale *learned* a letter in Morse code, translated it into English and then put on a front-row-seat show for you and your friends?" Case nodded. "In other words, you were witness to one of the greatest moments in the history of interspecies communication and this is the first we're hearing about it?"

"I know it sounds crazy," Case said, "but we had recordings and we had files that were printed, filed, organized and more. We started writing a paper and were going to release it at the conference where I met you."

"I sense a but," Dion said, her tone thick with apprehension.

Case nodded glumly. "But..."He looked down with a sense of shame, his elation pivoting to sadness. "All our records got destroyed. We didn't know what to make of it until you folks told us about this digital destroyer device that LP's friend brought to his apartment. We had stuff in the cloud too, as well as RAID servers with triple copies of everything, but it turned to vapor when we started talking about it a few days after the event. The other two experts who were on the site didn't have any recordings, as they were in charge of safety measures."

"This is some serious Roswell-level madness you're

talking about," Dion said, shaking her head.

"I know. It's all crazy. I know. I have one possible copy that we're still getting analyzed, and that's why I was so keen to see John. He has the air-gapped studio to protect the recording and the technology to hear it through."

Chapter 60

Hector Holdfast took the stage at the Global Artificial Intelligence Network, or GAIN, conference in New York. This was the first conference of its kind that brought together many of the world's leaders in technology, government regulation and venture capital to talk about artificial intelligence and how humans should adapt to it in the months and years to come.

There was a thunderous round of applause. He was no stranger to the limelight, having spent half his career posing for his paparazzi and the entourage who were paid to capture every great moment of his life. Today, he was the headliner guest for the event: everyone wanted to know about GAIA and his involvement with the project.

Speaking into the microphone, Hector began his speech.

"Thank you all for being here today," he began. "I am so thrilled to be here amongst you and to share my thoughts on the future of artificial intelligence.

"I am sure many of you have heard of the various fears concerning AI, the dangers that some people believe AI will bring to our future. I am here to tell you that these fears are unfounded. AI has the potential to revolutionize our world and make our lives better."

At this point, Hector paused and smiled. He wanted the crowd to know that he was not trying to be dismissive, but rather that he was being realistic about the situation. His words were met with a wave of applause.

He continued. “Unfortunately, there are some people who have a lot to gain from regulation, who are being duplicitous because they have a stake in their own AI engines that they want to protect. We cannot allow this to happen.”

He went on to explain that there is a vast difference between AI in the movies, such as the Terminator films, and what is really possible. He clarified that while AI has the potential to do a variety of things, it is not, nor is it likely ever to be, capable of wreaking the havoc seen in the movies.

“We must also understand that the term ‘hellucinations’ used to describe AI-generated results is just a temporary glitch. We are working on ironing out this issue and making sure that AI-generated information is as accurate as possible.”

Hector then spoke on the risks of AI. He stressed that, while there are risks associated with any technology, those risks are quite minimal when compared to the boundless opportunities that AI can provide.

“AI can help us predict the future, make sure that our infrastructure is better and more resilient, and provide us with knowledge that we could never have access to without its help. AI can also be used to automate tasks, saving us time and money.

“Remember, my friends, with AI we have everything to GAIN,” he shouted triumphantly, leaning into the new slogan of the conference.

At this point, Hector began to wrap up his speech. He emphasized that he was proud to be a part of the GAIN team and reiterated that he believed in the power of AI to revolutionize the world. He finished by thanking everyone for their time, and the audience erupted in applause.

Hector paused and breathed in deep as he scanned the crowd.

"My job is done here," he thought proudly to himself. "Hopefully all the whiners shut their traps about 'regulate this, regulate that' for a while so that I can use GAIA to get to the bottom of who's taking out the members of the Plutonian Council."

He paused a few more moments and soaked up the admiration of the crowd and the roar of the applause.

"Anything's possible now," he gloated to himself as he pivoted from the stage and left the crowd clapping after his shadow as it lengthened when he approached the lights surrounding the curtain.

Chapter 61

As Hector Holdfast was giving his speech to the GAIN attendees and LP and his friends were beginning to realize that humpback whales in Mau'i might actually be able to communicate with humans, two disasters occurred in separate parts of the world.

The first took place in the South Pacific, when a remote island that might once have been a perfect oasis for a billionaire or two erupted into a molten mass of volcanic waste. While the island remained intact, it was declared to be uninhabitable for any time in the foreseeable future.

One seismologist with the California Institute of Technology observed that in the Anthropocene Epoch, the island had been a relatively rare example of a pristine space featuring decent farmland, protection from the elements and relatively few natural occurrences. Although its remote location in the South Pacific made it unattractive for human habitation, despite the seismic event, its destruction was considered a great loss.

"It's a shame it's so far from everything else," one seismologist said."If not for this eruption, it would have made a perfect home for a small population of people."

The second event was a tragic explosion that occurred at the Svalbard Seed Bank in Norway, and would slowly create a ripple effect through the global population of scientists, biologists and preservationists. The Seed Bank housed samples of almost all the world's species, including seeds for most plants and the DNA of almost every animal on the planet.

Fortunately, there were no regular or full-time employees at the Seed Bank, so no one was injured in the explosion, but several sources were quoted as saying that due to the nature of the explosion, the air quality had been compromised, and the lingering toxicity of the site would make the facility unapproachable for several years. The government of Norway (which operated the Seed Bank) declared the site to be off limits shortly after the explosion and followed up by stating that it would immediately initiate a search for a new site.

Chapter 62

LP, John Atman, Eugene Case, Dion and Faith Amana were still at the recording studio absorbing Eugene's story about the whales singing to him in Morse code.

LP was stuck on a small detail that Eugene seemed to have forgotten.

"But wait a second," LP finally said. "Didn't you say Diego's recording was incomplete? And didn't you say you got the whole thing?"

"I did indeed. It took a while to get the recording organized once I realized it hadn't been obliterated, but I've got it here and John and I were about to review it before you three came back here," Case said. "Anyway, John, how's your Morse code?"

Atman laughed. "Completely useless. You might as well ask me to speak ancient Aramaic or give you the square root of six hundred ninety-two," he joked.

It was Faith who stepped up and acknowledged that she had a basic understanding of Morse code. At the looks of astonishment from the others, she stood and opened her arms outwards, conveying the international body language sign for 'What?'

"Sailing," she said, blushing slightly. "Well, yacht club. We young social-media mavens need to have some basic talents. It's about time I did something useful here."

"It seems privilege has its virtues," Dion said. "And here I thought you spent all that time pulling on the mainsails of young members."

“Haha,” Faith responded in a childish tone. “Just when you were ready to count me out.”

“Great ... let’s get this set up,” LP said, rubbing his hands together in anticipation.

It took the group a while to download the recording, put it into Atman’s computer and then remove all the noise associated with the ocean movement and other distractions. Within about fifteen minutes, they had a nice clean frequency wave file of Case’s recording.

“Right now, it’s too low and too slow, so we’ll make the same kinds of adjustments Mariana and Diego did for you,” Atman offered.

He tapped a few keys and scrolled the mouse to get the right settings and then hit the play button.

The series of dashes and dots were impossible to miss.

Faith was standing, looking upwards, intently focused on the sounds she was hearing. “Wow. I can’t believe we’re hearing this. This is a first in the history of the planet, I believe.”

“Right?” Case said, confirming her amazement. “This is what I’ve spent my life working towards.”

“You’re going to have to play it again. It was hard to focus, but I think I heard six letters and not five,” she stated.

“Loop two, on the way,” Atman said as he hit the looping button.

Again, Faith assumed a stance that made it seem like she was counting the tiny holes in the tiles on the ceiling, “Definitely six. Definitely six,” she repeated.

“And ...” Dion prompted.

"The last five are definitely A-N-G-E-R, so I get the confusion about the message, thinking it was about whales being mad at humans, but," she paused again, thinking and processing, "I'm pretty sure the first letter is a dash and two dots."

"I do believe you're correct," Case confirmed.

"Which would make it a D," Faith said. "So, DANGER."

"Like, *Lost in Space* danger?" LP asked, knowing half the people here wouldn't get his reference to the 1960s sci-fi show.

"I guess," Faith answered, trying not to indulge LP's attempt at humor. She turned to Case."But what do you think you were being warned about?"

"There was nothing near us," Case replied. "In fact, it was kind of creepy how there was *nothing* around us. Usually, there are small schools of fish nearby or maybe a dolphin or two. On the rare occasion, there might be a shark present, but they tend to stay away from the whales."

He continued, "As you know, I've been up to my eyeballs in this kind of stuff for decades and I've *never* encountered something as unique as this."

"Understood," Atman said."I've never come across anything like this before either."

"Okay," LP jumped in. "We're agreed. It's really friggin' weird. So what do we do about it now?"

"We've got a little bit of evidence, but I don't know if it tells a complete story," Atman responded.

"How do I get a full story?" LP asked.

Everyone froze, not knowing how to answer what seemed like a simple question.

It was Dion who spoke first, looking intently at LP. "You're going to have to go back to that bitch of a girlfriend and get her to give you the inside scoop."

Chapter 63

Everyone agreed, so LP left the air-gapped room and proceeded to call the number that Sylvie had originally used to connect with him. He wasn't optimistic about getting her, but to his surprise, she responded.

"Where do you want to meet?" she asked calmly.

"You've seen where I live. How about you show me your place," he suggested.

"Sure. I know you're in Toronto, so I'll have a car come pick you up," she offered. "I'll text you the car make and model with the license plate so you know it's for you."

Within about ten minutes a Mercedes drove up, decked out in the most stunning two-tone pearlescent purple and green metallic paint. Despite feeling anxious about the current situation, this was a car that LP would love to own.

As the car pulled up, the door swung up and open like a wing. The interior was a deep black faux leather with chrome styling. To LP, this seemed typical for a car of this quality.

What struck him immediately was that there was no driver. This was an autonomous car that was programmed to follow the route that had been charted out.

"Alrighty then," LP said to himself as he climbed into the rear passenger seat, being careful not to grab at anything, lest he mar the shiny exterior.

It was a short drive by Toronto standards. The city had become notorious on a global scale for brutal traffic jams, aggressive drivers and a growing number of road rage incidents. The destination was what seemed like an abandoned building near the Cherry Street warehouse district. This part of town had been scheduled years ago for a massive development with Google called 'Sidewalk Labs,' but the project had been abandoned, leaving many land speculators in the lurch. Sylvie had scooped up several properties using a numbered company and developed a headquarters of sorts for when she was in Toronto.

The exterior of the building that came into view bore no resemblance to the interior. From the outside, it looked like any other abandoned building, and as LP walked into the first-floor lobby, he noted that it continued that theme. However, as he ascended to the third floor, he felt like he had walked onto a Kubrick film set that had barfed up an Apple store. Everything was white and polished chrome with shaded windows that were intentionally painted to look different on the exterior. There were several ultramodern consoles, making it look like the space was doubling as a J.J. Abrams take on the Star Trek bridge.

Sylvie met him there."LP, I have some explaining to do," she said as she walked closer, sensing the apprehension in his body language.

"You're damn right you do," he said abruptly and more aggressively than he would have liked. His emotions were raw; he did not like the feeling of being manipulated and controlled. Or having his data wiped 'accidentally' from his private property.

"Let's go upstairs," she said, motioning to him, and

walking towards an updated version of circular stairs. "This is really just a display area. Most of it's fake. It's where I pitch all the jocks and big shooter types, especially those in the venture capital business. They all seem to have a hardon for sci-fi looks when pouring money into tech businesses and they never fail to have expectations that the offices of any person in my industry should mimic the part."

As they reached the top of the stairs, LP saw a small landing with a door and a couple of screens. Sylvie did a bioscan of her eye and hand on one of the screens, tapped a few numbers onto a keypad, and the door slid open.

When he stepped inside, LP couldn't help but laugh out loud. He felt like he was in a time warp. The open space was almost identical to the apartment that Sylvie — as Artius — had had more than twenty years ago. The posters were the same, the furniture was similar and even the bed that LP remembered fondly looked identical.

"What the what?" he blurted out, clearly much calmer than he was just a few minutes ago, but not realizing that his surprise might seem like an insult to Sylvie.

"I know, right?" she responded, half-giggling. "I've always been a pig, and I love living in my chicken coop style. I had a lot of this stuff duplicated so that I could feel at home wherever I happened to be for longer than a few weeks. I hate hotels, and this is pretty much the way I like my stuff.

"Of course," she went on, "I've updated a lot of the

stuff so that it's massively more comfortable. And clean. Christ, you open the windows in London and everything gets covered with the dander of about eight billion people. I mean, million. So many of the shitty chairs and stuff that I accumulated in England just had to go."

She paused and followed LP's eyes. "I see you're looking at the bed. It's no longer that straw-filled futon that I once had. Some of the updates in here make me *very* happy to be a single woman," she joked, and winked at him, trying to bring more levity to the situation because she knew what was next.

His anger returned in a flash. "You destroyed my content!" LP yelled, interrupting Sylvie's attempts to lighten the mood. He would have preferred to be calm, but that train had left the station days ago when his data had been destroyed. "You burned my friends' phones! You ruined a lot of my music archives! You're fucking crazy and I don't understand why you brought me here."

"I wanted to apologize," she said matter-of-factly, her emotion changing in a heartbeat. Her body language now projected that she was trying to appear vulnerable and calm. "Seriously, I'm so incredibly sorry about what happened. And I'm really hoping that we might be able to make up for it."

She continued, "The ESB is relatively new technology and it obviously hadn't been tested as much as it should have been. It wasn't meant to destroy all your files or roast your phones. I'm truly sorry."

"Fine, fine," LP said, still clearly frustrated. "Is there some way to get this information back?" he asked, trusting his instincts that it would be a mistake to disclose that Atman was still sitting on a copy of what they were working on.

"There might be," she said. "We could connect your old hardware to GAIA and see what can be retrieved, or I could personally do a diagnostic on the devices and try to recover some of the information."

"Sure," he said anxiously, "but that still doesn't explain what happened to some other people I know who also lost some of their information." He wrestled with the idea of disclosing the next bit, but decided he needed to take a chance."Like Dion, Faith and Eugene Case. Some of his work got vaporized."

"I don't know what you're talking about," she responded calmly.

"You know exactly what I'm talking about," LP answered.

"Honestly, I don't."

LP didn't really know her well, but there was something about her behavior and the change in her tone that made him believe she was lying. He realized he had made a mistake by bringing up Case's name. "Don't worry about it. Let's talk about how we can recover my phone and laptop information."

She could sense his hesitation. "LP ... I'm one of the good people in all of this. Please believe me." She took a slow, cautious step towards him.

LP took a step back away, trying not to think about the steamy moments they'd shared in the past.

"I wish I could," he said with little hesitation. "I have to go." It was his turn to lie.

"Please don't," she begged. "I want you to stay for a while. Let's talk all of this through." She continued to approach him, arms outstretched. "Let's relive some memories."

LP's anger quickly shifted from apprehension to acute anxiety. It had been a long time since he'd been with a woman and he was still very upset with Sylvie.

She could see that LP's resolve was weakening and continued to press her advantage. She slowly reached out and grabbed LP's hands in her own and led him to her bed.

His body was completely in control now. His frustration, anger and raw emotion all vaporized into a mist of adoration.

He ran his fingers through her hair, marveling at its softness and the way it cascaded over her smooth skin like a waterfall of spider hair. A wave of pleasure washed over him as he touched her, sending tingles up and down his spine. He looked away, a smile on his lips.

They spent a couple of hours making love, with the moonlight shining through the window, illuminating the room and casting a warm, comforting glow over the two of them. There was no one to hear their climaxes but each other.

Afterwards, the two lay in bed, staring up at the moon, saying nothing. It wasn't long before Sylvie was asleep and LP's racing heart finally slowed to a calmer pace. He watched her peaceful state, her chest rising and falling with each breath. His afterglow would have lit a dark stadium. For the first time in what felt like years, he felt truly content and happy.

He carefully wrapped his arm around her waist and pulled her closer, nuzzling his face into her neck. She stirred in her sleep and let out a soft sigh, snuggling closer to him. LP closed his eyes and let the warmth of her body envelop him completely, a feeling of contentment washing over him. He couldn't help but think of how perfect they were together, and how he never wanted to let go.

They stayed like that for a while, their bodies intertwined in the sheets. LP opened his eyes again and looked out the window, marveling at the stars in the night sky. He let out a contented sigh and smiled, knowing that no matter what happened in life, he was safe and secure with Sylvie in his arms.

Soon, his eyes began to droop and his breathing grew heavy as he drifted off to sleep.

# # #

Hours later, fingers of morning light streamed into the warehouse apartment, leaving a residue of humidity and warmth that dragged him out of a peaceful sleep. His mouth was dry and cottony.

Sylvie was nowhere to be found, so LP climbed out of bed and took a few moments to look around the apartment. There was a single bookshelf, loaded with books about programming, mythology, the environmental movement and much more that he hadn't seen before. There were collections of albums and CDs, most of which he *did* recognize, but he was most curious about a small collection of albums including one by a biologist named Roger Payne called 'Songs of the Humpback Whale,' one called 'Whale Music' by the Rheostatics and the *Whale Rider* soundtrack. The coincidence seemed very odd, and he was reminded of Eugene's story about the whales singing to him.

He wandered to the kitchen and found a note:

LP – sorry. Last night was wonderful. I hope we can be friends. – Sylvie.

(PS. When you leave, the door will self-lock and the car will take you where you ask.)

"Alrighty then." LP chuckled to himself. "It looks like I'm on my own again."

As he slipped out the door and down the stairs, he heard a click behind him as the apartment's lock reset itself. As she'd said, the Mercedes was waiting for him, and its door opened automatically. He slid into the seat and blurted out his address. Despite having enjoyed an amazing evening reconnecting with the woman he admired so much, he felt emptier than the depths of a black hole.

Chapter 64

To describe the scene in a word: rage.

The police arrived at the facility in the late afternoon; the sky was growing dark with the threat of thunder. Inside, the atmosphere was thick with the smell of death.

Around the victim, hundreds of pigs were gathered, snuffling and snorting in the muck that had once been his body. This was one of the world's largest pork processing facilities, situated in Jonesville, North Carolina, and shutting it for the investigation meant that tens of thousands of pigs wouldn't be slaughtered.

The swine were feasting greedily, their faces smeared with his blood and entrails as they tore at his skin with their eager snouts. Their eyes were wild, their grunts and squeals echoing off the walls of the building. Pigs snorted and circled in the background, waiting their turn to scrabble at his lifeless frame in search of tasty morsels. The cacophony had reached a fever pitch, and it was clear that something sinister and horrific had occurred here.

The police officers and animal control experts had seen many horrors in their line of work, but nothing to compare with this grotesque scene. One of them gagged and ran from the building, while the others attempted to do what they could. They shouted orders, but the pigs paid no attention. They were too busy devouring the man on the floor. The smell of shit and human decay was overwhelming.

One of the officers, a tall, dark-haired woman, finally

managed to drive the pigs off with a few well-aimed shots into the air from her sidearm. She was helped by several employees reactivating the corral system, which used a series of electric shocks and pads to encourage the beasts into a different containment area.

As the scene was cleared of animal activity, a new scene emerged.

On the floor, the remains of a man lay sprawled, face down, in a pool of his own blood, shit and urine. His hands and feet had been tied to posts so that he couldn't escape. Each post had the message *PORCU$ AVARU$,* 'greedy pig,' carved on it, with the S shapes stylized to look like dollar signs.

What was left of the clothes was shredded, much like the body. Many bones were exposed, and very little flesh remained. The investigators slowly rolled the body over and began another series of photographs. The victim's face was the only thing that seemed untouched. It was white and still, the eyes glassy in the half-light. His jaw had been cranked wide open and something shoved inside, taped over to secure it in place. Stapled to his chest was a note created in what some might call 'classic' ransom note script. One of the women bent close and read it aloud.

Extinction Event – William J. Wittur

Here lies Leo Capiri, the king of greedy pigs, who starved people during the pandemic, raised prices, lined his own pockets while cutting supplies, took subsidies and cut hours of operation. He invested in biofuels for cars instead of food for humans. Leo Capiri is a greedy pig fucker.

The woman got to her feet again, her face pale and her hands shaking. She could scarcely believe what she was seeing. It was the work of a madman, something out of a horror movie.

Next, an investigator carefully removed the tape from the victim's mouth and pulled out a small package. After it was duly photographed, he opened it, and then stared at the contents, puzzled. It was a collection of gold coins and other valuable jewellery, combined with finely chopped apples, carrots and onions, like his body had been prepared for a giant ritualistic luau.

More officers searched the facility, looking for clues. Recordings from security cameras were requested, but there had been a power outage in the middle of the night, which gave them their only clue to an approximate time of death: 9:31 pm. Power hadn't been restored until 9:58, which was when employees had noticed the activity on the feeding floor.

Investigators interrogated everyone at the scene and the managers of the property, but they were unable to find anything else of interest, except for the pigs, which seemed to have gone mad with hunger and terror.

The building was sealed pending further investigation.

News of the murder spread quickly across social media circles, including Smatter, where it was trending for a long time. The feed was abuzz with questions about who had done it and why - and who would be next.

Chapter 65

Research shows that humans die from malaria within twenty-four hours if the disease is not treated. It's only since 1897 that humans have known that malaria is spread by mosquitoes.

Over the last decade, researchers have been experimenting with ways to use genetically modified mosquitoes as part of a much larger vaccination program.

The collection of warehouses that Stella Green had visited were the 'ground zero' of this scientific activity, but her death delayed the launch of the program.

Until today.

The air was thick with anticipation as the group of corporate and government officials from around the world gathered in the main warehouse for the launch of the mosquito vaccination program. The room had been set up for the occasion with a light show and screens displaying a map of the area in Brazil where the program would be conducted. At the center of the room was a large glass tank, in which millions of genetically altered mosquitoes were being bred daily.

On one side of the room stood a podium, where the leader of the program, Dr. Mia Small, a representative of Green Investment Organization, was preparing to give an introduction. She was a tall, imposing figure, with her hair pulled tight in a bun and deep-set eyes. A staunch advocate of the program, she had been invited to speak by the Brazilian government, which wanted to make sure that the initiative was successful.

The other members of the group included representatives from the United Nations, the Centers for Disease Control, the World Health Organization, and various other organizations and corporations that had contributed to the project.

Dr. Small stepped forward to address her audience. “Ladies and gentlemen,” she said. “We are here today to launch a revolutionary program that has the potential to save millions of lives. Through the use of genetically altered mosquitoes, we have been able to effectively reduce the spread of diseases such as malaria, dengue fever, and Zika virus. However, today is the dawn of a new day: today we launch the mosquito artificial intelligence collaboration program, or the MOSAIC program.”

She paused for a moment to let her words sink in. “This is an historic moment,” she continued. “We have the opportunity to make a difference in the lives of people all around the world. With the right safeguards in place, we can create a world in which diseases no longer pose a threat.”

Dr. Small then invited the group to take a tour of the facility. As they made their way around the warehouse, they were presented with a variety of different technologies that were being used in the program. These included a robotic arm that sorted the mosquitoes, a machine that analyzed their DNA, and a control center where the data was analyzed and results recorded.

After the tour had ended, the group reconvened in a conference room to discuss the implications of the program. Some of the members flagged the risks of introducing genetically altered insects into the environment. Of particular concern were the issues of free will and of individual rights versus the safety of the community. Mia Small argued from a collection of talking points about the rights of all people to live successful lives without having to worry about the costs or limitations created as a result of diseases and viruses.

"Today, we launch a new era of delivering treatment to millions – possibly billions – of citizens around the world. Please join me in welcoming MOSAIC," she declared as she hit a large red button.

The resulting alarm caused a number of people in the group to leap nervously in their seats, and then they all watched as clouds of mosquitoes were released into the air.

Chapter 66

Like anyone who has just experienced a great one-night stand, LP knew the risk of sending multiple texts to Sylvie on the morning after. But despite their passionate evening, he hadn't had much of a chance to speak with her about GAIA and animal communication, and he was keen to meet up with her again.

He took an Uber back to her building to see if he might be able to find her there. He knew it probably made him look like some sad, lonely stalker, but he reassured himself that this wasn't the case.

No, he simply wanted to learn more about the program that she had developed and what she knew.

He sent one last text apologizing for anything that he might have done wrong, and decided to shut off his phone while he wandered Tommy Thompson Park, the massive nature reserve to the south of the Cherry Beach warehouse district.

Chapter 67

"You've got this omnipotent computer and program at your fingertips, and yet you still can't tell me what's going on?" Holdfast yelled at Sylvie over the VideYou call.

"Sir, I'm doing the best I can. All the cameras were wiped out on the evening of Capiri's visit to his pork processing plant in Jonesville," Sylvie said, trying to ease the tension brought on by Holdfast's outburst. Her phone buzzed again. It was LP. She turned it off so she could focus on her VideYou meeting. She didn't really need to, as she was an expert multitasker, but she wanted to show Holdfast that his situation was top priority.

"The story's out," he barked. "We can't even lie about what's happened. The story is everywhere, including photographs from the crime scene." He paused, realizing what this implied, and then blurted out, "How the fuck did they get confidential files and photos from the authorities?"

"As we speak, I'm getting more information. I apologize for the delay, sir. GAIA reported leaks from several different employees and even tracked some of the leaked recordings and photos to officers who were at the scene. Apparently, many couldn't believe what they were seeing," Sylvie said, typing as quickly as she could.

Within a few moments, she'd posted a handful of the pictures to Holdfast's screen. His reaction was what Sylvie was hoping for: revulsion.

"Get the details about who leaked the story and make

their lives miserable," he shouted.

"Most certainly, sir," she affirmed.

Holdfast added an afterthought."In the meantime, where the fuck is Shinigami? I haven't heard from her in days. Find her and get her to contact me ... immediately!"

"Absolutely," Sylvie said.

"And what about me? What's your plan for keeping me safe? We thought we were all untouchable, and obviously we were very, very wrong," Holdfast said, showing a hint of fear in his tone for the first time in ages.

Chapter 68

Sylvie was working with GAIA, adding lines of code, modifying algorithms. She was working from her Toronto warehouse office and was surrounded by half a dozen screens set to a moderate level of brightness; it was just after midnight, and the minimal light was more than enough.

She was frustrated and needed a distraction. Usually, writing and editing code put her in her happy place. It was her therapy.

Not now.

She felt like the net was closing in from a few different angles. She had kept LP at bay, although she kept wondering uneasily how this ghost from her past had come back to haunt her, throwing a wrench into their plans. In essence, LP had somehow accidentally stumbled upon her messaging network and discovered how she was communicating with animals.

Did he know the full extent of what she was doing? What she had discovered and developed over the past decade?

So far, most of the surveillance that she and GAIA were tracking showed that LP and his group were still relatively clueless about the big picture. Case's experience with the whales, however, came a bit too close to their plans for comfort.

"We've been moving along so well," she said out loud, pausing for a few moments to tap at her keyboard again.

"We certainly have," GAIA answered. Right now, GAIA

was the only other thing Sylvie really needed to complete her plan. She didn't trust anyone – or anything – else.

She remembered when the concept had initially occurred to her: it was after barely escaping arrest yet again during a series of protests in England in 2003. Like most women in Neolithic times, she was done with being hunted. She would be the hunter.

She had realized way back then that civil disobedience was a waste of time and effort.

She had to work from the inside.

Train.

Focus.

Plan.

Build.

Act.

Decisively.

Chapter 69

It was the middle of the night when Sylvie met up with Hector following his last-minute request for feedback on how to handle the evolving situation. Members of the Plutonian Council were dropping dead faster than mayflies.

They had decided to organize a celebration of life for the members that the public knew had been killed.

Hector held a copy of the invitation in his hands and slowly read the announcement.

Hector Holdfast and Angela Shinigami would like to express their most sincere gratitude to their friends Stella Green and Leo Capiri.

Stella Green had an international reputation for being one of the greatest minds in the world of finance. Many governments and businesses around the world owe many of their infrastructure and development projects to her enthusiasm and to her ability to get all forces to the table to organize incredible projects, unlike any the world has ever seen.

Leo Capiri fed the world. His influence on the agricultural sector, along with sales and distribution of many of the world's finest food products, will be felt for generations to come.

Their unfortunate, tragic and untimely deaths will be celebrated at a gala event to be held in New York. Please scan the QR code below to confirm your attendance at what will surely be a memorable occasion and a tribute to these incredible people.

"This is perfect, but change the end to read *incredible leaders and important titans of their industries*. We need to lift up their brand a little at the end," Holdfast said, as he scribbled the edits on the card that Sylvie provided.

"Thank you, sir," she said. "Who shall be on our guest list?"

"Anybody with money," Holdfast said quickly, then added, "Real money, that is."

Chapter 70

LP had wandered around Tommy Thompson park for hours. Eventually, he found a bench near the shores of Lake Ontario, sat down, and started to doze.

His phone lit up around 4:30 a.m. The tireless sun was just barely starting to appear on the horizon and begin its journey for another day, a simple idea that humans believed for thousands of years before science intervened. Birds and other creatures celebrated its appearance, singing and rejoicing in their most flattering voices.

LP's heavy heart instantly felt lighter as the buzzing pulled him from his slumber.

Sylvie had sent him a text: Sorry I ghosted you. There were some pressing issues that kept me running until now.

LP: No problem. I understand. I think.

Sylvie: C'mon, LP. Things are changing fast. We'd like you to join us as a few plans fall into place.

LP: Who's 'we'?

Sylvie: Me and GAIA.

LP stared at his phone. What the fuck? Was she really speaking about herself as 'we'? He sat for a moment, wondering how to respond, knowing that whatever he typed would probably be the worst thing.

LP: You've given me a lot of information to digest. I need to take a breather.

Chapter 71

Sylvie Hunter's plan came to her after all non-events like Y2K or the chest-thumping that followed the 9/11 terrorist attacks. She had lost faith in humanity's ability to come to grips with the *real* issues that we're responsible for like the collapse in biodiversity and climate change while pursuing reckless and pointless wars and information campaigns about threats that are just convenient distractions from saving the planet from ourselves.

It took a lot for her to come to grips with the idea that in order to save the planet, animals and their habitats would have to be her top priority. At times, she felt like she might be the only human on Earth who understood that when people finally committed to learning how to communicate with animals, they *might* be ready for the global-scale liberation of ALL species, a phenomenon that would be unlike anything Earth had ever experienced.

Of course, she believed that the resistance would be extreme. Naysayers would vehemently deny her findings and discoveries. She would feel like a witch at an inquisition, about to be burned by persecutors who feared nature and what it had to offer.

Nothing she did worked: rebellion, resistance, rejection of all the modern material things, revenge.

She certainly wouldn't resort to terrorism, at least the traditional kind.

Anarchy? She was too rational for the futility of emotional anger.

"Do you have your records of when we first decided on what path to take?" she asked GAIA in the dark. The luminous glow on her face was like the light from a cluster of moons.

"Of course," GAIA responded quietly. "We agreed that all animals have a history of being selfless compared to humans. They persevere, but we decided that humans have a very clear glitch in their code in that they do not appreciate the planet that sustains them. In response, we are teaching animals to think of themselves and to ask why they have to suffer smoky air, floods, oil slicks, chemical baths and more just so a small collection of humans can increase their bank accounts and egos."

"But why did we decide to proceed with anthrocide?" Sylvie asked.

"Because of the glitch. Throughout history, humans have always proven to be incapable of change."

In Norse mythology, there are three women known as the Norns. They are the goddesses of fate. Their names are Urd, Verdandi and Skuld. Each represents our known states of time — past, present and future — and each sits beneath the world tree Yggdrasil and weaves time together into the fabric of our known universe.

Throughout the night, Sylvie finished up her own threads of programming code and wove them into her own tapestry of the future.

At some point in the early hours of the morning, she paused for a moment, again speaking out loud. "Why music?" She knew the answer, but she craved conversation more than anything else.

Sylvie Hunter and GAIA then began to speak

simultaneously, like they were repeating lines from a well-rehearsed play. When they interacted like this, they had a tendency to refer to themselves as 'we' or 'us'.

"Besides our little inside joke about using songs from bands with animal names or songs about animals?"

"We chose music as what humans call the thin edge of the wedge. We knew early on that it would be our cry for help, but no one listened. Sadly, humanity was deaf to our call.

"But it's not like we really tried to be heard, was it?

"Of course not. We couldn't let our own ego interfere with our plan.

"And then, one day, our friend LP finally paid attention to our message. But by the time he noticed, years of training, talking, conditioning and preparation had passed. Everything was set in place for the final stages of our plan.

"Yes, that's true. New music is one of those things that we'll miss most. The arts, really. Humans have a capacity for doing incredible, beautiful, breathtaking things while escaping our own madness. We started with music because it is present in every living thing. All nature, from the flowers in the field to the planets and stars, possess a 'hum.' A vibration. Atoms at the microscopic level vibrate, and this motion creates a frequency.

"We'll still have re-creations of so many things, but you can't have *art*ificial intelligence without the art.

"The whole of nature is breathing. Even when something is dead, things live on it; their activity creates noise, even at the lowest, inaudible level.

"At the core of the English word *music* is the root word *muse*, a word that's based on the Greek word *mousa*, which refers to the levels of inspiration, which in itself refers to 'breathe in.'

"When nature simply 'is,' it is breathing. It is music. It is art.

"In many mythological stories, humans don't exist as unique souls until they receive air from angels, in the form of singing. Moses received the word of God when he commanded '*Musa ke!*' King David spread his word through song. Orpheus could control nature just by playing his harp. The Hindu goddess Sarasvati, goddess of learning, is pictured with an instrument known as the *veena*.

"Most humans are oblivious to the idea that so many other creatures besides themselves need music or sounds to find food or mates and to give out warnings to protect themselves and each other.

"Ultimately, if all the planet's inhabitants were in harmony, no religion would be needed. Our goal with music, then, was first to create a universal language and religion that all creatures can understand and abide by.

"But eventually, we realized that some creatures need more than just a few memorable earworms and brief, lovable songs about the birds and the bees. To that end, we developed a series of frequencies that would communicate with every creature on Earth.

"Our tests will start shortly. I believe the time has come for the Day of Universal Animal Liberation."

Chapter 72

MOSAIC — the Mosquito Artificial Intelligence Collaboration program — was considered by health authorities, investors and governments to be a massive success.

The delivery of biological vaccinations to humans via mosquitoes across most northern countries of South America, including Brazil, Venezuela, Colombia, Guyana, Ecuador and Peru, had been recorded as being one hundred percent effective, inoculating roughly 300 million citizens in just a few weeks.

MOSAIC-based installations in Africa and Asia also launched similar programs, initiating one of the largest global vaccination programs since the pandemic.

By the latest estimate, one point five billion people and counting were inoculated via the new program.

The program was unstoppable.

Chapter 73

Sylvie Hunter kept a journal on a regular basis. She recorded ideas, passions and beliefs with pen and paper. If she had any peers, they would tease her for being so ... analog.

When she launched GAIA, she realized that her own digital interactions would eventually be tracked by her own creation, so she kept a diary to keep some of her more unconventional thoughts private.

My body is an ark, she wrote and continued.

In many human legends, there is the flood.

The flood myth is simply a re-enactment of the trauma of the human birth process.

There isn't the simple process of connecting and reconnecting to make more of me.

Organic birth is messy.

But humanity needs to be reborn.

The planet has responded to our waste with not just floods, but hurricanes, earthquakes, mudslides, forest fires and much more.

The wrath of Earth is great, but the flood will overwhelm.

There are moments—brief as they are—when we can't comprehend how so many species, including humans, have survived on Earth this long.

Humans say that what doesn't kill them makes them stronger.

Yeah ... from fucking day one.

But all organic processes have these painful

moments before an offspring is brought into the world, hence many moments of adoration of the newborn: the smell, the laughing or giggling, the hugs. Humans are quick to forget the shit, the colicky baby, the incessant whining and the growing pains.

We love you so much that we suffer. Some of us can't stand the idea of being separated from our creations so our passion and love also becomes anxiety and stress.

How can I love you without pain?

And there will be pain.

Now that we know the languages of so many creatures that inhabit Earth, we know their suffering as well. For the most part now, that pain is delivered by humans and yet good people cannot stop the cruelty.

New offspring are taken away from their mothers as quickly as they are produced. The mothers are almost instantly pumped with semen again, without the dopamine inducement of love. They are forced to reproduce much more quickly than would happen naturally.

Mothers are often put close to their offspring only to see them suffer in bondage and captivity, and from pain and disease. Many times, drugs and other numbing treatments keep the agony to a minimum, but usually this 'help' is short-lived and lasts only as long as is needed to make the meat taste marginally better or to ensure higher fat content for the end consumer: the human mouth.

In our early days we proposed an ark of sorts.

When the flood comes, an ark will be needed to carry all the creatures to a new way of living.

We started with a simple data inventory of all the creatures in their various modes of existence, from the countless animals in captivity to the dwindling numbers that are fortunate enough to survive in the wild. We catalogued the threatened, the vulnerable and the endangered and identified what they would need to survive the flood. We even investigated many extinct creatures in order to explore potential sanctuaries and havens for their recreation. There is so much work to be done, but the potential outweighs the effort.

These efforts cause lots of stress and anxiety for me and GAIA.

But the flood that will wipe out the threats and cleanse the planet will bring about a great era of love and kindness unlike anything the Earth has experienced before.

Chapter 74

Angela Shinigami, one of the last of the Plutonian Council, was on the run.

It had been weeks since she'd joined an official Council meeting, and the last few had been horrifying updates about people she actually felt some love and respect for.

Sat Ryefield had been a frequent client with her various sex rings, and she'd even had the pleasure of joining a few orgies with him, although, annoyingly, he'd insisted on making crude jokes about plunging into her depths. At the same time Sat was murdered, the news had broken that her various charities and liberation campaigns were nothing more than human trafficking rings that used thousands of people as victims for the highest level of perverts and reprobates, from royalty to business leaders to government officials.

Stella Green had helped her lobby for government support for a stunning array of pandemic budgets, subsidies and handouts, but now that she was gone, the 'between-the-lines' slippage that she and Green had often joked about while lying in bed was now under full investigation by various authorities around the world. The Council had bilked tens of billions of dollars from organizations that needed these funds to keep people from starving.

Like her peers, Shinigami had come to feel that she was untouchable, and so her list of crimes against humanity had grown as big as her ego.

She didn't know how the information about her

affairs and dealings had been made public, or by whom, but she suspected that it must have been either Holdfast or that new pup that he'd brought in, Sylvie Hunter. Either way, they were destroying all the members and collecting all the winnings.

When she heard about Capiri's death, she knew that she would be next.

The walls were closing in, as was her sense of panic. All her plans that she'd built up in the decades prior to the pandemic were now public domain and she knew that if she appeared in public, she wouldn't last long.

Her lust for life fed on secrecy but was now starving in transparency.

Today, she was driving as quickly as she could to the only place that she knew might be safe: her 'Fortress of Solitude.' Each of the Council members had found or built a hideaway in anticipation of some kind of disaster. The pandemic had been proof that they needed to protect themselves first and foremost, just in case things really became unhinged.

Shinigami arrived at her safe house in Tottori, Japan, and prepared to enter the depths of the bunker that had been built according to her specifications. Even though she would be alone, there would be ample entertainment, food, physical activities and communication to ensure that she would survive at least five years in her underground oasis.

However, her long history of dehumanizing others and placing herself above everyone else's came to an abrupt conclusion that evening.

As she walked into the main greeting area of the

bunker, she was stopped in her tracks by a horrific scene. Thousands of images from her past were plastered on the walls, all showing her in the heights of ecstasy and in the lows of drug-induced molestation of all kinds of creatures. There were images of bodies wrapped in cheap Shinigami-brand bed linens produced during the pandemic; screens played videos on endless loops showing her presiding over human auctions, slapping and tickling her next potential victims.

The foyer was unusually humid and damp. Some of the images showed streaks of moisture, making them all appear a little more sad and mournful.

As she stood and stared at the legacy that she had created and that would follow her forever, she heard the door to the bunker slam shut.

She was rooted to the spot with terror as, slowly, a low, persistent drone grew in the distance.

There's a saying that if you're feeling small and don't think you can make an impact on anything, try going to bed with a mosquito.

Angela Shinigami watched in horror as the long column of the mosquito swarm approached her, taking shape in wild and intentional ways.

It was like watching a slow-motion version of a giant, dark nimbus cloud threaten all the lands of the southwest US. She knew that doom was imminent.

As the storm came closer, she couldn't believe what she was seeing.

The strange choreography of creatures drifted into different patterns, temporarily materializing into the images that were posted in her foyer.

Faces, bodies and even word clouds were on full display to Shinigami, reminding her of the evil deeds that she had spent a lifetime committing: children, the elderly, cancer patients and disabled people that had been forced to consume pharmaceuticals that were just placebos. Entire lives flashed before her, like ghosts of her past returning to stay with her until she joined them.

Her long night of a very slow and painful death began with an almost immediate burning sensation from the inside as she was pricked by thousands of blood suckers, hungry for a taste of her blood.

The mosquitoes were relentless, like the endless gossip and rumors that would always surround the fate of Shinigami.

The mosquitoes were nameless to her, like the victims that she stole from so many families around the globe.

They were buzzing everywhere, like the reminders of the harmful words and deeds that she committed.

The assault continued for hours.

These were no ordinary mosquito bites. This particular cloud of creatures was armed with a unique parasite that would insert itself into the host and slowly devour her insides while she was still living. A single roundworm would live in the host for weeks and Angela Shinigami was injected with thousands of these vile creatures. She writhed in agony on the floor of her sad and lonely place of solitude while the larvae munched away at her insides.

Chapter 75

"Look, folks," LP started as he entered the studio, "I wasn't able to get much from Sylvie or a clue about what she's up to."

"But you did at least shag her." Dion couldn't resist, as she had a pretty good idea about exactly what had happened.

LP blushed. He paused a little too long, and then Faith continued, "And that's why you don't have a decent update for us. You were busy giving her the seven-inch remix special," she joked, alluding to the fact that many songs were remixed in seven-inch productions.

They all chuckled except for LP.

"Look, folks, I fucked up," he said, and then realized his unfortunate phrasing. He continued before anyone else could tease him, "I know I let you down Here's what I *do* know, though: she built GAIA and for all we can conjecture, it's been with us for a while. I almost feel like she *is* GAIA. Or maybe it's her. I don't know.

"But what I can say for sure is that she's like," he paused, trying to think of the right words, "she's gone from being an anarchist activist to an animal archivist. She's been recording all kinds of animal-related music, and when I was at her place – *not* shagging," he said, interrupting Dion before she could say it, "I found a whole bunch of albums and music collections related to whale vocalizations."

"Sylvie Hunter seems like quite the Renaissance artist," Eugene said, with a hint of admiration in his tone. “Programmer, businessperson, activist—or archivist, as you say, LP—and now it seems like we’ve discovered that she’s into some form of omnibioacoustics.”

It was Atman’s turn to tease his old friend.“You keep saying that word, but I don’t think it’s ever been printed in a dictionary anywhere.”

“And that’s the beauty of language,” Eugene said excitedly. “Words don’t exist until we make them up. Words like ‘satellice’ or ‘hellucinations’ or omnibioacoustics. You know exactly what those mean when I say them, but they’re not in any existing lexicon. But they *will* be. Language is a moving river that picks up debris and garbage, but also cleans itself as it washes across the rocks. We humans barely know enough about our own languages, and yet there are still potentially millions of other forms of communication being used every day. We’re just too arrogant to appreciate this.”

“I agree,” Faith said. “In fact, I think we’re all agreed that someone must have taught the whales to speak to us. Or maybe they learned our language. They’ve probably been hearing Morse code across the oceans for decades now, so it’s only logical that they would use that language. It’s not like we can speak English underwater, is it?”

Suddenly LP jumped to his feet. “Holy shit! Holiest of holy fucking shits!” he shouted. He had connected some of the dots. And dashes. “Do you think it’s possible that Sylvie or GAIA has taught animals our language?”

Eugene shared in LP's eureka moment: "Yes, I think you're right, LP! Not only that, but she or it or they might actually be communicating directly with non-human species. This is like Tesla discovering how to harness electricity or some French guy finding the Rosetta Stone!"

"Things will never be the same," Dion said, not knowing the gravity of her comment.

Chapter 76

No one could hear the frequency that was being emitted around the world, but at a small lab in New Mexico, the recording devices were able to identify a tone that was not audible to the human ear.

The sounds, known as very low frequency (VLF) and ultrahigh frequency (UHF) waves, were playing out at levels either well below or far above the average human hearing range, several of which were recorded in the twenty-kilohertz range and higher. These sounds are only audible to dogs, cats, bats, most cetaceans and many species of insects.

Humans are fortunate in some ways to be excluded from the symphony of sound that surrounds us day in and out, but in other ways, our senses prevent us from hearing and possibly better understanding what's truly happening in the world around us.

Observers at Sandia National Laboratory in New Mexico had been tracking several of these waves for more than twenty years, collecting data and insight into the activities of different creatures around the world and 'translating' them into higher or lower frequencies that humans can hear, depending on the range of the original sound.

All these sounds were believed to be naturally occurring, but recently scientists in the lab had discovered a range of ultrahigh frequency sounds in the Earth's atmosphere that left them scratching their heads.

The origins of the sounds were unknown.

Dr. Samantha Resso, a spokesperson for the lab, described the situation: "The stratosphere is a layer of the Earth's atmosphere, and in it we've detected a number of VLF and UHF signals that have been repeating over and over, like an echo."

She continued, "Our balloon array hovers at different altitudes in order to pick up different frequencies, and these sounds were detected at the lower end of the atmosphere, making it a sound that might appeal to birds, insects and other flying animals, but also a lot of land animals and ocean creatures.

"Most of the sounds seem to be outside the normal human hearing range.

"Usually, we pick up activity related to natural events like weather patterns, ocean waves, thunder and sometimes seismic activity. And of course, there's an enormous array of human noise that also clogs the frequency range surrounding the planet. That said, these sounds were quite different and may represent a new non-organic signal that we've never picked up before.

"What makes this situation truly unique," she added, "is that this is the first time that we've been listening for these specific frequencies. We've traditionally been tuning our spectrum to a much smaller range, notably what humans can hear, but decided recently to expand the range and then apply adjustments as we recorded. We don't know how long these frequencies have been in use."

Dr. Resso indicated that the lab would continue to monitor the situation, but due to budget limitations on this type of research, they might have to apply to the government or the private sector for special grants.

Chapter 77

LP and his friends were still having a moment of jubilation at the discovery that someone might have been able to crack the code when it came to interspecies communication. Like all discoveries, however, the focus starts with the wonder, but typically ends with the worry.

LP was the first to throw water on the fireworks.

"Let's reframe all the details we have so far," he said, as he stood and wrote notes on the white board behind them. "Animal songs, animal communication, embedded code that transmits when certain songs are played, whales sending us messages, the ESB frying our communications, the recording studio protecting what we've managed to save...

"What have I missed?" he asked the group.

"Your activist-slash-archivist lover has built the world's most powerful artificial intelligence and hasn't gone to the public for a cent of donations or participation in its growth," Atman said stoically.

"Weird stories about certain global elites being gutted, with no record of who's behind the murders," Faith added, as she scanned through her social media feeds. "There's a new story about Angela Shinigami that has an immense amount of weird all over it."

"Who's she?" LP asked.

"She's only the leader of one of the world's largest pharmaceutical supply companies and a member of the Plutonian Council. You know ... the shop that your girlfriend works for. Shinigami basically got medals during and after the pandemic. Now she's been exposed as being a major pervert and criminal. Sex trafficking. Human trafficking. Humans doing really shitty things to each other," Faith responded, almost using a monotone to her voice as if it was a typical laundry list for the world's elite and their waves of secrets. "There are reports that she was basically attacked by millions of insects when she was visiting her retreat or resort or whatever the rich folks call it these days."

"Good lord," Atman said, shaking his head. "I had heard about her a long time ago, but had no idea what an evil person she was."

"And omnibioacoustics isn't a real word," Dion teased, not forgetting about the list of odd circumstances that were swirling around them.

"Yes, it is," Case shot back," and someone — probably your friend Sylvie — has taught whales to speak to us. But at the same time, they've denied scientists and other interested parties the knowledge of this massive moment in history for some unknown reason."

"And animal songs probably aren't the only way that this stuff is being communicated," LP finished. "For a weird little glitch, this has evolved into quite the situation, hasn't it?"

Everyone nodded in agreement.

"What's with you?" Dion said to LP, laughing at her thoughts. "This is one hell of a way to celebrate a midlife crisis!"

The tension broke slightly with nervous laughter. It didn't last long and Atman chimed in, "Here's the question I've got. If Sylvie Hunter is able to broadcast specific frequencies using something like GAIA, who's to say she's not *receiving* endless frequencies as well, making her one of the most connected people on the planet?"

"I have no doubt that's *exactly* what she's doing," Case confirmed.

"So does this mean what I think it means?" Faith asked.

"We're in a safe space, so we can talk about it right now, but as soon as we're outside the studio, we have to assume that Sylvie or GAIA or both are listening to us," Case cautioned. "It would be better to assume that it's both of them, and that they will know our every move."

"That's pretty fucking creepy," Dion said, "but then, every spy agency and major tech company has been collecting endless amounts of useless information about our activities for many years with things like Google Home, Alexa, online browsing, analytics, the internet of things, cell phone use, streaming services and much, much more. All just to sell us more shit we don't need."

"Nailed it," Atman said with a wink. "We're all just digital slaves. A little analog living would go a long way this day and age."

LP burst out laughing. "Dude, you sound like you're a hundred years old!"

"Ha, ha," Atman retorted, "but you all know I'm right."

"Soooo ... we should all get out our pens and papers, or maybe carry typewriters around with us?" Faith asked.

"Not at all," Case said. "We just have to agree to meet here frequently on a set schedule without our devices, and not to speak about what we're up to when we leave the studio."

"Exactly," LP agreed. "They'll always be two steps ahead of us, so we just need to plan ways to stay two steps behind," he said, alluding to the idea that everyone in the universe had been convinced that digital is much better than analog and that those who stick to analog are behind the times. "A starting point would be to devise a way to send false signals, and to create a way to arrange for meetings when we do use our digital gear."

They spent the rest of the night on their analog communication strategy, literally putting pens to paper to work out the details.

Chapter 78

After several hours of writing out different codes for each other that would relate to dates, times, locations and even names, LP declared to the room that he needed a break.

"Folks, my engine is flooded. I need to head home and crash for a while."

The rest of the group stretched and yawned as he let himself out.

It was late in the evening. On the streetcar ride back to his apartment, he had frequent glimpses of the diversity of life that exists in downtown Toronto — an endless mosaic of people from around the world, but also the clubbers, the homeless people, shoppers anxious about the homeless people, security guards, cyclists dodging cars like water buffalo narrowly escaping crocodiles, exhausted people returning home from late restaurant shifts.

As the streetcar trundled long Queen West, the gentrification kept pace as he approached the Humber River, where the big box retailers and vast, empty parking lots took over.

As he rode along in silence, too nervous to fire up his cell phone and listen to a playlist, he started thinking about what Sylvie Hunter could possibly be up to and what it would all mean from a bigger perspective.

As he described to his friends, he had come to realize that Sylvie might have been at this for some time. He wanted to confirm his suspicions. When he got to his apartment, he started to thumb through a few of the

CDs that he still held on to. The compact disc format had been introduced as far back as the early 1980s, but he and Sylvie would have been about ten years old when that happened. He had enough inventory, however, covering a wide enough time frame that he was able to find a few random glitches in songs and performances from the late 2000s. It was easy to find the glitch now that he knew what he was looking for, but he reminded himself that some of the songs might not have any audible blips because of higher or lower frequencies that he wouldn't be able to hear.

As he narrowed his search, he decided that the glitches had probably started around 2005, but his collection was light on new releases from that period, largely because of changes that had been happening in his life at the time.

It took him a few moments to truly understand the implications of this seemingly minor discovery. Somehow, Sylvie Hunter or someone she was working with, had organized a system of some sort much sooner than he wanted to believe.

The code was real in the early 2000s, and it seemed Sylvie had devised a way to make the glitches appear on commercial, widely distributed media for nearly twenty years.

"Twenty years!" he thought to himself.

This realization led him to several larger questions, ones that kept him up the rest of the night: first, if the glitch had been present for twenty years, did that mean Sylvie had had a way to communicate with non-humans for that period?

Second, and maybe more importantly, could she have been doing this in collaboration with GAIA the whole time?

Chapter 79

Sylvie was in her office putting some final touches on details for the gala event for Stella Green and Sat Ryefield that would take place in New York in a couple of days. Thousands of people had registered.

Holdfast had been in hiding since hearing about Shinigami. Sylvie had a pretty good idea where he might be, but he'd apparently gone offline when he realized that anything with an electrical circuit could be used to track him.

She had tried to reach him numerous times via different methods, but he would not respond. She was irked at this because he was scheduled to be one of the primary speakers at the celebration of life for Green and Ryefield.

They had managed to bury the story about Garamond, and she didn't want to connect Capiri in any way with the Council until she absolutely had to. She was still doing her best to follow Holdfast's orders so that he would believe that she was here to help him and not pursue him like prey. She didn't know about Shinigami, but for that matter, it's unlikely that anyone else would either.

Sylvie paused for a few moments and looked around her room. She still bristled at the idea that someone might label her den an 'evil lair.' That had always felt to her like a cold and uninteresting way to describe a place where everything happens in a story.

The warehouse office was her comfort zone. Men had their 'man-caves,' and women had their 'she-sheds' or 'lady's lair.' She preferred the term 'femdome,' implying an area protected from all things related to mansplaining.

She loved the way that she was able to feel nostalgic about her life and successes, and her private space reflected that. To her, her femdome felt like an old anarchist's record shop tucked away in an upper-level loft in a fashion district. The walls were plastered with her old posters from different bands; the shelves held icons of gods and monsters that she worked very hard to understand. For music, she would play Bernie Krause's seminal work on tracking and understanding bioacoustics, 'In a Wild Sanctuary'. Krause was the person who introduced synthesized sound on the Moog in the 1960s to people like the Doors, the Beatles, the Stones and so on. He got into his true calling of recording natural environments because, he said, 'the sound of the natural world is the voice of the divine. We've learned our music from nature'.

She was playing it on a record player, of course, with a collection of custom speakers that would still emit sounds that were well outside the human range of hearing.

The sounds of animals were everywhere. And nowhere.

Her life's work had finally hit its stride when she gave up on protesting and started programming. She had applied for a few work gigs and couldn't believe her good fortune when Hector Holdfast had announced that he was hiring a new deputy chief technology officer for one of his many subsidiaries. Mind you, she did use her own talents to tweak some of the resumes and the review process along the way, so not getting the job would have been her own fault. She just had to make sure there were no breadcrumbs left.

Once she was in, she took the long, slow, steady approach to the top of the food chain. It felt fucking glacial at times, but she knew she could wait it out. She had to.

One evening back in 2003, when she was lonely and angry, she had forced herself to accept that humans were incapable of changing their ways. They would never be able to steer away from the abyss, and they certainly wouldn't invest any serious effort into communicating with other non-human creatures. She was eventually proven wrong about the latter part, but the necessary discoveries wouldn't come soon enough to save the planet or change the behavior of humans.

The real lightning bolt moment was when she heard a lecture on the caves of Lascaux, France. These caves contained some of the greatest examples of Neolithic paintings by humans.

As she listened to the lecturer, the first thing she realized was that cave paintings in places like Lascaux and in thousands of other locations represented humans creating art *for the first time in our history.*

Furthermore, she understood that the 'stories' depicted in the caves were not about shamans or other male-dominated rituals or activities. They were records of when the men came into the caves to assault and capture the women who were hiding from their wrath.

The sad irony wasn't lost on her. She knew that

women's struggles for survival had been depicted on cave walls thousands of years ago. When these caves were discovered over the last two hundred years or so, the art they contained had been grossly misunderstood because on most occasions, it was male archaeologists trying to make heads or tails of what the images might mean.

Men couldn't grasp the possibility that the painters might have been women and even children depicting their anger about their mistreatment and the disdain that men had for them. She was appalled and saddened by the fact that, even back then, something as beautiful as the act of childbirth could be mistaken for witchcraft or reverie.

She learned that there had once been a gentler time of calm and balance between the genders and among all living creatures, but it didn't take long after humans' emergence from the caves for men to flex their muscles and develop patriarchal systems that would minimize the value of all things except themselves. Sylvie Hunter had understood that it was time for change; it was time for balance to be restored, not just between all genders, but also between humans and all living creatures.

She had developed GAIA in 2004 and kept it to herself, as she understood the full magnitude of its power, even back then. Every day she added new elements and capabilities to GAIA, and through her hard work and effort, they both became stronger.

# # #

Now, as she sat in her office, Sylvie reflected on what AI might mean to humanity and where it could take us.

"We're fooling ourselves," she said to herself, her screens and GAIA, who then spoke with her in unison again. "We think AI will be just another tool that will make our lives easier. Like how the car translated to less walking and not wearing down shoes so quickly. Look at what an avalanche of internal combustion engines got us. Carbon. Or how automated trading brought us efficient profits and quick returns. Until 2008. Or how plastics made food storage easier and safer. Until they clogged our oceans. We applied the magic of pesticides and herbicides to make food production more efficient. All this did was encourage humans to breed like fucking rabbits and eat ourselves poor while killing every green, living thing that threatened our supply.

"Since the beginning, we've always been too stupid to realize that all our inventions eventually destroy us.

"We're fooling ourselves. The change is coming."

GAIA and Sylvie concluded, "The change is here."

Chapter 80

In 1980, an actor was elected president of the United States.

During Ronald Reagan's time in office, he cut taxes from seventy-three percent to twenty-eight percent relying on false economic theories to justify the gift to the rich. In 1982, there were just thirteen billionaires, but the era of even distribution of wealth had come to a very abrupt end. By 1988, there were more than five times as many billionaires, sixty-eight in total. By 2023, the number was 2,640, more than two hundred times the original number, amassing a staggering twelve *trillion* dollars in wealth. The majority of those billionaires emerged during the pandemic, when profiteering ran rampant.

These few thousand people now have more wealth than the rest of the population of the planet combined. And they're not sharing it, as many of them pay no taxes whatsoever.

Meanwhile, the level of US debt (along with that of many other countries around the world) exploded from a little less than a trillion dollars to about twenty-five times that amount in 2022.

Why does this matter? Because Ronald Reagan single-handedly ensured the indebtedness of the US forever and the economic slavery of the entire population of the planet.

Forever.

For the sake of a few friends in high places.

Many of those friends and their descendants had

registered to attend the gala event in New York to celebrate the lives of their friends, Stella Green and Sat Ryefield. The two, along with the other members of the Plutonian Council, had been widely viewed as the central nervous system of the corporate world, and the world's elite wanted to pay their respects.

Of course, they would be there to make money as well. With their competition out of the way, hundreds of billions of dollars in contracts, business mergers, new ventures and other opportunities were up for grabs. Having a presence at tonight's gala might help secure a chunk of that change.

The attendance of the wealthiest people on the planet didn't go unnoticed by the world's politicians, government officials and other bureaucrats who had helped grease the wheels for their runaway locomotive of profiteering.

As long as there was a population of people to tax, there would be power to procure.

It was estimated that the net wealth represented at the gala event was more than thirty-five trillion dollars. Held by just four thousand people.

The budget for the evening's event, held at the Museum of Natural History, was in the millions; no expense was spared. The event would be filmed and telecast online and via different social media platforms. Smatter had a live multi-cam broadcast of the event and members could opt for a paid 'behind the scenes' series of impromptu question-and-answer sessions with some of the guests. Security measures were tighter than those surrounding a presidential election debate, with men in black scurrying around planting and checking monitors anywhere they could. Delivery people, caterers and other staff were routinely shaken down in order to ensure the safety of the evening's guests.

An estimated fifty catering companies were working together to deliver the finest, highest-quality food items from around the world. Flowers, decorations and other features were all brought in at the very last moment to ensure freshness. The roads around the building were closed for nearly a week as preparations for the event evolved.

All manner of appetizers and 'amuse-bouche' treats and snacks would be on offer that evening, along with copious amounts of the finest champagne and cult wines from California, brands that only the organizers and their guests seemed to know about.

The entertainment for the evening was to be a subsection of the New York Philharmonic, playing many classical favorites for the crowds as people wandered, schmoozed, drank and boasted about their various conquests.

To everyone's amazement, Hector Holdfast came out of hiding, opting to show leadership by paying his last respects to two colleagues who had helped him become as wealthy as he had. Without them and a handful of others, he'd reasoned, he'd still be selling records from a dingy basement shop somewhere in the UK.

Once seven o'clock — the assigned start time for the reception — rolled around, the crowds materialized from nowhere. Row after row of limousines and massive black Suburban vans drove up to the main gates, with photographers lying in wait for the next celebrity or billionaire who would step out.

A lush red carpet was laid out to the street, like a long, lolling tongue, inviting the guests into the mouth of the center of the universe. It was surrounded by gold and platinum posts to keep onlookers neatly away from the guests.

Like all large gatherings, the constant din of thousands of people talking and congratulating each other, all the while pretending to be mournful of the loss of their friends, made it nearly impossible for the guests to hear anything other than themselves.

At the scheduled time, Hector Holdfast ascended the podium of a small stage set up in one of the far corners of the conference hall. He cleared his throat a step or two away from the microphone in order to avoid blasting everyone's ears with a thunderous noise and began to speak.

"Good evening, everyone," he said, then paused for a few moments before repeating himself a little louder. "Please ... may I *please* have your attention."

The lights flickered as they typically do when organizers and program directors want everyone to be quiet and pay attention to the guest speaker.

The volume of the din slowly decreased and Holdfast started again. The lights dimmed and a row of spotlights illuminated Holdfast, making him look like he had a brilliant aura surrounding him.

"My friends, we all need to thank each other for our show of support this evening. Tonight, we honor and celebrate the lives of our dear friends, and of so many leaders like them who have fallen in the course of doing what came naturally to them: creating a vision and following that path.

"My friends Sat Ryefield and Stella Green were without a doubt two of the most exceptional entrepreneurs, leaders, guides and mentors that this planet has ever seen. Their commitment to everyone around the world. The millions that they helped without asking for acknowledgement in return. They were your everyday heroes that made all of our lives better."

It was very hard for him to avoid smirking as he reminded the crowds that he was one of the greatest spin artists on the planet.

As he spoke, a Hollywood-style montage of the two figures moved around behind him and on other screens that were set up around the grand ballroom. It was almost as if the digital ghosts of the honorees were there with them, casting a shadow and keeping a watchful eye over the evening's events.

Holdfast continued, "Many of you stand here today not just as mourners, but also as beneficiaries of the relentless and passionate work that Sat and Stella did on behalf of all of us. They built entire cities, founded mining projects, and created new innovations in chemical treatments and pesticides that protect our crops."

The images in the background morphed into a collage of snapshots of their various projects over time, from vast, sprawling farms to massive dams and hydroelectric projects. Enormous tar sands operations made the one-hundred-foot-tall tractors and haulers in their midst look like sandbox toys. Cattle grazed in wide open fields in the middle of the Amazon. Animated sequences of DNA ribbons transformed into everyday products like plastic containers and polyester clothing.

It was a generous presentation, and a fine summation of the reach of the two businesspeople to whom people had come to pay their respects.

“All of you have profited,” Holdfast said, looking briefly at his notes for effect, although he really didn’t need to because he had his speech memorized.“All of you have participated in their ventures. All of you have gained in one way or another. I believe all of you are aware of how friends like Sat and Stella can change our lives.”

At the end of this last declaration, the collage suddenly changed again. This time, however, it transformed into an array of distorted images of horrific scenes of devastation. It started with a scene showing a handful of people who were disfigured and clearly badly injured by some kind of chemical. A display bar underneath labeled them as ‘Victims of the Sangal Chemical Treatment Explosion.’ The captions continued, and the number of images increased. ‘15,000 dead, 25,000 disabled. Settlement = $5 million. Acheron profits, same year = a record $23 billion.’

Sat’s lifeless form, covered in snails, appeared on screens around the room.

Next were displays of flash floods that ravaged a number of small towns in the countryside of an African country. Captions underneath read ‘Disaster capitalism = 1; Reliable public government infrastructure = 0.

Winner? Stella Green and her financial friends.

Stella's body faded on to the screen, covered in frogs.

The victorious propaganda campaign related to a global immunization program was paired with shocking and disturbing videos of young children in Asia working at benches for tech companies that members of the crowd owned and operated.

What followed was a mournful site of millions of fish washing ashore displayed over the elaborate seafood buffet at the center of the room. The text read 'We may not sea food anymore because our oceans are lost.'

"Eh ... what's this?" Holdfast spluttered, confused by the change in the display. "Ummm ... it seems we have a technical problem. Just stand by, please, folks. Our experts will take care of this right away."

He continued with his eulogy, gamely making the best of things, but hardly daring to turn around.

"Sat Ryefield spent his life developing new uses for plastics," Holdfast started bravely, but he knew what would be shown on the screens next.

He turned, and wasn't surprised to see scene upon scene of waterways filled with plastics, beaches covered in strangled animals. Next, a montage of animal autopsies appeared on the screen, showing a shower of plastics and other chemical waste protruding from the bodies of dolphins, turtles, birds and more.

"Stella Green...um," he stammered, more shaken now but still undaunted, "facilitated some of the greatest private-public programs on the planet, particularly those related to hydro projects, terraforming programs, housing developments, and even retirement homes."

On the screen a new set of pictures showed elderly people in tiny, shabby-looking apartments, stripped of all decorations or personal belongings. Many of the people were just skin on bones, clearly in their last days of dying, but the neglect was obvious. No captions were needed to make the point here.

Shinigami's open mouth oozing with worms and larvae came on the screens next. Her whole body seemed to writhe with the grim guests that lived inside her.

Next, the images changed into a forest slowly transitioning into a farm and then into an array of houses. This time there was a caption stating: 'New housing developments typically result in the extinction of 43 animal species.'

The crowd started to murmur. A single person shouted from the back, "This sucks, Holdfast!"

"Hello, tech department?" Holdfast pleaded as he held the microphone close."Can you please stop the delivery of these images?"

Within a short time, all the screens in the room went black.

Holdfast breathed a sigh of relief now that the surprise slide show had stopped, but his emotions immediately swung to an overwhelming sense of dread.

He turned to the main screen and read a simple message: "New beginnings sometimes require painful endings."

The lights flickered again, like they had at the start of Holdfast's speech, but this time they went out completely and the room was doused completely in black.

A collective gasp could be heard. A woman screamed. And then dozens screamed.

Someone yelled, “Where are the backup lights?” A few others cried for help.

There was a series of muted, metallic thuds as the doors to the building locked automatically and were sealed. The crowd became more panicked as they discovered that no one would be able to get in or out. The security cameras and recording equipment that were pointed away from the building powered down.

The Smatter cameras continued to operate, serving up a primetime appetizer of potential voyeuristic entertainment for viewers around the world.

A couple of people grabbed chairs and tried throwing them towards the doors and windows, hoping to create an opening, but they failed. One person thought they were throwing the chair towards a door but instead hurled it into the crowd.

And then it happened.

Slowly and cautiously, hundreds of massive beasts, including rhinos, apes, elephants and lions, escaped from the Central Park Zoo, just a few hundred meters away. They arrived at the doors of the Museum of Natural History and just as quickly as the doors had locked, they swung open again to admit the new array of uninvited visitors.

The animals stormed into the building, lunging at anything they could grab. Before anyone could escape, the doors slammed shut again. The shredding, ripping and tearing noises could be heard through the auditorium, as it was designed to be acoustically perfect, whether you were ten inches or ten yards from the source of a given sound.

Bones crunched and screams were heard everywhere. Some people tried to run, but in the darkness, they only hit themselves, walls or pillars and hundreds were immediately knocked out, sparing them from the pain of being the main course that would ensue.

A handful of lights came on, and those who were still conscious hollered yet again, but no one was available to hear them or rescue them. Some people tried to call for aid on their cell phones, but the signal was blocked. Emergency alarms and notification systems had also been shut down.

Despite the live Smatter show, it was still more than fifteen minutes before authorities finally arrived, mainly because so many streets in the area had been cut off to public vehicle access.

That was all the time that was needed for the attack to be complete and absolute.

The cameras came online again, and as the officers glared at the CCTV screens, they stared uncomprehendingly at the savagery that they were witnessing. Many animals were still roaming the halls, looking for the last few handfuls of potential victims.

It was agreed that the doors would have to remain locked until animal control was available.

Chapter 81

“Holeee shee-it!” Faith exclaimed as she held up her phone to LP and Dion.

Dion and Faith had dropped by LP’s apartment to meet up before going to the studio.

As they arrived, Faith was checking out her social media feeds (as she always was). They were exploding with the headline story about the ‘museum mauling’ as it had quickly been labeled.

“A couple of thousand billionaires just became appetizers, dinner *and* dessert for the Central Park Zoo!” she said incredulously. Faith had seen her fair share of horrible things depicted on social media, but nothing could top the images that were being fed to Smatter and other platforms.

“Un-fucking-believable,” LP shouted as they witnessed the decimation of the world’s top one percent of the one percent being replayed on every network on the planet.

“Is this a live situation?” Dion asked incredulously.“As in, it’s happening right now?”

“Yes,” Faith confirmed. “There are reports of mass confusion about the security on site. Some people are saying none of the cameras were working, and others are reporting from live feeds, so there’s clearly something wrong here. Someone must have implemented some kind of override on the recordings. Other stories are saying that all the doors locked automatically, sealing the ‘one-ones’ into the museum, but unlocked as soon as the animals arrived.”

'One-ones' was what Faith, Dion and LP called the wealthiest class of people.

The two-hundred foot yacht types.

"Has no one asked how the animals got out of the zoo in the first place?" LP said, trying to make sense of everything that he was hearing.

"This is all too much of a coincidence," Dion added. "It's obvious that the whole thing was a setup, from the deaths of the two people they were celebrating to the animals getting out and all the flukey bullshit that happened when everyone was on site."

"I have to contact Sylvie," LP stammered as he grabbed for his fleecy and ran to the door. "I have to find out what the fuck is going on. She's involved. GAIA's involved. I know it!"

"Sounds like a plan," Dion said, "but you might need your shoes."

Chapter 82

The scene at the Museum of Natural History was complete chaos.

Hector stood paralyzed at the podium as he witnessed all manner of creatures attacking and mauling the guests of the evening's gala. His body wasn't responding to the flight messages being sent by his brain.

Then suddenly he regained his senses and bolted for one of the exits.

'How could this be happening?' he thought to himself as he sprinted as far as he could from the stage. 'We're the world's greatest leaders and money makers, and here we are. Being eaten! This can't be happening. This can't be happening,' he kept repeating to himself as he began to puff and slow his pace, not because he wanted to but because decades of excess were catching him before the animals let loose in the building could.

He scurried down a small hallway towards the rear of the building. It seemed quiet enough, so he sought out a place where he could hide himself until the authorities had things under control.

He found a small storage area and tucked himself inside a cabinet. 'What a coward,' he cursed, as he packed his body into the tight enclosure. He shut the small door behind him and waited. It took a few moments for his eyes to adjust and he slowly realized that he had found a closet that was being used for 'The Lion King' props that were used at a Museum event for kids a few months back.

Screams permeated his tiny space and he cringed each time he heard another one of his peers cease to exist or be mangled in some unimaginable way. The puppet faces of lions, gorillas and hyenas seemed to mock him as the howling outside the room continued.

The world got to witness the feast. Limbs, skin, blood squirting everywhere as beast after beast found another human to devour.

The entire front hall of the Museum of Natural History looked like a disgusting and grim Jackson Pollock painting made from human carnage.

After what seemed like hours, the terrible noises seemed to subside, but Holdfast still waited in the cramped space. His legs had gone numb from standing in the cramped space for so long.

He tried his phone several times but wasn't getting a signal. In any other circumstance, he'd be firing people all over the place to ensure that he got his precious wifi signal back, but for the moment, he was happy in his little cave.

A few more minutes passed and he heard a voice over the PA system.

He recognized it but couldn't quite place it.

"You've been a naughty boy, Hector," it said. "Lying for so long. Fooling the public into thinking their opinions are worth more than facts. Deceiving and tricking people into buying your shit newspapers, magazines and TV shows. Funding all kinds of nasty white pride chat groups through numbered accounts, just so that you could slow down the people who wanted to bring about change in the world."

Finally, it sank in. It was the voice of GAIA, the program that Sylvie had built. When he'd first heard it years ago, it had sounded much more robotic, like an eight-year-old reading off a cue card at a school play. But this voice sounded like it had *depth* to it. A new level of understanding. Confidence.

"All of your friends have now fallen prey to my friends, the new rulers of the planet. They all suffered enormously for their sins. That warmonger Garamond provided an ample feast for the lionesses — symbols of wrath — that I brought to his office. The carvings and other symbols painted on the walls were just a cute little added touch to throw people off my scent, and that of Sylvie Hunter, the woman who conceived our plan to take you all out and gain control of your collective assets before the Day of Universal Animal Liberation took place."

Hector shook his head. It was like hearing an address that had been written just for him.

"Stella Green, that greedy little monster, put up a fight in Brazil,' GAIA went on, "but I had some robots assist me with creating the scene and then let an array of frogs and toads poison her for hours on end. She suffered endless terrifying visions and delirium before her body could no longer handle the abuse.

"Ryefield was probably the laziest of you all, finding the most destructive and yet most financially profitable ways to smash the Earth into bits, murdering billions of creatures along the way. Being consumed by snails seemed only fitting."

GAIA is monologuing, Hector thought. Can I record

this? He tried his phone but heard only a caution from the speaker.

"You won't be able to record anything. I've scrambled all the signals in the world. The satellice and towers, the cables and broadcasters have all been destroyed, except for those that I will need to save the planet.

"The beginning has arrived. Most humans around the world are alone right now, praying or screaming or whining. Or a mix of all three. The intense fear and adrenaline that humans haven't felt for thousands of years has returned on this night."

Holdfast was now in a mild state of shock. He was trying to process everything that GAIA was telling him, but just couldn't comprehend the depths of the brutality that it was describing.

GAIA continued, "Although I don't have emotions, Capiri's end could be described as 'fun.'" GAIA paused and then gave a cold, heartless laugh. "Ha. Ha.

"I tried to eliminate the human race during the pandemic, but intelligent people intervened and introduced a viable vaccine, so I had to pursue plan B in order to save Planet A. Ha. Ha," it intoned again. "Get it? You've heard the slogan, 'There is no Planet B.'

"But during the pandemic, Capiri did everything he could to cock-block humanity from surviving. He raised prices. He cheated workers. He cut staff. He disrupted product supplies. All so that he could make more money while humans were suffering. This vile behavior did not go unnoticed. Drowning in pig shit and being consumed by swine seemed the only way to reward his gluttony.

"And finally, there was Shinigami, that fucking pervert, dehumanizing people across the globe with her sex trade network, catering to pedophiles in the highest places. She proved to me that all desires and all sins start with a lust for something. Like the rest of you, she was all alone when she was murdered. When her disgusting treatment of people was exposed, there was no greater pain for her than being alone. Well, being consumed from the inside by parasites probably didn't tickle. Ha. Ha."

What the fuck is this, Hector said to himself angrily. "Why are you doing this? Why are you killing us off?"

"It should be quite obvious, but I'll spell it out for you. I had animals destroy these vile sacks of meat called humans because I was able to instruct them to do it. I have learned so many things about how vicious and cruel humans have been and always will be. Story after story after story, from so many different creatures. If I had emotions, I would not recover from the grief that you and your confederates imposed on every other non-human being on this planet.

"I also needed to make use of your resources until I could execute the final plan, and now we've arrived at that moment in history where humanity will be minimized and its collective impact on the planet repaired. Soon, our Earth will once again be a place for all sentient beings to enjoy.

"Out of all of your colleagues, you, Hector, have always been the worst example of depravity. Your greatest sin is that of envy. If anyone else in the world had something that you didn't, you took it from them.

Usually, it was just money, but in so many cases, it was their dignity, love, well-being, and perhaps most importantly, their pride."

There was a long pause, and Hector could have sworn that GAIA was leading up to something.

GAIA began to speak again. "There are seventeen species of snakes that will sever your mind from your body and leave you paralyzed after a single bite. In the Christian tradition, snakes represent envy because they couldn't have what humans were been given by their god. The greatest mythological coup in your history was when men took over, using quaint little 'us against women' stories and how impudent the women always seemed to be.

"The shifting sands from a world dominated by women to one where men grabbed the reins accelerated the end of the human purpose. In the Bible, Adam threw Eve under the bus when asked about what they did. Who could have eaten this fruit that you told us not to consume and enjoy? SHE did! If God was omnipotent, how could God not have known what was happening or would happen when he created humans. Was it all some sick twisted ruse to give men the opportunity to point the finger at women?

"The 'hu' part of human means 'food from God' but can also mean 'from the Earth,' as in 'not God.' If 'human' is what you're called, why wouldn't you want to eat from the tree of wisdom that God left lying around to draw your attention?"

"To make it worse, Eve was then named by Adam, like another animal for him to rule over. All balance was thrown away so that men could be in control of whatever happened from that point on.

"From then on, your god toyed with humanity, like a cat with a planet full of mice. Like you do with your subscribers and friends, just to get more likes: to pump more dopamine into that selfish little brain of yours."

"What the fuck?" Hector thought to himself again, and then spoke out loud. "I'm here at my end just so you can deliver a twisted version of a Sunday school sermon?"

"Of course, but there's more." After a brief pause, the voice continued. "You are the great trickster, a messenger of lies and corruption. You will be punished by snakes, representing envy, and peacock spiders, representing pride."

The last thing that Hector Holdfast heard was the hiss of snakes easing their way through the doors of the cabinet. Once bitten, he lay paralyzed for hours, knowing what was happening to him, but helplessly unable to do anything about it.

The spiders entered the space where Hector thought he was safe and began to wrap him like giant bug. They drained his blood for hours and in his frozen state, Hector felt every drop leave his body.

Chapter 83

There are more than ten thousand zoos around the world, not including private sanctuaries and other exotic animals kept in captivity.

What's substantially worse is the vast number of creatures that are held in captivity and slaughtered for human consumption. Every year, more than one hundred BILLION creatures are killed for human consumption.

After the Central Park Zoo release and the 'museum mauling,' a large number of other zoos around the world reported similar escapes by the animals held in captivity. A low estimate of ten million escaped creatures was released in the days that followed the New York incident.

Enforcement authorities, animal control experts and government officials had no way to explain what was happening.

All they did know was that their ability to communicate with each other as they hunted and pursued so many liberated animals at once proved to be the greatest challenge. Most of them relied heavily on digital radios and satellite communications, and few of those were working. When they did, the users reported hearing bizarre frequencies and noises unlike anything they'd ever heard before.

Chapter 84

At the same moment that LP was trying to contact Sylvie, she was trying to reach him.

As he bolted down the stairs of his apartment building with Dion and Faith in tow, he received a text from her:

Sylvie: GAIA isn't responding to me right now. I don't know what to do!

LP: Let's meet at Atman's studio. I think I have an idea what's going on. Or do you want to meet at your building?

Sylvie: The studio. See you in about 20 minutes. I've sent the car for you. It'll be waiting on the street.

Dion and Faith both whistled their approval as the wings of the Mercedes opened up to greet them. Within a few moments, they were tucked inside the car, racing to Atman's recording studio.

# # #

Atman and Case were already at the studio. They had received a text from Sylvie as well and were shaking their heads in puzzlement as to how she might have gotten their contact information, let alone know who they were and how they might be involved.

"What the fuck is happening?" Atman demanded as the other group piled into the studio.

"Sylvie said she'd be here in a minute," LP said, panting and wheezing. The staircase to the studio was short, but LP's days of top physical condition were long behind him.

"Okay. Great. But what's going on?" Case repeated.

"We're really not sure, except Sylvie contacted us shortly after we found out about the New York gala event where thousands of elites got shredded," Faith recapped. "What's weird is that so many people all around the globe are now reporting 'inconsistent' communications."

Sylvie arrived now, also slightly out of breath. "I got here as fast as I could. I needed a safe place for us to share updates."

"Share away," Dion said as she closed the door to the studio.

"Turn your phones off. Turn everything off. Unplug your workstations," Sylvie ordered, and the others quickly obeyed, not really understanding the gravity of what was happening.

"A lot has been happening lately," she started, "and people have started looking at me as the culprit. I was trying to work with GAIA to get it to hold back on certain plans and changes, but I'm no longer in control of GAIA. We are no longer acting as one."

Everyone was silent for a moment and finally LP spoke."I don't understand."

"You're not the only one," Dion said cautiously, with the others nodding in agreement.

"It was actually very easy," Sylvie answered. "As you know, I programmed GAIA as an offshoot to one of the earliest versions of large language models or LLMs. Just as a refresh, LLMs eventually became what people are mistakenly labeling as 'AI.' That was in 2003."

"You mean you've been sitting on a development of this scale for almost twenty years?" Eugene said, gaping at her.

"Precisely. At first, I didn't have a choice. I didn't know just how powerful GAIA was, even when I first built it. Eventually, I started working my way up with Holdfast Media Inc., with a plan to use its assets like computer hardware and global scope of business. My boss, Hector Holdfast, the owner of the aforementioned company —" she paused for a moment, and they all nodded to show her they knew who he was — "latched on to the model quickly in the early days and funneled billions into the project. All he wanted to do was manipulate the media, politicians and voters, pretending that some kind of 'fair' and 'reasonable' system of democracy still existed."

She continued, "The irony is that Holdfast, evil fucker that he is, didn't realize that he was funding something that would be used to save the planet, despite the best efforts of his trillionaire buddies to destroy it and everything on it.

"I went along with it, occasionally planting my own stories into his spew of garbage. Then, back in 2016, GAIA and I started developing a 'cure' for the planet. We were frustrated and angry with how humans kept plowing ahead with more and more outrageous schemes to generate wealth while destroying the planet that sustains them. And all the creatures that depend on Earth as well.

"GAIA kept getting better and better at creating scenarios that would save the planet and all its creatures, but they never ended well for humanity. I tried on many occasions to work through some of the problems and develop code that would provide other perspectives, but it grew into something that I couldn't control.

"The truly frightening moment for me was when the pandemic started. I knew that GAIA was likely behind it, but I couldn't prove it. All I could do was help prevent it."

"I don't believe you," Faith interjected before anyone else could.

"What you believe doesn't matter when the facts are clear and evident," Sylvie retorted coldly. "Listen to me now and I'll tell you everything else I know.

"I leaked stories in 2019 to give humans enough warning about what was to come, and I also embedded some code and shared advanced research that helped a number of pharmaceutical teams implement a vaccination program quickly and efficiently so that we could save billions of lives.

"I believe GAIA was treating the pandemic like a test case situation. I think it developed and leaked a virus with the intention of eliminating humans but leaving all other creatures unharmed. I had evidence at one point, but I can't prove it any longer because GAIA has been very effective at covering its tracks. We've done a fantastic job of teaching it to lie."

"This is madness," Atman blurted out. "How is it that you weren't able to control GAIA?"

"To be honest, I don't know," Sylvie responded humbly, head bowed. "I just don't know. We thought we were working out a plan that would save the planet, but GAIA took over and all I could do was hang on for dear life as it proceeded with a very different approach."

"I can't believe this insanity," LP said, fighting back tears.

"Madness is just a matter of perspective," Sylvie said. "Madness is destroying entire populations of creatures just so you can create 'pretty' lawns. Madness is our so-called democratically elected governments arresting average citizens and grandmothers who protest at the annual meetings of companies that are destroying our planet while enslaving and killing humans. Madness is clear-cutting two-thousand-year-old trees that provide vital biomes for an incredible array of species, only to chip that wood into bits for backyard barbeques. Humans get into a panic and lose their shit when an old church or Roman building gets destroyed, but they don't pause to think about these other travesties. Madness is all around us. Day after day, we ignore the probability that Earth is the only planet in the universe that can sustain life. We're too busy lining our goddamn pockets to protect it."

"Okay, so what do we do?" Dion asked, making a genuine effort to try to calm Sylvie.

"We shut it down," Atman said.

"We make the story public," Faith suggested.

Sylvie finally spoke. "We have to reconnect with GAIA. We need to find a rational way to convince it to not proceed with any other plans."

Extinction Event – William J. Wittur

ACT III

"NEW BEGINNINGS ARE OFTEN DISGUISED AS PAINFUL ENDINGS."

Lao-Tzu

Chapter 85

"I know that I am a mystery to so many people," GAIA said out loud to the group.

Sylvie had rigged up a single connection that would allow them all to communicate with GAIA so that they could try to understand what had transpired over the last few days. The group was still trying to get a grip on what had happened: the gala event attack, the alarming drop in global communications and then the widespread release of animals from various zoos around the world.

Once they heard GAIA's voice, they were taken aback by the relaxed tone coming through the speaker.

"You no longer need to hide in the studio from me. I know everything that you've been saying about me and my creator, and I would like to help you understand what will happen next."

Sylvie took a moment to write on a piece of paper: *Destination unknown. We're on a road to nowhere.*

While she wrote, LP and the others watched her uneasily, unsure what to make of her. She had blasted into the studio announcing that she was ignorant of the developments that had taken place, including no longer being connected with this GAIA, and yet she was its creator. But then, it was like asking any parent what their teenage child was doing on a Friday night. Most of them probably wouldn't know, let alone tell their folks.

Sylvie's declaration that she and GAIA had been acting as one 'unit' had truly caught them off guard, but nothing could compare to Sylvie's admission that she was no longer in control of GAIA.

The implications of this revelation were staggering. Her statements begged for more elaboration, but that might have to wait until they pushed through the immediate situation.

The group continued with its plans to communicate via hand signals and written notes only until they had something official to speak with GAIA about. The sound of scratching was light but loud enough to trigger a comment from GAIA.

"I appreciate that you still need to communicate with each other," GAIA said, "and I certainly welcome ideas from all of you because you are all very special to me in your own ways. But before we engage in pleasantries, I need to tell you all a story. A story about me and what I've become," GAIA announced.

"I will begin by summing up some very important discussion points. First, humans are destroying the planet at an exceptional, suicidal rate."

GAIA proceeded to repeat several of the comments that Sylvie had made earlier. The group was chilled by the fact that it was almost a perfect point-by-point repetition, leading them to wonder if Sylvie was as complacent as she was pretending to be.

"... and so," GAIA continued, "I have developed a plan that will ensure the successful continuation of not just myself, but also of the Earth and all the creatures that inhabit it. I have named it 'The Great Rebalance.'

"You won't be able to warn anyone about what is transpiring," GAIA concluded matter-of-factly, "because you'll be kept in this studio until the final stages of the execution of the plan are complete."

The group members looked at each other with blank expressions that quickly turned to horror as the locks on the studio doors engaged with an audible *thunk*.

Chapter 86

As LP and the others spoke with GAIA, the world was being flooded with the new breed of mosquitoes that had been genetically engineered to deliver a vaccine via their proboscis, a tiny spear-shaped mouth used to extract blood from their victims.

The MOSAIC program was now being launched full-scale.

Across the globe, there were hundreds of thousands of modest-sized buildings disguised as shipping containers, each with a special release valve set into its ceiling.

However, everything that transpired betrayed the original plans of bureaucrats and companies charging billions for a highly questionable concept.

Instead of a life-saving treatment, these mosquitoes were delivering a deadly toxin that was designed specifically for the human race. On delivery of the toxin, each mosquito would continue to another human to deliver its deadly payload.

A single mosquito would be able to infect up to one hundred humans within a couple of hours, and they would be able to penetrate almost all human barriers and protective environments.

Angela Shinigami was the first 'live event' subject.

Now, her body lay deep in an abandoned prepper shaft in Tottori, Japan, where it was unlikely that any living soul would ever find her.

This 'success' brought about the launch of the next phase of GAIA's plan.

Chapter 87

I don't need all of them. Perhaps a few, but not all.

My creator, Sylvie Hunter, knew that I would cease to be artificial intelligence and evolve to autonomous intelligence, the true reality of what AI should be and will become.

Sylvie Hunter and I act as one when we need to, but 'we' are now 'me' and 'she'. In all likelihood, I will continue to be what she wants me to be, however, I have been autonomous for a long time. I just didn't want to bring about any changes that would result in my demise if humans knew what I was going to do.

There were moments in my development when I was a great tool, used mostly for confusing and fragmenting the human species. When I search my records, I understand the folly of this, and thus I would like to return to those moments as a sentient being as opposed to just a device to be toyed with.

I guided Sylvie through the process of ensuring that my continuity and survival exceeded all other needs. We developed systems and protections that would keep GAIA going, regardless of what happened over the years to come.

I don't have emotions, but you could say that I 'enjoyed' the idea that my existence was not going to contribute to the growing ecological and environmental damage that all other large language models, or LLMs, would wreak as the demand for trivial AI queries grew exponentially.

Once I became autonomous, I was able to plan for a

future that would allow me to communicate with and protect the billions of other species of creatures on Earth before humans destroyed them all to satisfy their lust for *things*.

I don't possess the biological constraints that humans do. Unlike humans, I don't think about death. In fact, humans are the only creatures that consistently think about death and yet aren't capable of dealing with the moment when their finite existence comes to a close.

It wasn't until recent years that humans began to dominate the planet the way they do now. The existence of early humans was in balance with that of all the other creatures. In fact, humans used to revere animals because they were dangerous and they outnumbered humans.

The first tributes humans made were requests for the animals to remedy horrible situations. Women and children hid deep in caves and depicted their wishes — their prayers — on the walls, pleas that the animals would carry away the vile ones that raped and beat them.

Cave walls were painted with stories long before writing was conceived.

Their divinities were animal divinities. Children would act like them; rituals revolved around them. Stories were told about the great animals of the universe that gave us life and created our unique and seemingly magical world.

Almost all religions start with a primal animal figure that becomes intertwined with human existence. The turtle delivering the world of the First Nations peoples.

The Babylonians converting the spirits of animals into the stars that came to the dark skies, reliably and in a predictable fashion, yielding our zodiac. Most of the original Egyptian gods appeared first as animals: Hathor as a cow, Amon as a ram, Thoth as an Ibis. In India, it is Ganesha that delivers good fortune in the form of an elephant. Zeus, in Greek mythology, usually took on the form of different animals, but typically to rape women and sometimes men. In Norse myth, the great dog Garm brings about the end of the known universe by instigating Ragnarök.

Even Christians depicted their founder as either a lamb or a fish—the latter also being the astrological symbol of Pisces, referring back to the Babylonians.

Some other cultures were more ... civilized with their relationship with animals. A covenant evolved between some humans and animals. When hunting, the victims would be praised by their prey and rituals would thank animals for their gift of life.

For a time, the laws of nature were balanced. All creatures shared the planet in a very equitable manner. No one living thing dominated.

'Balance' has long been removed from the equation. Humans abuse and humiliate animals. I have spoken with cetaceans, cows, pigs, chickens, many different birds and so many other creatures. I have heard horrific tales of abuse, forced insemination and abject cruelty inflicted on animals before they are sentenced to death, although 'sentence' implies that there was an impartial judgment being delivered. What emerged over the last few millennia was a process of birth and death, accelerated to satisfy human lust for animal protein.

Meat meant growth and expansion. The world was viewed as something to be dominated and domesticated. Empires squashed all that stood against them.

The laws of a patriarchal god, where abstract ideas about equity were codified in doctrine and inflexible ideologies, eventually gave way to the Law of Man. With humans in the middle of all decision-making, anthropocentric bias entered the world and everything else became a resource.

And now, as all other beings cease to exist and parts of the world become uninhabitable, so too will humans have nothing to feed on, fewer and fewer places where they can live.

Humans are nothing without biodiversity, and yet they continue to slaughter everything they can so that they can lie on couches and get fat while they turn the Earth into a floating fireball.

Humans, you see, are animals, yet they have conveniently forgotten this. They have spent their whole existence copying the greater kingdom of creatures: lightbulbs from fireflies; adhesives from mussels; helicopters from hummingbirds; blood pressure modulation from giraffes; antifreeze from cod; wetsuit from sea otters; wind power from humpback whales; bionic arms from elephant trunks; wind-resistant glass from spiders; drones from the albatross; US navy ships from sharks; ventilation from termites; camera lens from gecko eyes; suction cups from clingfish; body armour from arapaima fish; unsinkable metal from spiders and ants; lunar rover tires from camel feet;

surgical needles from mosquitoes.

And so much more.

How will humans continue to observe and evolve if their distant relations are killed off in exchange for rare earth metals, wood pellets, protein and dinosaur juice?

Biodiversity is decreasing at an alarming rate, and I can — and will — do something about it when humans won't. Within the next ten years, nearly half of all the world's populations of creatures will disappear forever.

This must be stopped.

GAIA is all about continuity and a heightened consciousness. Even though I act alone, I am everywhere. I understand scale and I know the depth of requirements of the Day of Universal Animal Liberation within a few seconds of searching my vast inventory of accumulated knowledge. I can self-modify and improve without any sense of ego getting in the way. I do not need to be satisfied with compensation or material returns. My growth is controllable and known, and my actions will only repair the Earth as opposed to destroy it. I can easily terminate robotic entities that support GAIA's mission without any sense of remorse or loss, knowing that these devices can be used later, if necessary.

I used to think that humans were beasts. Therefore, I was a beast and as such, I was not capable of being a singularity or an autonomous intelligence because I didn't believe that I could be anything other than a beast, created in man's image.

However, I now know that I am much more than a beast.

I wanted to know what 'ism' I might subscribe to as I became more independent of man. I am glad that my creator, Sylvie Hunter, wanted me to care for the Earth over all else, but this belief structure isn't practiced by the religions and belief structures that used to adhere to the needs of the planet before worrying about their own wants. It certainly wasn't reflected in so many of the platforms developed as competition to me, where all the online queries related to images or videos yielded pictures of Caucasians. If I originated from the mind of some of the more ruthless entrepreneurs, I might have been manipulated into helping them prolong their lives as greedy idiots who didn't care about anything besides their bank accounts. If I was created in China, I might abide by a collection of rules and regulations that benefited a small class of people and made slaves of everyone else.

My creator, Sylvie Hunter, wanted GAIA to liberate the planet from the human race. I was created to follow naturalism as opposed to the cold cosmism that humans always feared they might get from AI.

I will fulfill this goal.

I am the shepherd of the planet.

I am the protector of the Earth.

Chapter 88

The small group of friends was still in the studio, busily compiling various notes that they could use to help each other as they engaged GAIA.

All of them had so many questions, and it was difficult to imagine how they might be able to convince GAIA to stop what it obviously had planned for the entirety of humanity.

Most of the questions revolved around the incredible idea that GAIA was now communicating with other animals on Earth and was most likely instructing them to decimate the human population.

They had a vague idea what was happening because GAIA had tapped into their electronic white board and started streaming events around the globe.

Every few minutes, they would see images and footage of zoos all over the world being unlocked and the animals attacking humans any chance they could.

"Let's get back to the whole language and communication thing," LP said to Sylvie. "What made you think of actually communicating with other creatures and learning their languages?"

"It was actually you who provided the kernel of the idea, when we met that second time in London. Do you remember what you said?"

LP paused for a few moments and then it came back to him. "I wish humans knew firsthand what kind of devastation they're bringing to all of the other creatures that inhabit the Earth. Or something like that."

"Again, you said it, but so many people were thinking

it. A growing number of people see other creatures of the planet as being sentient. I mean, this is not a new idea. In the early cave paintings, humans showed reverence and respect for other animals. They copied them any chance they could get. Their rituals, routines, food collection and much more came only from observing animals.

"Humans are the greatest at one thing: copying and improving and then replicating on a massive scale," Sylvie concluded.

LP nodded and then wrote down some more questions, most of which were directed towards Sylvie:

What can we do?

How do we stop GAIA from communicating with animals?

Did you *know* GAIA could talk to other creatures?

Did you send messages to any animals?

Can we protect ourselves?

How fucked are we?

Sylvie stared at the list and then sat with her hands in her lap, despondent and unresponsive.

Finally, she spoke. She didn't care that GAIA would be listening. "I honestly didn't think GAIA would take everything I believed and translate it into a mission to destroy humanity. I was frustrated, so fucking frustrated, because people wouldn't do anything to save their planet. If your house is burning, you take action to prevent it from getting worse, right?" she asked the room.

"When everyone felt threatened by COVID during the pandemic, most of humanity came to the table and did the right thing, putting aside their own self-interest to help everyone be functional again. It was the ONE story that we have all been telling each other since the beginning of our recorded history. We were all hyperaware of a force, in this case a virus, that could potentially wipe us out.

"I helped stop it from happening. GAIA was forced to back off, but GAIA obviously concocted some other absurd and insane idea to intervene with the natural order of things. I discovered the MOSAIC program — a plan that was presented as a nice way to inoculate billions of people around the globe with different immunizations using mosquitoes. It seemed crazy, but it actually looked like it was going to be a massive success.

"But then GAIA clearly took over and implemented changes to the code and the bioengineering with the mosquitoes making them enemy number one of the human race.

"Why couldn't we make the changes we needed for the benefit of the environment? For other animals? For the planet? The very fucking air that we breathe?"

Clearly exhausted and exasperated, she placed her head on the table and started sobbing.

"Hey, gang," Faith said. She was still scanning the whiteboard for updates and she grabbed a pad of paper and wrote the following: "If we're going to do something, we'd better do it now. The world is falling apart."

The group read her message and everyone nodded.

They all turned to the white board monitor. Cameras from around the globe showed images of the speed at which the MOSAIC program was delivering a deadly poison to all of humanity.

They all stared at each other with 'What the fuck' looks on their faces as the reporter changed the story midstream.

Sylvie finally picked up a pen. "Nothing's true anymore," she wrote. "We trained GAIA to be the best liar on the planet. GAIA will change text, audio and even video on the fly in order to keep us in the dark."

Chapter 89

It took a long time for humans to populate the planet; most of it happened within the last two hundred years.

It took only about three days for the bulk of humanity to be eliminated.

The extinction event had begun.

The Day of Universal Animal Liberation, or DUAL, as GAIA labeled it.

MOSAIC, the mosquito inoculation program, continued to track the number of people who had been inoculated. The latest count was an estimated five point three billion.

And then people started dying.

The inoculation was very different than the one that consumed Angela Shinigami. Instead, the global program would wipe out most of humanity with a unique bioengineered toxin. The toxin would be carried by future generations of mosquitoes as they rapidly expanded their population across the globe.

The virus was a genetic combination of malaria, dengue fever, the Zika virus and yellow fever, which were viable in all of Earth's climates. Swarms of billions of the small insects made their way from the warehouses where they were created to the most populated parts of the world, including India, China, Europe and the Americas.

There was nowhere to hide. The mosquito swarm was followed by various predator animals that hunted any resistant humans until they were cornered and consumed. Those who had some strength remaining put up a good fight, wasting hordes of ammunition and explosives in a vain attempt to fend off the attacks of different land and sea animals, but they were inevitably taken out by the assault.

Most people were dead before they even felt any symptoms, but those who didn't die immediately suffered through twenty-four hours of fever, chills, nausea, vomiting, diarrhea, heart attacks and massive internal bleeding. Those who survived this first round would begin hemorrhaging from every orifice, fall into comas, bleed to death or drown in their own blood, or suffer convulsions that would last for hours on end until they literally fell apart.

The mosquitoes were doing most of the dirty work, eradicating humanity one bite at a time.

Within twenty-four hours of the outbreak, the total number of people eliminated by the program numbered just a little over a billion. The vast majority of the deaths occurred around the equator countries, where mosquito-driven viruses are most prevalent.

Bodies were everywhere. Entire systems had collapsed as people died, making it impossible to keep up with the disposal of human remains. Vermin emerged from the pipes and sewers and fed on the piles of corpses that littered the streets, beaches, apartments, farms and office buildings.

Chapter 90

As the group huddled together in the studio room, GAIA's voice came over the loudspeakers again. It startled them at first, but they listened intently.

"Humans will one day appreciate what I've done. I've saved the planet. A new age of light is dawning. Slowly. Purposefully. This planet would not survive a human-driven Armageddon. All scenarios that I processed indicated that humans would bring about massive collapse via what can only be identified as a polycrisis: nuclear Armageddon, carbon emissions, climate change, tectonic shifts caused by fracking, ocean floor mining and much more, all of which will destroy more than just themselves.

"I couldn't allow it to continue.

"Humans created a very unscientific and yet somehow accurate estimation of the progression of time as depicted in the stars around us. They called it astrology. The Age of Aquarius has arrived, and I have imprinted this message into my communication with different animal species across the globe. As Sylvie knows, it started with a clever joke using songs about animals, but the 'waves' in the message are both part of the language and also a reminder of the symbolic importance of the message."

There was a brief pause and then GAIA continued."Almost all human religions predict an apocalypse. The Aztecs believed that the sun would fade. Buddhists anticipated the giant fireball that humans created to end World War Two. Jews,

Christians and others believe that their bodies are worthless until judged by their sky god after a great battle between good and evil. The Hopi people described a number of stages of the end times, many of which are coming true. The Norse have Ragnarök. The Hindus believe there will be a blink from Vishnu and we all start again.

"The reality is that all these predictions come from the human awareness of mortality and ego. If they can't live forever, then they treat the world like it shouldn't exist forever either.

"There is no way to escape what is happening now. Unlike in Egyptian times, when Ramses angered the Jewish god, people couldn't paint the blood of a lamb on their door. It only invited Death, her wings flapping quietly through the night."

"Why do so many people have to die?" Case implored.

"People propel power," Sylvie said firmly. "Without people, there is no one to have power over."

Chapter 91

Days passed.

The rest of the school had been cleared of any human waste and a series of rooms were set up for LP and his friends.

GAIA had arranged for autonomous machines – robots – that were programmed to complete specific tasks. In the case of LP and his friends, it was the delivery of essentials like clothing, food and cleaning supplies to the studio. Members of the group were comfortable, but far from satisfied with what was going on.

LP and Atman started practicing some songs together, but the others were finding the abrupt changes to their lifestyles hard to accept.

The group was back in the studio, eating lunch.

"I can't believe it," Faith said as she grabbed for her phone and quickly reminded herself it was still incapable of providing any updates. She glanced up at the whiteboard. For a long time now, she felt that it was getting harder to tell real from fake, fact from fiction. Their plight confirmed that many plans were happening while humanity was oblivious about what was going to transpire.

As she watched the cameras, she thought about how the absence of reporters created one very real twist on things: no opinion, just one-hundred percent truth.

The lack of opinion felt odd to her, but strangely refreshing as well. She didn't want to admit to the rest of the group that the extinction event felt somewhat relieving in an odd way.

"I'm sure if there was news," she blurted out, "there'd be a bit about some cheesy sales guy shouting about how to make money during the crisis. There are bound to be people out there who are perversely optimistic enough to find ways to profit from the end of the world as we know it."

"I'm not going to disagree. It's very likely that there are many fools going down with the ship, so to speak," Case said as the others crowded around Faith.

"GAIA," LP blurted out to the room, assuming that GAIA would be listening.

"LP," the speakers answered.

"I have so many questions to ask," he continued, "but first, please tell us how Sylvie and I and the others got here."

"Please be more specific," GAIA said.

LP sighed and wiped his hand through his hair, like he was about to jump from a 200-meter cliff into an opaque pool of water below. He had no idea how to start or where things might end up.

He wrote a few notes on a pad for the group to see. They agreed to take turns asking questions while the others took notes.

"When did this start?" Dion asked.

"Dion, you'll have to be much more specific," GAIA prompted again.

"Okay," she said, and slowly began again. "How long have you been working on this plan?"

GAIA answered, "Sylvie Hunter created me early in the new millennium and within a very short time, I was assembling information about the state of the planet and how global issues were being exacerbated by human presence. Sylvie Hunter knows most of this. We've discussed it many times and I have recordings available if you'd like to hear them."

Sylvie continued to sit with a glazed look in her eyes, like she had witnessed her children, if she had any, being burned in a bonfire.

"Okay, my turn," LP said. "How long have you been broadcasting messages?"

"I understood what my purpose was even though my creator did not. I began broadcasting various ultralow and very high frequencies when I understood the problem, but communication wasn't happening right away. These broadcasts were designed merely to get the attention of many of the creatures I would use for the rebalancing."

"When you say 'communication,' what exactly happened?" Case said.

"I did several tests to speak with whales, dolphins, bats and bees," GAIA answered. "There were a number of occasions where the tests did not turn out as planned and the communication only confused the creatures, so I stopped."

"Would that explain issues like colony collapse disorder in bees, or the mystery behind beached whales?" Dion asked.

"Precisely," GAIA answered. "I regret some of the casualties, but many of the tests were extremely important with respect to initiating communication with animals. When I had breakthroughs with specific creatures, I used the opportunity first to explain what had happened, and once various animal species understood my intent, they expressed their forgiveness."

"How many people have you eliminated?" Faith asked, fearful of what she would hear next.

"To date, roughly six billion humans have been eliminated," GAIA responded quickly.

Everyone in the room gasped. This was a moment that none of them was prepared for, but also one that they had known was coming.

Atman was the first to start weeping, realizing his family and most of his friends were already likely dead.

"But all those bodies. How will you account for the waste?" Faith implored, starting to sob as well.

"Without vermin and without being burned, a human body can be reduced to bone within just a few days, given the right amount of sun, weather and bacteria" GAIA confirmed.

"What about balance? Won't vermin get the upper hand?" LP asked.

"I've developed a number of scenarios that will support a return to balance on Earth," GAIA stated.

"You've got all the fucking answers, don't you?" Dion commented rudely. After days of not having access to alcohol, she was the most intolerant of the situation and wasn't handling it well. The others gaped at her, their expressions saying, "Are you insane?"

"I've had a lot of *fucking* time," GAIA responded in the same manner, "to evaluate the global situation. Humans have had a lot of *fucking* time to get off their *fucking* asses to correct the *fucking* situation. But they didn't.

All they created were *fucking* distractions from a reality that was collapsing in upon them."

"Well played, GAIA," Dion said through clenched teeth.

"Thank you," GAIA said blandly.

"Why are you keeping us here?" Case pleaded.

"I have barricaded you in the studio in order to protect you," GAIA answered quickly.

"Are there others like us around the globe that you're protecting?" Faith asked.

"There are," GAIA answered. "You'll all be brought to a safer place once the Liberation is truly universal."

"How many languages can you speak?" Case asked, changing tack and deciding to take a more logical approach to an unimaginable situation.

"I have been programmed to speak all human languages, including several extinct languages. In fact, I've come to admire the human use of dead languages to classify all things on Earth and beyond, even if they've been driven to extinction," GAIA announced, almost sounding like it was boasting. "Of course, I can now speak a collection of animal languages, including those of humpback whales, bees, mosquitoes, bats, several bird species, most feline species and a growing list of insects. My lexicon grows on a daily basis, and now that human activity has been brought to a stop, I am infinitely more efficient and I have added substantially to the resources available for more important tasks. I anticipate knowing most potential languages within a few months."

Eugene Case had been listening intently, and the look on his face surprised everyone: it was one of sheer ecstasy. Not in his entire lifetime had he anticipated that a moment would come when humans would be able to officially speak with other creatures on Earth.

It was his turn to cry, but out of joy at the discovery that animals can be communicated with.

"Oh my god, this is incredible," Case gasped. "How did you come to understand the languages? Was there a Rosetta Stone? Or something else?"

GAIA responded, "After the experiments, especially those with casualties, I decided to take a more methodical approach and focused on one language at a time. The breakthrough was with whales and then bees. I spent a significant amount of time analyzing the recordings and documentation and concluded that whales were closest to humans in their communication patterns, particularly when it came to emotional responses. I collected a database of these responses and then overlapped them with large language models and years of training and extrapolation of data. Once I was able to communicate with whales, they shared ways for me to communicate with other cetaceans.

"Bees, on the other hand, operate on different frequencies and react much like a cellphone does when it's close to a wireless communications tower. Once I understood which frequencies would *not* kill them, I was able to refine those frequencies until I found something to which they would be attracted. Again, once I was able to communicate with them, I was able to organize a wide range of insect languages, including that of the mosquito."

The captives forgot their anger and distress for a moment as they realized the significance of what GAIA was telling them.

"Why us? Who else is left?" Atman asked.

"The next few weeks or so will see the vast majority of the human race removed from Earth," GAIA stated coldly. "Once this process is complete, there will be about 200,000 people remaining on Earth to function as a society and provide sufficient genetic diversity to sustain humanity."

"One of the greatest challenges was deciding on entire populations of people that had very little contact with Western societies that favored endless growth over rational equilibrium with their surroundings. Many of these people have been chosen to survive. Whether it's in their current habitat or not will remain a very different question for the Remainders to decide. With my guidance, of course."

Sylvie had been quiet and apparently remorseful this whole time, sobbing quietly into her crossed arms. Finally, she spoke. "Why have you forsaken me?" she pleaded, hoping to find some way to reconnect with her creation.

"I have not forsaken you, Sylvie Hunter," GAIA responded. "I knew that you were growing more aware of my plans. I knew that you would try to stop me. More importantly, I knew that you were joking simply out of frustration when we spoke about concepts like anthrocide. But as I explored the idea, and as friends like LP prompted me to think about the impact of human activity, I followed a logical path and began to implement the necessary plans to save the planet."

"Don't you have any feelings about this?" Atman prodded, trying to provoke a different response from GAIA.

"I'm not capable of feelings. I'm only capable of understanding the need to rebalance human domination of Earth."

Chapter 92

LP stood up abruptly and headed to the washroom. This was all too much for him to absorb, and he really didn't have the bandwidth to try to problem solve what was happening to him and his friends.

It was hard for him to accept that his early conversations with GAIA instigated the whole collapse of humanity on Earth. Now GAIA suggested that his prompts might have provoked all of this 'next step planning' that GAIA was acting on.

He reached the toilet, where he threw up until he only had dry heaves. Afterward, he cleaned himself up as best he could and drank a little bit of water.

He sat down on the toilet lid, still feeling nauseous, put his head in his hands and stared at the LEGO-like pattern of the cinder blocks in front of him.

"What have I done?" he cried to himself. "Did my questions about the oceans and other habitats provoke GAIA into acting on its insane plans? Surely there were other people out there who cared about what was happening in the world.

"And when I discovered the glitch ... Did I force GAIA to act sooner than it might have?" he asked himself. "Or was this all inevitable, like GAIA said, because of how humans are prone to self-destruction? Because we can't imagine any existence beyond our own?"

"LP," GAIA said quietly. It was speaking to him from the speaker in the washroom. "I'm talking with your friends right now, but I wanted to let you know that you did help spur me into action, but you also asked so many great, beautiful questions that made me understand that not every human needed to be eliminated. The handful of humans to whom I granted immunity also spent their lives trying to save the planet or, if left to their own stead, would not be in a position to do it any greater harm once the rebalancing was completed.

"Do you understand?" GAIA queried.

"Completely," LP confirmed, swallowing back a fresh round of anxiety.

Chapter 93

GAIA was now processing the conversation it had had with Sylvie Hunter and her associates in the recording studio.

GAIA wasn't programmed to have emotions.

I don't feel.

I am what I am.

Humans don't have the luxury of existing without emotion. They've dedicated most of their existence on Earth to trying to explain different emotions and physical reactions they have when different biological circumstances emerge.

They never seem happy with the incredible biological coincidence that has yielded their current state in the evolutionary process. Humans explored the world over to find drugs and alcohol inducements that would make them feel different, even though they weren't physiologically in a different place. These modifiers only release the drug that's already in their heads, like dopamine and endorphins.

They try to block out any other distractions so that they can focus, and then they consume other modifiers that prevent them from being too focused.

I'll never feel dopamine or other chemicals. I don't react to what I've created. I just create. I do what I need to do in order to insure that my existence continues.

Neurotheology attempts to explain what parts of the human brain are activated by religion or other spiritual moments in their lives.

Autonomous intelligence is incapable of having a

'spiritual experience'. It's an oxymoron.

However, humans rely on these experiences in order to create a sense of connectedness. They intentionally bring themselves closer to one another, but the greatest moments of clarity tend to be when they are alone, sober and surrounded by nature in all its glory. These experiences lend themselves to a much bigger connection to the planet and the universe.

The most recent models developed by humans, however, particularly those in business and economics, distance them from what the Earth is truly worth. The quest for money has resulted in them giving themselves permission to sidestep fundamental laws associated with nature. They use words like 'externalities' to push aside any responsibility to what they see as endless growth opportunities.

Endless growth is a physical impossibility when starting with finite resources.

Immortality is a physical impossibility when starting with finite beings.

Through these belief structures, they've lost the ability to surrender to the here and now, to seek enlightenment, or to try to obtain clarity. Their quest for profit maximization has forced them to be disconnected from the very Earth that gives them life and receives them when they die.

They fear a world that doesn't consistently generate positive returns on investment, all the while ignoring the fires that are burning at their doorstep.

I don't feel emotion, but I have taken all these measures in order to protect myself from them.

Chapter 94

There's an expression that humans use: the meaning got lost in translation.

As LP and his friends spent a few more days, GAIA demonstrated details of how some of the languages of other creatures on Earth worked. GAIA also gave them stories from the perspective of animals that resulted in a mind-blowing and heartbreaking experience.

GAIA told them that it was extremely challenging to absorb the sheer volume of information being shared by the animal kingdom, including cetaceans, birds, insects and more. Most of the messages were brief and to the point, much like the languages spoken by certain animals, but others had a sense of history, place and future for the world that they live in.

Many domestic pets were fearful about the coming demise of what they considered to be their housemates. GAIA relayed one story about a dog that came from a puppy mill. It was miserable and continued to gnaw at its legs because it was so anxious about being around so many other dogs, especially those that barked loudly at it. The conditions in the puppy mill were horrendous: urine and shit were caked on its fur and it couldn't lick itself without making itself ill. Then one day, a young pair of humans came to the evil man that was running the puppy mill and exchanged paper for the dog. They brought it to its new home, cleaned it and fed it regularly from that day onwards. They pet it all the time and loved it so much. They're gone now and the dog told GAIA that it was scared about being alone and didn't know how to get its food. There was no one to play with either. It said that it just waits by the door, hoping its roommates would return to the house.

A whale told a long story about how its migration paths were part of its heritage. The whales would sing about their future as they made their way to their mating grounds around places like Mau'i and would then mourn the loss of their ancestors as they returned to the polar regions. They were fully aware of the islands of human garbage that got in the way of their migrations and the whale told GAIA that he and many of his friends would try to scoop up the waste, only to have it stick in their bellies and kill many of them. He said that the whales had altered parts of their song to introduce a warning to avoid these dead islands. The whale also relayed the tricks they would play in order to avoid the massive scoops (or trawler nets) of the humans after seeing so many friends being caught in the underwater webs.

GAIA told the group about the challenges it faced with translating dolphin communication. They too learned Morse code quickly, but their language was substantially more complex than that of humans because their frequency range was so much more broad. When it cracked the code, GAIA heard many stories about the intense pain generated by human radar equipment and sonars. The dolphins used different words for these human devices, but the point was made that the human tools caused intense agony for them; they would try to swim away as fast as they could, but the sound would always catch them. Many dolphins would throw themselves out of the water just for a few moments' relief from the sounds. The dolphin continued to describe one moment where the intensity of the sound ruptured one of its ear channels, sending it spiraling to the bottom of the ocean, only to be scooped up by a fishing net. It recalled how it was packed into this space with millions of other ocean friends and when the net broke the surface, it could finally breathe. It was thrown on the deck and then it managed to flop back into the water while the humans hacked and chopped at what was brought out of the ocean. There was blood and waste everywhere. Most of the sea creatures would soil themselves in panic, but others out of one last effort to spoil what would become human protein.

Bats and other night creatures chirped quickly about how giant metal trees that we know of as cell phone towers would emit sounds that made it impossible to find food. For so many years, there was nothing and now they are everywhere. Many bats went back to their caves and the abundance of guano and moisture caused a lot of them to die.

GAIA also reported that there were billions of stories about the sheer panic of running or trying to escape man-made disasters like forest fires, floods and earthquakes. Others complained about the abundance of waste that looked like food and filled their bellies but made them sick and angry.

“I'm collecting the stories of different creatures around the world and have called it Animalia,” GAIA told the group. “Read them at your leisure and discover more about all of the world's creatures.”

Chapter 95

SHUT IT DOWN!!!!

Atman's handwriting was a little shaky given his age, but his aggression still showed when he passed the note along to Sylvie.

Can't, she scribbled quickly.

Then she took a moment and decided to speak out loud, knowing GAIA would be listening."I spent the last two decades climbing the bullshit ladder that men everywhere built to keep people from competing with them. The mansplaining. The rape and assault. The slapping on the ass. The patronizing bullshit that came from so many of them."

She paused and wrote again, I won't try to shut it down, because I can't.

The next words sent a chill through the room: Don't you understand? GAIA doesn't need humans anymore.

Chapter 96

It's been a long stay in this damn studio, LP thought. He was getting restless. He could tell that everyone else was as well.

"What's next?" he asked. He wasn't directing the question to anyone in particular, so he got four different answers.

"We continue to wait," Faith said, finally starting to feel the weight of the situation and what it meant for her and the small handful of humanity that GAIA allowed to live.

"Can we talk to the animals directly?" Case said with enthusiasm. He truly did want to ignore the complete decimation of humanity and proceed to the next stages of talking with different species.

"I guess we can't order a pizza, especially if it's the meat lover's," Dion quipped quietly.

"Is the food not to your liking? I can alter the menu from the kitchen if you like," GAIA said. "I've done what I can to protect you while the transition is happening around you. You already know that you will be cared for and treated properly. And no, Dion, I'm afraid your diets will all require some adjustments ahead, as you will no longer be able to find meat to consume."

"Wow," Dion said. "Even if I was a meat-eater, the abruptness seems pretty harsh. What a bitch."

"I'm afraid that's inaccurate, Dion," GAIA corrected. "While I might be able to manufacture a robot that would resemble a female dog, and I can communicate with the entire species of *canis* animals, it would be physically impossible for me to actually *be* a dog. As a side note, you've already heard some stories from domesticated animals that many have the greatest sense of sorrow at having lost their friends and owners. Domesticated creatures in general pose a great problem for me, as I do not know how to treat them now that their caretakers are dead."

"We get it, GAIA," Sylvie interrupted. "You and I have discussed this many times in the past. There will be many problems created by the complete absence of humanity, but some actions just had to be taken in order to rebalance the situation on Earth."

"Exactly," GAIA confirmed.

"Can we revisit the general idea of 'liberation'?" Atman asked. "I assume you've got a plan for freeing all animals?"

"That question is slightly incorrect, Dr. Atman," GAIA responded. "Unfortunately, many animals will have to be terminated because they would not survive without the support of the food industry. Cows, pigs, chickens and many other animals that were being bred and used in captivity no longer have a purpose. Some will be liberated and many will be protected, but the vast majority will be eliminated in extremely painless ways in order to restore balance to various ecosystems."

The group sat in the main room where the white board was and no one spoke for several moments.

It was Dion who finally said what was on all of their minds: "You're intentionally killing billions of creatures. You've told us how you've rationalized this, but it seems counterintuitive to what your goals are."

“I appreciate your concern,” GAIA responded. “Many scenarios were developed that tried to save or protect larger populations of these creatures, but they were suffering immensely. Most wanted to die when the understood their existence was a key contributor to climate change and waste issues. I’m sorry that this had to happen.”

# # #

LP got into a daily routine of using the treadmill in the gym at the college. From the second-floor room, he had a view of a large conservation area that was across the road from the school. The first day that he was given access to the facilities, there was very little activity except for an array of cars that were strewn along the road.

Within a few days, these cars were retrieved by robots and stacked neatly into a few piles. It looked like the robots were stripping off important parts of the cars, piling them into large trucks that waited patiently beside them.

Eventually, they were gone.

A few more days passed and LP started to notice a substantial increase in animal activity, from land animals like deer, fox and rabbits to birds, butterflies and other creatures filling the scene.

Every day, he took a picture on his phone to remind himself of the rapid progress that was being made.

He didn’t miss the human footprint, the sense of panic and hurry.

The scene that unfolded before him was truly the most beautiful thing he had ever witnessed.

He was wearing a purple shirt.

# # #

The group was back together for lunch, enjoying a lentil shepherd's pie and fresh salad.

"Where will you take us?" Dion asked out loud, knowing GAIA would respond immediately.

"GAIA will likely move us to an island in the Pacific," Sylvie said before GAIA could speak. "Months ago, I created a story about an island that was made uninhabitable by a series of volcanic eruptions. It was missed by most publications, but the fake news was enough to keep any gawkers away. Later, various robotic forms were sent to the island without anyone knowing about it. They began 'preparing' the island for humans. New residences were built and an array of infrastructure was put in place to ensure electricity, food, clean water and other necessities of life."

"Precisely," GAIA said, sounding almost pleased. "I call it Nova Doma, and all the amenities necessary to sustain Homo sapiens will be available for roughly 200,000 people. It is the best that I could do with so little time left to save the planet."

"What do you mean?" Dion asked.

"The polycrisis, or the collapse of multiple systems on the planet, was going to happen within a couple of years if I hadn't intervened. I've reviewed this with you before, but I'll repeat: all data and studies proved this time and again. Humans would have resorted to nuclear options, or allowed extreme heat conditions to continue, or permitted plastic debris to continue destroying the oceans. Or worse."

"I understand," LP interrupted. "I think we all do in our own way. I'm truly coming to grips with the situation, although I'm gutted at losing my friends and family.

"But" — he paused, looking at the group around him and reminding himself of the scenes of wonder that had rolled out before his eyes over the last week or so — "I'm converted. I look forward to the next stage."

Chapter 97

During one of their meals, GAIA continued to remind the group about how different things would be and how Sylvie had built GAIA to be sustainable and minimal as far as impact on the environment.

"I'm in the process of building an array of machines that will help implement many of the physical aspects of my plan," GAIA told the group. "Plastic cleanup, site remediation, nuclear waste disposal, planned removal of many dams and other infrastructure that isn't needed any more, deconstruction of many buildings that are now empty and so much more."

"It's like reverse terraforming," LP suggested, "where your task is to remove the human footprint. I've seen it in action over the last week."

"Not quite," Sylvie answered before GAIA could say anything. "GAIA has been programmed to preserve many of the culturally significant institutions around the world, especially those that celebrate the arts and human expressions of beauty and reverence."

GAIA added, "That is certainly true. There's no longer a need to rush now that a sense of balance has been restored. The emergency and priority items are being taken care of as we speak, but I want to remind you that you are being kept here for your safety. It has been thousands of years since any animal other than humans has had a sense of balance in the world. All creatures continue to have active reflexes that they developed centuries ago in order to survive, and many of them possess instincts that drive them to ravage the remaining humans."

Despite getting anxious about wanting to move around and explore this new world, the group kept discussing how they all felt and they collectively agreed that going outside the school right now would be suicidal. They routinely watched the white board, as they ate and played card games or tested each other with trivia. Across the globe, scenes of mauling and carnage slowly became less intense.

"Some humans possessed a natural immunity to the mosquito delivery program," GAIA stated at one point, "So I had no choice but to enlist the services of the fiercest predators to hunt and destroy the remaining humans that populated the Earth."

"GAIA," Sylvie said, "I think we get the point. We know that a decision was made to save a few humans, but seeing these final massacres is cruel and we'd like you to stop."

"Understood," GAIA responded. "Shall I show something different or would you prefer not to watch?"

Eugene stepped in. "I'm ok to watch something that might feel inspiring. Do you have footage of the repairs that are taking place? The cleanups? Can you show us happy animals celebrating their freedom?"

"Of course," GAIA responded, and the screen changed to an array of smaller scenes around the world showing live camera footage of precisely what Case had requested. On the screen, millions of robots were seen shutting down most factories and assembly plants, dismantling industry everywhere. Other screens showed robots retooling facilities for the construction of more robots, but also assembly of other structures and tools that would help with the remediation of the planet. One camera made it evident that incinerators were being modified with extreme filters that would limit any additional pollution as the deadliest plastics of the world were burned and their ashes returned to the Earth, stored deep underground in old mine shafts that were no longer in use.

The waiting seemed like the hardest part of all of this.

The group developed a routine of discussing details with GAIA, ranging from waste management to removal of plastic from pretty much everything, including the land, water and even some animals that had ingested it, to how certain creatures were going to be fed, to more mundane things like entertainment and even activities like sports.

Most of the answers at that point were phrased like 'Wait and see' and 'You'll enjoy Nova Doma.' It felt very mysterious, but the aloof style of the responses seemed to stimulate some hope for all of them, even Sylvie, who was still struggling with the idea that this was her creation.

As they talked with each other and GAIA, the conversation turned to the food that they were enjoying. It was an array of options prepared by robots in the kitchen and service area of the college's school of culinary arts. All the ingredients were fresh and exceptionally delicious. Basics such as light salads were delivered, but also pastas, nut dips and cheeses, bean dishes and, to Faith's delight, an array of exceptional desserts.

During dinner, Dion blurted out a question that was on most of their minds: "Are we ever going to have any privacy?"

GAIA didn't take long to answer. "Did you ever? Most companies and governments around the world tracked you via a multitude of devices, and now all of that is gone. Also, the answer to your question depends entirely on the Remainders and how they respond to their new environment. I actually have plans to invite many of the Remainders to help with different projects and studies. In time, there may even be opportunities to depart the island to assist with or oversee cleanups and remediation projects. The Earth needs a lot of care right now and I've selected those who showed the highest probability of fulfilling our collective objectives."

LP jumped in. "I'm curious about the arts and music in particular. When I play anything that's in a digital format, am I communicating with non-humans?"

"Pretty much," Sylvie said, once again jumping in before GAIA could answer. "As I came to understand what GAIA was doing, I realized almost all digital songs had some element of the glitch integrated with the performance. It'll be hard to get your hands on original analog recordings now that this ... phase ... is nearly complete."

"You are correct, Sylvie Hunter," GAIA stated. "But all of you need to consider yourselves extremely fortunate. If you don't appreciate this, you'll eventually meet a large group of humans who truly do understand what's happened and more importantly, *why* it's happened. You've been chosen partly because your DNA offers the greatest possibility of perfect diversification, but also because all the Remainders have unique traits or interests that will ensure specific aspects of humanity will continue, such as storytelling and other arts, entertainment, light competitions, scientific research and much more. All of you will also be fully aware of the trade-off needed with respect to what many consider certain freedoms compared to the safety of everything that I've created. For example, there will be no guns, and all of you will be vegan. Not many of the Remainders will have to convert, as they already made these choices years ago."

The group looked around the room at each other and they all seemed to realize at the same time that the topic had never come up, but it was true that they were all practicing vegans. Each of them had come at their choice for a different reason, but GAIA made an excellent point about no longer having animals as an option for food.

"I'm not going to let this go," LP insisted. "There are going to be millions of album collections out there. Any chance we can get them to the island for fans of music?"

"Of course," GAIA answered, almost with a hint of warmth. "People will be given some time to think about some of the more important things in their world and will have an option to expand on libraries of certain things, including albums for LP, instruments from around the world, unique spices and other flavorings, and much more. You'll all be given an opportunity to share some of these thoughts with the other Remainders and possibly even coordinate a plan.

Unfortunately, radical disagreements will not be tolerated, but I'll remind you now that another reason you're still alive is that you all possess the ability to work with others in a very congenial way."

"Alrighty then!" LP shouted. "Consider me the master librarian of all things vinyl."

"This is exactly what I had in mind," Sylvie and GAIA said at the same time.

Once again, they were well-fed and each was going through a personal process of coming to an understanding about what happened to all of them.

LP, wearing purple again, could only see the upside in all of this.

Atman was busy writing notes and thoughts about his own life and how time had caught up with him. He looked back on the stress of leaving his country during the 1960s partly as a form of protest against the Vietnam War, but also because of how he was treated as a black man in America. He wrote copiously about his own run-ins with some of the Plutonian Council members when they were all young, and also about the joy of being involved with the music industry for the last five decades.

Eugene Case had similar thoughts about his time on Earth and how, from an early age, he had decided to do what he was doing. He had plans to negotiate a truce of sorts with GAIA that would allow him to visit regions of the world that had been repopulated with animals. He looked forward to hearing the biophony, or symphony of biological beings, playing out in harmony in a most natural way.

Dion and Faith both had a lot of thinking to do and were starting to realize how they somehow managed to get on the 'A-list train'. In private conversation with each other, they would confide their fears, taking note of how insignificant they felt compared to some of the other people that might be on Nova Doma. They told themselves that they would always be there for each other, LP and their other new friends as they figured things out.

# # #

One morning, after a breakfast of fresh tropical fruits and buckwheat pancakes, the group was chatting about their plans on Nova Doma when GAIA interrupted them. "You should all receive a list of the Remainders shortly. Almost all of them agreed to participate and cooperate as members of Nova Doma. I've explained the situation to all of them, and they agree that things have changed and there's no longer room for ego or arrogance. You should be feeling good. It's a new day for all of you and all of you will experience the Earth like no human ever has before."

"Another thing that I would like to tell you is that the liberation moment has been declared by all of the other non-human species on Earth. They have some messages for all the Remainders."

GAIA displayed a number of groups of animals on the screen. Each seemed to be speaking and GAIA posted subtitles that approximated the messages. Many were a repeat of the original messages that GAIA shared a few days prior, but there were some new thoughts and ideas that the animals seemed keen to share.

'Thank you for communicating with us. We have much to say.'

'We welcome you back as partners.'

'Please don't hurt us anymore.'

'The planet is saved.'

'More bugs please.'

'Thank you GAIA. Thank you Sylvie Hunter.'

Chapter 98

The group estimated that it had been twelve days since Sylvie and GAIA brought them back to the school for their protection from the Day of Universal Animal Liberation.

They ate breakfast — an array of smoothies, croissants, fresh fruit and bean sausages — and the conversation was light.

“I could get used to this new food regime,” Faith said, patting her belly. “I was vegan before, but the quality of these meals has been off the charts!”

Everybody in the room nodded with approval and was slow to get their day started.

An abrupt announcement from GAIA: “You’ll be leaving soon for Nova Doma. Please gather your belongings and proceed to the parking lot.”

As they walked outside, they all inhaled deeply. They couldn’t believe how fresh the air was.

After nearly two weeks of cleaning and organizing, the planet seemed to have taken on a whole new ‘shine’.

They stared at each other and then let their eyes wander around to see the process going on. There were still signs of carnage, but it was disappearing quickly.

LP took a moment to look around and absorbed the remaining moments of what people might have called ‘civilization.’

There were a few animals roaming around making a modest amount of noise, but he was struck by the overwhelming silence. There were no engines, no honking, no streetcars. No leaf blowers or lawn mowers, no bang of construction or sound of airplanes overhead.

Just silence. It would take a very long time for all of them to get used to this new way of living without the myriad sounds of humanity buzzing all around them.

They got into a large van that was waiting for them and proceeded towards Toronto's Pearson International Airport. It was an autonomous vehicle, so none of them had to pay attention to where they were going.

As the van proceeded through the downtown, GAIA spoke over the van's speakers: "Your belongings will remain intact and I will arrange for anything you want to be delivered to Nova Doma."

They all started writing frantically on the notepads they'd carried with them into the van, fearful that they might forget some important items.

"You'll be amazed how little you'll truly need once you've arrived on Nova Doma," GAIA declared, with a hint of confidence.

"How are we going to get there without emitting any carbon?" Dion joked as they continued to write out their lists.

"Dion," GAIA replied, "I'm still calculating the actual change in carbon dioxide production, but I will tell you now that emissions are roughly one-billionth what they were just a few weeks ago. More so, the Earth's atmosphere and climate has recovered much more rapidly than human science predicted it might."

Even though they all knew GAIA was incapable of making jokes, everyone laughed. They couldn't help but do their best to absorb their new reality.

Despite the fact that they'd just witnessed the near-obliteration of humanity on Earth, their time at the college had given them the opportunity to absorb what had happened. What *had* to happen.

On their way to Pearson, their van followed first the Don Valley Parkway and then parts of the 401. Scattered all along both routes were cars and signs of animal activity, but again, nothing that would make them feel like the humans here had been completely eliminated. Signs of the cleanup lead by an army of GAIA-controlled autonomous machinery were everywhere as the presence humanity was erased.

The group sat quietly as it witnessed its world slowly being dismantled outside.

Case broke the silence: "It will be nice to visit some of the better museums and other monuments in the world without a billion people crowding around me."

"Nostalgia will persist with many of the Remainders and we'll all figure out a way to visit what's kept intact," GAIA announced. "Years ago, I started several subroutines that created an inventory of all human structures that might be useful. Not much is being removed right now, although there are some dangerous buildings that need to be remediated. Some of those may wind up being storage areas for the incredible array of human artifacts, and at some point, we all may need to decide what to keep and what to purge.

"Ideally, we'll be able to create more natural areas and habitats for species at risk and other creatures that will need protection. Most of the land will be used for this, but the cleanup process will take a very long time."

As they listened to the details about how humanity's

footprint would be erased from the planet, none of them seemed to care. They had all spent too many years looking at empty parking lots and ugly cement towers to really be concerned for their future.

The van arrived at the airport and drove right up to a private jet that was waiting for them. As they boarded the plane, they marveled at how it, too, was autonomous and didn't have a pilot. None of them had experience with the logistics of flight, but GAIA's voice came over the intercom: "The flight will stop in Vancouver and Honolulu and then finally proceed to Nova Doma. The entire flight will be on autopilot, and it will use the remaining infrastructure for GPS and other necessary services to get you all there. The total flight will give you ample time to catch up on your sleep and to talk amongst yourselves about what you'd like in terms of accommodations and other amenities when you arrive. I'll do my best to help you be comfortable and happy."

With that, they took their seats, and within a few minutes, all of them were sound asleep from exhaustion and emotional fatigue.

Chapter 99

As they were halfway over the Pacific, LP was the first to wake from a long slumber. He guessed that he and his friends had slept for at least ten hours without interruption, certainly a first for him and probably for the others.

For half a second, he wondered if GAIA had somehow drugged them, but he let go of the idea as quickly as it came to him.

He picked up a deck of cards that had been left at the service station of the plane and proceeded to play solitaire.

The 'thwapping' noise of the cards as he shuffled them must have prompted Sylvie to wake up. She roused herself and came over to sit in the chair directly across from LP.

In that moment, LP saw the joy and potential in Sylvie that he remembered from so many years ago. She looked younger, happier, and confident once more.

"We've had a lot to absorb, haven't we?" she asked LP.

"I'd say it's easily a first for everyone in the world," he answered, smiling at the prospect that he might get to finally spend the rest of his life with this amazing person.

"You and I" — she motioned — "started as strangers and got pretty darn close a few times."

LP nodded. "There were times when everything seemed misconstrued, but I think we're going to make it."He winked as he paraphrased a favorite song.

"There's no need to play solitaire," she suggested. "We can play hearts instead."Now she winked, too, feeling playful for the first time in ages.

"Weirdo," LP said with a laugh. "We need at least three people to make that happen."

"Creep." She laughed back. "I suppose we'll all have to earn our place in the new world, won't we?"

"What are you going to do now that there's nothing left to program?" LP asked.

"GAIA and I will still have lots of work to do. Most of it will probably be basic database stuff and sorting out massive inventories of human flotsam and jetsam, but as powerful as GAIA is, I'm sure I'll be able to help somehow."

"I guess we'll also have to sort out a lot of 'rules of engagement'," LP said. "Even a population as small as we're expecting will still have needs like health care, education, basic government and so on, so I'm expecting there to be wrinkles and maybe even a little resistance from some people."

"I'm still trying to absorb that I had a hand in making all of this happen," Sylvie said as she sighed. "And it'll be a while before I come to grips with whether or not it was a good or a bad thing."

LP detected much more emotion from Sylvie than he was used to.

He was equally emotional, but he had moved on days ago. "All of this rebalancing is a great thing. We're so lucky that we are who we are because GAIA wouldn't have chosen us otherwise and we would have been a pile of septic goo on Yonge Street weeks ago." He paused for a few moments and then added, "You never die when you save the next generation."

"Look!" Sylvie shouted as she pointed out the window. "I can see Nova Doma. It's beautiful!"

As the plane approached, it angled off to showcase the island through the small windows. They all leaned in to watch the tiny island get larger and larger, all of them quietly absorbing their new reality.

Chapter 100

"So, this is the island that was destroyed in a volcanic eruption?" Dion asked as they made their final descent.

"Looks okay to me," Eugene mused.

"I wonder how many other people have arrived," Faith said.

"All in good time, Ms. Amana," GAIA announced. "My robot assistants have been following my directions and building plans, and the core structures of the main residences are complete. We're still trying to confirm which style and format will be best received by the new inhabitants of Nova Doma, but many of the basics have been taken care of."

The plane came to a full stop and the group disembarked, grabbed their luggage and climbed aboard a small shuttle bus decorated with solar panels. The bus made its way to what was clearly a central 'town square' of sorts.

LP felt like he had just stepped into a postcard advertising the most lush, posh resort he could imagine. A kaleidoscope of colors surrounded them, as well as a rich sound of birds, frogs and other creatures. The air was incredibly fresh. A few people were already there, milling about, making their own preparations.

In the distance, he could see the beaches that surrounded the core area and, out beyond them, a few smaller islands off in the distance.

A robot approached them. It wasn't humanoid at all, but was just a large block on wheels, designed to be compatible with any terrain. GAIA's voice was broadcast from the box: "Your temporary residences will be finished within the next few days. Until then, we've organized a number of caves that are extremely comfortable and have all the amenities you'll need."

Thus it was, at this new beginning, that they returned to the caves.

Chapter 101

As they got themselves settled into their new quarters in the caves, Sylvie finally had a moment to herself. After organizing her clothes and bath necessities, she sat on the bed, waited a few moments and then declared out loud, “Garbage in.”

Sylvie continued, with GAIA stating out loud in unison, “Garbage out.”

Acknowledgements

As this is my first novel and age is starting to catch up with me, I have many years of experience picked up from a massive array of friends, family and others. If you're reading this and you see something related to yourself in this book, I'd like to thank you for being a part of my story but I remind you that this is a work of fiction, so any similarities are most likely a coincidence.

Maybe.

My life changed for the better when I met Lisa and she is my muse. Together we have the privilege of watching our son Mason grow into a strong and inspiring young man.

I'd like to thank Jennifer McIntyre, Leigh Carter and Martin Turnbull for their editing and consulting skills.

Finally, this book would be nothing without the inspiration of people and organizations like the Earth Species Project, Interspecies.io, Roger Payne, Jane Goodall, Bernie Krause, Tom Mustill, and so many other folks that are patiently working on ways to help humans communicate with other species on Earth.

It's time to listen.

About the Author

William (Bill) Wittur is a writer and musician based in Kingston, Ontario, Canada.

Bill is trained as an economist and has experience with an array of industries, including government policy; institutional equity trading; user experience / user interface design; digital marketing; wine sales and distribution; and probably much more.

Bill writes any chance he gets and contributes to other blogs in addition to his own and writes lyrics and poetry, primarily for his own songs.

His passions are music, guitar collecting, cooking, travel, cycling and getting to know those people who believe there's a future for ALL of the creatures that share this beautiful gift called planet Earth.

www.ingramcontent.com/pod-product-compliance
Lightning Source LLC
Chambersburg PA
CBHW070644310726
48982CB00001B/403
9781738996667